FIRE AND ICE

Michael's mouth was warm and firm against her own, all too real and demanding. And then his tongue tickled her lower lip. A flood tide of longing raced through her veins in hot, unexpected need. She moaned. Fire of a wholly different sort licked her as his tongue darted inside to touch hers. So intimate. So provocative.

His arms slid around her and tightened, pulling her closer still, pressing her to his chest. The contact inflamed her further. Her fingers locked at his collar, clinging as he kissed her as no one else had ever dared.

Certainly not the hesitant, hopeful suitors from the world she'd left behind in Boston.

Not even her husband.

Dear heaven. Her husband. She was a new widow, her husband dead less than a month.

Shame, scalding yet icy-cold, doused her to her toes. She broke away from him, her breathing ragged and uneven. . . .

BOOK YOUR PLACE ON OUR WEBSITE
AND MAKE THE
READING CONNECTION!

We've created a customized website just for our very special readers, where you can get the inside scoop on everything that's going on with Zebra, Pinnacle and Kensington books.

When you come online, you'll have the exciting opportunity to:

- View covers of upcoming books
- Read sample chapters
- Learn about our future publishing schedule (listed by publication month *and author*)
- Find out when your favorite authors will be visiting a city near you
- Search for and order backlist books from our online catalog
- Check out author bios and background information
- Send e-mail to your favorite authors
- Meet the Kensington staff online
- Join us in weekly chats with authors, readers and other guests
- Get writing guidelines
- AND MUCH MORE!

**Visit our website at
http://www.kensingtonbooks.com**

THE CHRISTMAS KISS

Elizabeth Keys

ZEBRA BOOKS
Kensington Publishing Corp.
http://www.kensingtonbooks.com

ZEBRA BOOKS are published by

Kensington Publishing Corp.
850 Third Avenue
New York, NY 10022

All Kensington titles, imprints and distributed lines are available at special quantity discounts for bulk purchases for sales promotion, premiums, fund-raising, educational or institutional use.

Special book excerpts or customized printings can also be created to fit specific needs. For details, write or phone the office of the Kensington Special Sales Manager: Kensington Publishing Corp., 850 Third Avenue, New York, NY 10022. Attn. Special Sales Department. Phone: 1-800-221-2647.

First Printing: October 2003
10 9 8 7 6 5 4 3 2 1

Printed in the United States of America

Prologue

September 1859
Boston, Massachusetts

"This cannot continue." Rising desperation burned Amelia Lawrence's throat raw and hurried her steps along the boulevard. "It just cannot."

Her summer-long *visit* to her aunt and uncle's home in the Berkshires had garnered her everything but the healthy change and favorable consequences she'd been seeking. Regardless of their assertions to the contrary, from the very beginning she'd been treated as a poor relation.

A poor relation!

Amelia Lawrence, the toast of Boston society, reduced to caring for her uncle's disrespectful brats and catering to her aunt's disparate whims. She groaned aloud. It was unbelievable. It was intolerable.

It was only too true.

Leaves tinged with bright red, golden yellow, and blazing orange glowed high above her head as she hastened along Milk Street. The joyous colors mocked her pain, twisting regret deep inside to pierce her heart. Not so long ago, the same sight would have heralded anticipation for a new round of delightful plans for soirees and entertainments amidst an entire army of suitors, culminating with Christmas revels.

But that was before her fortunes changed.

Before her whole world changed. She bit her lip, heedless of her mother's oft-repeated admonitions to remain calm in the face of all obstacles.

Ladies do not show their distress, Amelia. You are a paragon in society—you must set the tone for the others. With your lineage you must always be aware of your station . . .

Set the tone. Stay aware.

"Station, indeed," she murmured.

Those had been her mother's strictures prior to shipping her only daughter off to the mountainous wilds as an unpaid servant and subsequently allying herself with a butcher.

A butcher.

Amelia could hardly credit the topsy-turvy careening of her world. They could wrap her new stepfather's occupation up in fancy phrasing and call him a meat wholesaler all they liked, but Amelia was quite certain the drawing rooms on Beacon Hill were abuzz with the news that one of the Adamses of Boston, a Daughter of the Revolution and descendant of signers of the Mayflower Compact, had allied herself with a common tradesman. An Irish butcher, no less. Despite her mother's protestations of happiness, Amelia herself could hardly credit it if she were not currently residing in the butcher's house.

A breeze lifted the hair from Amelia's nape, cooling her damp skin and turning the glowing mantle of autumnal glory into derisive whispers of the life she had been cruelly torn from, never to enjoy again.

A burst of laughter proceeded a merry party of girls

emerging from a shop across the busy street. Amelia ducked into a small alley of the main street of Boston commerce lest any of the party prove to be among her former acquaintances. She could not bear to be the recipient of speculative glances or pitying looks the way she had been when news of her brother's scandalous embezzlements and flight to parts unknown had first played across the lips of Boston's finest.

If only she could hide herself so easily from the thoughts inside her own head and the wounds still pricking her heart and her pride.

That was the worst of it. Truly. Her pride.

Though she would be loath to admit that to anyone, even her closest friends, Tori and Lenore. Her whole life, up to the point that stuck sharp and fast like a knife in her back, had been a series of incidents designed either to flaunt or heighten her pride in herself, her family, her elegant looks.

Her future . . .

Her destiny was not now, and never had been, in her hands.

She released a breath, more sob than sigh; the sound mingled amidst the rustling, whispering leaves. Her shadow stretched ahead in the alleyway, elongated and impossibly shaped as it tapered away to nothing. Just like her prospects. It was almost comical. Or it would have been, if only the entire story had happened to someone else.

And that only made matters worse.

She leaned against the stone wall of an old and elegant garden, all too easily able to picture the parties and soirees this space would harbor amidst its welltended rhododendrons and box yews. Biting back her self-absorbed sorrow as it fought for release, she swallowed hard and faced her situation. She was no longer a society maiden expected to sigh and wilt and drape herself in feminine malaise from some balcony while her suitors vied for her attention, offering her all manner of sweetmeats in an attempt to lighten her mood. This year there would be no one trying to tease a Christmas kiss from her beneath a clump of mistletoe in an attempt to gain her agreement to a match.

How terribly spoiled she'd been.

The breeze that had teased her nape whipped stronger, pulling strands loose from her sedate chignon until wisps of inky black tangled about her face. Gray clouds filled the sky over the buildings around her. The weather was changing.

How quickly. How quickly everything had changed. How desperately she wanted to change it again.

She bit her lip again.

Change happened with haste, didn't it? There was nothing sedate or dignified about it. It just . . . happened. If only there were some way she could force a change in her destiny, to make a fresh start.

The thought quickened her heartbeat and tightened the twisting in her stomach. For a moment she felt on the verge of a precipice that would see her out of her current situation. Then as quickly, the wind died and the first spatters of rain began to fall.

"That'll do it." She pushed away from the garden wall, leaving her dreams of change and her remembrances of yesterday to battle among themselves. She'd already accomplished her goal for this day, trading a few of her tea gowns and walking outfits for pin money at the secondhand shop near Commonwealth

Avenue after refusing her stepfather's offer to give her an allowance.

She ducked her head and hurried her pace as she returned to the corner of Milk Street, almost at a complete run. Her lips curved over a laugh. She brushed past a stranger, barely avoiding a collision with him, and ran full tilt into a newspaper cart, knocking it, herself, and the papers to the ground with a thump.

Amelia Lawrence, former scion, Boston's finest arbiter of all that was fashionable and acceptable, sat in stunned silence as the rain pelted her from above. The cart's owner was nowhere in sight and the stranger who'd precipitated her fall had thankfully rounded a corner and disappeared. There was no one to witness her less-than-graceful performance.

"Oh, Amelia, how low you have gone." Derision laced her humor as she pushed to her knees and gathered the papers back onto the cart. When she bent for the last of the spilled issues, the wind blew again, swirling the pages open and she read the advertisement even as the ink began to run.

Proper gentleman seeks a wife to grace his grand estate and fill his life with elegance and charm. Contentment secured.

Her breath caught and the precipice rushed toward her again as further details of his suitability and an address completed the piece.

She gathered up the major pile of white-and-black muck and bundled it under the cart; it was ruined, for all intents and purposes. Then she rummaged in her bag for a coin to leave for the cart's owner, should he ever reappear. With one paper under her arm, she raced down the street with an entirely new goal in mind.

Change happened with haste, didn't it?

So be it.

One

Curled in a chair by the windows of her bridal suite, Amelia Lawrence prayed for dawn. And inspiration.

Time was running out to decide exactly what to do about the body on the bed.

"Amelia Lawrence *Mitchell*," she corrected aloud. Her new last name felt leaden on her tongue as her shuddering whisper barely echoed across the hotel room. She rubbed her arms to chase away shivers caused only partly by the dreary coal lumps long since turned to ash in the brazier. The silk shawl she'd retrieved from the dressing room provided little comfort. She sighed and turned her gaze outward.

Wagons rumbled past on the streets below. Doors opened and shut in the hotel's muffled depths. Daylight had yet to struggle through the clouds and smoke that hung over Chicago like a pall as they had throughout her week-long visit to the bustling shores of Lake Michigan.

An ominous portent in retrospect. But who could have known?

"Mrs. Robert T. Mitchell." She tried her new moniker

again. Equally foreign, yet just formal enough to bolster
what little confidence she had left in her new circumstances. She squared her shoulders under the cool silk
covering her nightgown. What decisions were left to
her had been made hours ago, really. She awaited only
the touch of dawn to begin.

Her eyes slid across the gloom to the figure of
her new husband on the bed. Her bridal bed. His
deathbed.

> *Proper gentleman seeks a wife to grace his grand estate*
> *and fill his life with elegance and charm. Contentment*
> *secured.*

She'd looked forward to sending the news of her
marriage to a man of wealth and power to the papers
back home once this very day dawned. Lord forgive
her, she'd composed the note several hundred times
on her long trip to Chicago. She could almost laugh
at her self-absorbed naivete. What was the proper
form for advertising one's new husband was wed and
dead within the span of a few short hours?

She swallowed back the hysteria threatening as her
throat burned.

Who among her friends back in Boston would believe that she could feel so very lost over the death of
a man she had known for only a week? Or think her
loss was not rooted solely in the prospect of social disaster? She could not expect even her mother and new
stepfather to show her more understanding than she
had shown them when she'd learned of their match.

Robert Mitchell had been kind to her. He'd proved
a proper gentleman indeed, if a little older than she'd

envisioned. Still, she liked the humor twinkling in the depths of his deep blue eyes. The rumble of laughter as he'd refused to take himself too seriously. And the way he'd listened to her, really listened to what she had to say, not just looked at her like an ornament he was interested in obtaining. She'd grown quite fond of him in the few days they had spent together.

For the better part of a week, Robert took her to dinner and the theater and acted the perfect gentleman. For long hours they'd sat in the lobbies of each other's hotels sipping tea, or walked along the promenade overlooking Lake Michigan, talking about their lives. Getting comfortable with one another. Deciding whether they could face the future together. This week had proved to be one of the most peaceful in her life. Until the most unnatural, comfortless quiet had settled over their wedding night.

Contentment secured. She'd actually come to believe that maybe it could be true, even if Robert Mitchell had a few more gray hairs than she'd ever pictured in her dreams of a future bridegroom.

"And so they wed and lived happily ever after." Her voice caught as she whispered the ending to the stories her nursery maid had told her every night before blowing out the candle. Her head throbbed.

She was not going to cry, not again.

Robert's ever-after had been too short. When he hadn't answered her. When she had taken his hand and looked into his eyes and realized they were already fixed on the world beyond, then her tears had flowed. But they had been as much or more for her as for him. The shock had sharpened her thoughts and stopped her from panicking or screaming for help.

Her husband was beyond any earthly assistance, just as her father had been when she had gone into his study a decade before and found him slumped in his chair.

She was alone. The fate she had seized and made her own had crumbled around her despite her efforts to control it. What happened next would once again be determined by others, by strangers, by the dictates of fickle society and its expectations.

Would the rest of the world recognize a wife of only a few hours? Would they even recognize the marriage as legal, given that they had not spent their wedding night together? Should she pack her things and strike out to find the elderly couple she had met on the train from New York and seek their assistance as they had insisted she promise to do if her plans did not work out?

It would have been so easy to slip away from the hotel and this dilemma. Use her tickets home and what little cash she had found in Robert's wallet to return to Boston, as if the simple ceremony in the judge's chambers had never occurred. Too easy. And so very dishonorable. So very like her brother's reaction to scandal.

But the thought never tempted her as it had him. She would not play the coward. She could not join Jonathan in running from responsibility for the choices she had made, no matter how unfortunate.

She was Mrs. Robert Thomas Mitchell of Warm Springs, Illinois. She would take her husband's body home. Home to lie beside his first wife's, overlooking the lake where the loons' cries echoed, just as he'd described so vividly. She owed him that much respect. She wanted there to be no question over the validity of their marriage, nothing to stop her from doing just that, and so she had kept her long vigil through the night.

Surely Robert's heirs would reimburse her and provide the means for her to return to Boston with her dignity intact.

The faint tapping on a door down the hall caught her attention. Her wedding night was over at last. Time to face the morning. Time to face the mourning. She could have laughed out loud at the wordplay, but she pressed her lips together, lest whoever she discovered in the hall think her mad or hysterical. The throbbing in her head surged with the effort.

"Help." The burning in her throat made the sound more a croak than a cry. Her limbs protested as she pulled herself out of the chair and crossed to the door.

"Please." Genuine panic spurred the urgency in her plea as the emotions she had held at bay throughout the night surged through her. She peered down the hall at the startled maid delivering a breakfast to another guest. "I think there's something wrong with my husband."

An hour later she stood in the center of the chamber while the local doctor attended Robert and the officious hotel manager hovered in the doorway. Carstairs, she believed he'd said his name was. He no doubt wanted to make sure that news of the tragedy in the bridal suite did not reach the rest of his guests.

"He's gone, I'm afraid." The doctor, a man who looked to be not much younger than Robert, straightened from his examination, perused her briefly, but didn't quite meet her gaze. "Most likely his heart. He would not have suffered. There was nothing you could have done. It looks to have been instantaneous. I am very sorry for your loss, Mrs. Mitchell."

Even knowing the words were coming, even telling herself he had been dead throughout the night, hearing the doctor make the official pronouncement sent a wave of shock through her.

"I am sorry for your loss also. Is there anyone we can contact to come for you, Mrs. Mitchell?" Carstairs, the portly hotel manager, said in an unctuous tone just barely above a whisper as he pulled out a handkerchief and mopped his brow. "One of the staff will dress him for you."

It had taken her a moment to realize the man was addressing her. More leer than concern lurked in the gaze he passed over her, making her conscious of her pale peach satin nightgown, white silk shawl and her hair still loose over her shoulders.

It didn't matter.

She shook her head and clutched her shawl tighter as she returned her attention to the figure on the bed. "There's no one in Chicago for either of us."

Most likely his heart, the doctor had said as he shook his head and pulled the sheet over Robert. He looked at her at last, a glance of sympathy tinged with a twist of skepticism as he donned his hat and handed a bottle to the maid, whispering some instructions.

"Mrs. Mitchell? Mrs. Mitchell?" The manager was still talking to her, but she kept her gaze locked on the bed she had shared with her husband, if only briefly. It was the questions in the doctor's gaze, the words he *hadn't* said, that held her horrified.

"We can help you with arrangements for a funeral if you like," the manager offered.

His heart. Contentment secured.

Did the doctor and the manager believe the rigors of having a young bride had done Robert in? Had they? She couldn't seem to pull her gaze from the bed. Somehow, throughout the night, it had never occurred to her that she might indeed be the cause of Robert's demise. That if they had not wed, he would not be lying there right now.

"I want to take my husband home," she managed at last.

"Of course." Mr. Carstairs sounded relieved; this problem would soon disappear from his midst. "We'll make all the arrangements. And we'll move you to another room so you can rest in the meantime."

She could only nod her head as a rising tide of guilt broke over her.

"Shock," the doctor said to the maid, a girl hardly older than Amelia.

"You stay with Mrs. Mitchell, Mariah," Carstairs said. "For the rest of the day, if need be. I will assign your duties to someone else."

"Very good, sir."

The door clicked shut as Carstairs and the doctor made a hasty exit.

"I'm so sorry, Robert," Amelia whispered. A shiver shook her body and made her voice quaver. She hated feeling so weak and defeated.

"Don't be sorry, miss. I mean, missus." The maid came to stand beside her. "Mr. Mitchell was very happy. He told me so when I brought him his breakfast that morning ye first came to Chicago."

"Really? Mr. Mitchell spoke to you about me?" Amelia couldn't keep the skepticism from her voice as she finally looked away from the bed and focused on the maid. "Mariah, is it?"

A touch of her old imperious manner from the days she'd reigned over Boston's drawing rooms must have crept in, too, as the young blonde blushed from her neck to her ears and looked away. "Aye, although I beg yer pardon for intruding on yer grief, Mrs. Mitchell. Shall I find ye something a mite warmer to wear while we wait for Mr. Carstairs to send up the keys to yer new room?"

"Don't apologize." Amelia said as another shiver wracked her. "I did not mean to sound harsh. I am cold, but I would very much like to hear what my husband had to say about me and our . . . er . . . brief courtship."

The maid brightened at Amelia's more approachable tone. Her hazel eyes shimmered with sympathy when they met Amelia's. "He didn't say much, other than he'd met his future wife and ye were someone he was proud to be with, someone he hoped he could make happy and help find the joy and love ye deserved. Someone he knew had a good heart and would make him happy for the rest of his life."

Amelia glanced over at the bed. He thought she had a good heart. No one in Boston had ever said such a thing about Amelia Lawrence. No one. The magnitude of her loss struck her from an entirely new perspective. Tears hovered. "Robert said all that the day after I arrived?"

"Not all. Most he told me yesterday when I helped him move up to this room from his other one. He was fair bursting with pride that you'd agreed to marry him."

Mariah walked over to the dressing room door as she talked. "He said ye'd made him the happiest of men. And that's quite a gift, I'm thinking, for anyone, any day. Especially if it turns out to be yer last."

She was a gift, even for his last day on earth?

A notion she'd have to think about. Later.

Amelia felt immensely grateful despite her inclination to dismiss all the kind words as the maid stepped into the dressing room. Her head ached and another set of shivers shook her, but the guilt had receded just a bit. She'd given Robert happiness for a short time, at least. That was a small comfort.

"Ye haven't much in the way of clothes suitable for mourning." Mariah emerged with a simple brown wool gown, one Amelia had worn several days at a time during her journey here. "This looks a little worse for wear, but it will at least be warmer than yer nightwear."

There'd been a time when she'd given her cast-off gowns to charity, sometimes even before she'd worn them once. Now she felt embarrassed by her obviously strained finances. And the circumstances that brought her to this match. "I didn't just marry Robert because he promised to take me to his grand estate, you know. I wasn't just here for his money."

Heat burned her cheeks. What had possessed her to make the statement aloud?

"I know that, Mrs. Mitchell." Mariah's no-nonsense tone accepted even those words. "He told me that, too. And I can see ye have that good heart he spoke of." She nodded and laid the dress over a chair. "My sister works in a dress shop not far from here. We'll get ye settled for a lie-down in yer new room and I'll send for her. We'll have ye in proper mourning by tomorrow, don't ye fret."

She turned her attention to the drawers of the bureau and opened them to bring out the petticoats and undergarments Amelia would need to face the world as a wife in mourning. Cold and weary, Amelia marveled at the maid's efficiency. After over a year of dressing herself when Jonathan ran off with the bulk of her mother's money, it felt odd to have someone fetching her clothes for her. Odd and strangely comforting, as if Robert were still looking out for her through his friend.

"You don't think he minded that we were strangers before last week?" The question fell from her lips before she could call it back. What was possessing her? Amelia Lawrence would never speak so familiarly with a servant, no matter how friendly she seemed. Amelia Mitchell seemed a far different creature.

"He said he knew ye were the one for him through yer letters." Mariah looked up. "For what it's worth, my mum came here from London to marry without ever laying eyes on my dad. He worked in her uncle's butcher shop and my great-uncle arranged it all. They've been married going on twenty-five years now and have six of us to show for it."

"Thank you," Amelia said as she finally let go of the shawl she had clutched through the long night, and started to dress. Her thoughts careened. A butcher. Maybe her mother had made a good choice. Would she and Robert have had a chance to be so happy, despite their age difference? Neither of them would ever know.

A knock at the door proved to be another maid with the key to a new room. One where she could sleep. Alone. As alone as she had felt for most of the last year. Indeed, for most of her life.

The two days intervening between Robert's death and her departure from Chicago passed in a blur induced by the emotional strain and the laudanum Mariah dosed her with, following the doctor's directions.

Now, dressed from head to toe in full, unrelenting mourning black, Amelia left the hotel for the first time since her marriage. The wide silk moire skirts might not be up to the latest Boston styles, but Mariah's sister had been quite pleased to trade it for one pale pink satin ball gown and to sketch others in her small collection in exchange for the black, net-covered bonnet, kid gloves, and demi-boots to complete the outfit.

Accompanied by the maid and the hotel manager, Amelia alighted from a carriage provided by the undertaker and stood in front of the train station, a cavernous brick-and-granite building. A noisy crowd of people from all walks of life swirled past them, leaving her feeling more than a little lost and quite dizzy. Her head still pounded. Her throat burned.

"Do you feel all right, Mrs. Mitchell?" Carstairs caught her elbow in his meaty grip as she swayed. "Why don't we find a seat indoors? The stationmaster is a friend—I am sure he can find us a quiet place to await your train. You are so very young for such a sad trip all alone. I only wish my duties at the hotel could spare me long enough to give you comfort on your journey."

"You have been too kind already, Mr. Carstairs," she managed.

The thought of being alone with this man made her queasy, as if she did not feel poorly enough already. Something about the obsequious Carstairs and his leering glances made her exceedingly uncomfortable, despite her gratitude for all the assistance he had rendered in arranging for her to travel home with Robert's body.

She'd observed that men often considered widows easy conquests; her brother had sought to give them comfort often enough. She hoped she was misinterpreting the hotel manager's attentions—her own husband had barely been gone two days. It must just be the effects of the opiate and her headache that skewed her thoughts. Still, the man's fingers lingered on her arm.

"I must say that Mr. Mitchell was a lucky man." Carstairs's eyes narrowed as he peered at her more intently. She shivered, despite the bright sunshine. Carstairs had tried several times to see her alone since Robert's body had been sent to the undertaker's. Luckily, Mariah had been there and pleaded exhaustion and grief for her.

"If you will pardon my being so forward," he continued, "black becomes you, Mrs. Mitchell. You have a fragility that is quite endearing. I do not believe you will be alone in your grief for very long. And if you should return to Chicago—"

"I believe Mr. Lindstrom, the undertaker, would like a word with you, sir."

Whatever Carstairs was about to propose was mercifully cut off by Mariah's timely intervention. "I'll take Mrs. Mitchell inside while you two gentlemen make the rest of the arrangements for Mr. Mitchell."

Carstairs turned a malevolent eye on the maid but released Amelia's arm at last. "I'll see you inside, then."

"I hope your championing me will not cause you trouble later," Amelia said to the maid as Carstairs waddled over to the undertaker and his helper standing next to the hearse bearing Robert's casket.

"He doesn't bother with me much." Mariah wrinkled her nose in much the same way Amelia's friend Lenore had been wont to do a couple of years ago whenever she was compared to her sainted elder sister. Amelia felt a pang of loneliness for the circle of young women who had once practically lived in each other's pockets when they had all been the cream of Boston society. How very different their lives had turned out to be from the ones they had anticipated so eagerly only a short time ago.

"My brother Danny works as the doorman." Mariah dismissed Carstairs with a shrug. "He let that one know back when I first started that if he tried anything with me there'd be consequences."

Mariah smiled and looked her up and down. "He was right, though, with yer hair and fair coloring, dark colors suit ye."

"Thank you." Amelia felt more relieved than she could admit, even to the maid she had come to think of as a friend rather than a servant. She felt so shallow worrying about her looks, under the circumstances. "I suppose most women have a care for the impression they make, no matter what. I don't want my husband's family and neighbors to think poorly of the choice he made."

"No need to worry on that account. They'll see yer good heart same as he did."

Amelia doubted that. Robert Mitchell and this loyal little maid had been the only people who had ever looked at Amelia Lawrence and seen a good heart. The future she had lost came rushing back at her with that thought and she swayed on her feet.

"The hotel cook packed you a nice basket with a full jar of tea." Mariah linked her arm with Amelia's and guided her up a set of granite steps toward the wide glass-and-wood doorway into the train station. "There's some water and meat pastries to last ye on yer trip. And some nice apples my mum sent along, too. Ye be sure and eat more than ye have these past days. It would ruin the effect if ye was to faint dead away at their feet when ye arrive."

The black net veiling on her bonnet billowed out as they entered the cavernous building with its vaulted ceilings. The smell of the trains permeated the bustling room despite the amount of space. Hot metal and machine oil—a nauseating mix.

"Over there are some benches, missus. How about we wait there for Mr. Carstairs and the undertaker to get yer husband settled on the train." Hefting the basket on one arm, Mariah put her other around Amelia for support.

They headed through the crowd inside the building. All these people going about their business, arriving and departing. Snatches of conversations cut through the din. Greetings, farewells, complaints, and worried utterances—if only she did not feel so wretched, this was exactly the kind of place she normally would have found fascinating. Not as sophisticated as Beacon Hill drawing rooms, but it was guessing at the real stories of the passersby that would have fascinated her in other circumstances.

"Promise you will come home for Christmas." A pretty young girl dressed in the latest fashion was pleading with a handsome, if somewhat rumpled, man standing in too intimate a proximity to be anything other than a relative—although he did not look to be of the same station as the girl from the roughness of his ill-fitting clothes. A lover perhaps? She shuddered at the turn in her thoughts brought on by Carstairs's avid ogling.

"I beg your pardon," Amelia murmured as she stumbled and accidently brushed the man's arm in passing. Once she was settled on the train she would feel better, she assured herself. No more laudanum, no matter how her head pounded or her throat ached.

Promise you'll come home for Christmas.

The plea burned into Amelia. No matter how rough he looked, at least that man had someone who cared about him. Someone who would miss him. Her own Christmas was sure to be a very bleak one at best. How selfish of her to worry about that when her husband would never see another.

"Must you leave today, Michael? You only just arrived. Promise you will come home for Christmas at the very least?"

A widow, draped in black and leaning heavily on her maid's arm, brushed by with a barely audible "I beg your pardon" as she headed to a pair of benches near the Illinois Central ticket booth. She was not from around here, the lawman's side of U.S. Marshal Michael Thompson's brain noted, her accent crisp and cool like the autumn breezes outside.

"You know I can't make promises."

Michael chuckled as he looked down at the small pout settling on his little sister's face. The velvet-trimmed bonnet she had clamored for on their shopping trip yesterday framed her heart-shaped features to perfection and made her eyes seem enormous. "Keep practicing, Katie. By the time you come out, you'll be ready to wind even the most hard-hearted of suitors around your thumb."

"Then you must have no heart at all." Miss Katherine Eugenia Thompson's lips pouted further outward, but humor twinkled in the depths of her green eyes as she looked up at her brother and smiled at the compliment despite her attempt to wheedle the impossible from him. His heart tugged. At sixteen, her beauty already rivaled her mother's. Those future suitors would never stand a chance against the combination of her intelligence and charm.

"I made it home for your birthday," he reminded her as the crowd from an arriving train swarmed past them. He guided her over to the bench near the one occupied by the slender widow. "And have stayed for almost a week. But I must get back to work."

"You stayed but a few days and the last time you were home was just for overnight. Papa is not getting any younger, you know." Katie's pout returned and this time her complaints very nearly echoed the same ones used by his stepmother only last night when he'd made his farewells.

"Katie." He let the warning ring clear in his tone as he raised a brow to quell the list of arguments he felt certain she'd memorized to convince him of the need for his return to the city to take his place in their father's law firm. He'd heard them often enough from her mother's lips over the past three years or more.

And they echoed all too often in his own mind.

Katie looked away for a moment, fixing her gaze on the myriad people swirling past them. She put her gloved hand on his and looked up at him in earnest. "I didn't mean to vex you, Michael. I know you get annoyed when Mama plagues you with these questions."

"Your mother is just concerned."

"We all miss you so." Katie frowned again. This time genuine concern knit her brows together. "I barely remember Will. I could not bear it if something happened to you. And it would shatter Papa."

I barely remember Will.

The knife edge of pain, always close at the mention of their elder brother, twisted at her words. She'd not even been ten when Will's murder changed the course of Michael's life.

"I'm doing this for Will." He put his hand over hers and squeezed. "Papa understands. And so did Eugenia at one time."

"Mama says it is time for you to give up your quest and settle down. Did you not find even one of the women she introduced to you this week interesting?"

"Interesting?" He rolled his eyes. He could hardly connect that word to the parade of simpering debutantes his stepmother had produced during his brief visit. "Only if I am concerned with gossip or matching colors and fabrics, depending on the season."

Katie laughed aloud. "Is there anything more to life?" she mocked.

Knowing his sister had a passion for classical painting and had been indulged with an array of tutors to rival his and Will's, he doubted she would ever lack for intelligent conversational gambits.

"The 9:15 to LaSalle, McLean—" The stationmaster's call forestalled any further conversation, "—Decatur, Centralia and Cairo, boarding on Track Three."

"That's me." Still holding his sister's hands in his, he signaled to the Thompson coachman waiting discreetly by the wide station doors. The widow and her maid stood also, joined by a portly man with hair slicked over the top of his pate in an attempt to hide a growing bald spot.

"Take good care of her, Arthur." He waited until the coachman joined them.

"You can count on me." The coachman he'd known for most of his life tipped his bowler. "And you take care of yourself, young sir."

"Don't forget to write." With her eyes suddenly wide and a few wayward curls escaping the confines of her bonnet, Katie looked far more the little sister he remembered than the young woman of sophistication she was becoming.

He squeezed her fingers a final time and kissed her cheek. "Take care, sweeting. Don't break too many hearts while I'm away."

"If you don't come home for Christmas I'm going to walk around with a branch of mistletoe tied to my head and let strangers kiss me at will," Katie declared.

"The look on Eugenia's face might be worth the risk

of surprising you in mid-celebration." He laughed. "No promises."

Katie's grip on his fingers tightened. Tears hovered at the corners of her eyes. "Just promise you will come home to stay soon. That will be enough."

He couldn't really promise even that. But she was too young to realize it. "Anything to put the smile back in those eyes. Thanks for coming to see me off."

She threw herself into his arms and gave him the same hug she had been giving him since she'd been old enough to toddle across the nursery floor. "Take care, Mikey," she whispered as she clung to his lapels.

"All aboard the 9:15 Central Illinois to—" the stationmaster began his final call.

With a last squeeze he pulled back and reached for the valise the coachman handed him. "I have to go."

He had to run to make it to Track Three as the large engine began to belch huge clouds of steam. The widow he'd noticed earlier was pulling her hand from the grasp of her escort. The man seemed reluctant to surrender her fingers.

Even beneath the black netting, Michael could see she was very young to have suffered the loss of a husband. Young and quite pale. Perhaps she was mourning the loss of a parent. His sympathy surged. Though he'd been just eleven when his mother passed away, he remembered how lonely and adrift he'd felt.

"Thank you again for all you have done, Mr. Carstairs. I'm sure I can manage from here."

"Let me at least see you aboard the train."

"No." Her answer was short and horrified as she waved off his attempt to take her arm.

"Could I be of assistance?" he offered. "I could escort the young lady to her seat."

So strong was the flora scent laced with sweat permeating the portly gentleman, he must have bathed in it. No wonder the widow looked bilious. The man hesitated, "Well—"

The maid accompanying the pair brightened at his intrusion. "That's very generous of ye, sir. That will solve all concerns, don't ye think, missus? Here's her luncheon basket—I'm sure the hotel cook packed enough to spare a bite for ye if ye have the need."

So the young lady was a widow. He accepted the basket the maid offered him with a broad smile for the amount of information she'd packed into so few words. He didn't bother to explain that his stepmother's cook had prepared a similar basket for him already. Nor that he'd given it to a ragged-looking girl about Katie's age outside the building. Once he stepped onto the railcar, he wanted to blend in with the other passengers. Not appear as one of the privileged.

"Last call for the Illinois Central 9:15. Last call." The stationmaster's bellow halted anything else the man might have said.

"I can't miss this train. Thank you for your offer, sir. Good-bye, Mr. Carstairs." Panic edged the widow's voice as she clutched Michael's arm and they took the final steps to reach the railcar.

He put his hands on her narrow waist and lifted her up onto the steps just as the train started to move.

"Good-bye, Mariah," she rasped. Billows of steam blowing back from the engine swallowed the pair on the platform as the car lurched forward at an increasing rate.

The benches in the passenger car were crowded. He found a spot in the front for the widow, next to a kindly-looking woman and her two children who scooted over to make room for the younger woman.

"Thank you so much for your kindness." A fleeting smile touched the weary features of the woman who could not quite meet his questioning gaze as he settled her basket on the floor beside her feet. She was definitely from New England, judging from her clipped speech, if his university days in Boston were any indication. Dark circles rimmed her eyes and her lips were quite pale. She must have really loved her husband to suffer so.

He touched his hat. "No problem. I'm sorry for your loss."

She nodded her thanks again and he strode to the back of the car. Throughout the day he kept his eye on the drooping shoulders of the widow. She barely glanced out the windows at the landscape passing by. Even as the car emptied and the woman and her children departed in McLean, she stayed almost rooted in place next to the car wall as they sped through the heart of Illinois.

It was approaching dark when they finally neared his destination. Had anyone missed him? Luckily the comings and goings of a ne'er-do-well drifter were of little interest to most folks. He'd gotten off the train in Decatur long enough to drop his latest report in the post. Now he'd continue the hunt for the last of his brother's killers and the money they'd stolen in the process.

He couldn't help wondering how much farther the little widow had to travel in her sad journey.

Two

Motion.

Mmmm. Rhythmic. Soothing. Amelia drifted amid fluctuating patterns, rising and falling.

Salt tinged the air.

Had she gone on a sea voyage?

Papa had taken her on a trip to Charleston once. Jonathan had stayed home with the mumps. She'd had Papa all to herself.

The memory made Amelia smile despite her discomfort. Had he invited her to accompany him again?

Somehow that did not seem quite right. This was different.

She was chilled through and through and her throat felt hot and sore. She needed a good strong cup of tea, a fresh blanket to ward off the chilly sea air, and a valiant lieutenant to help sharpen her flirtation skills.

She opened her eyes and struggled to focus. She was very tired, more tired than she could ever remember being. How odd, but then she seemed to think she'd been ever so busy lately. Doing what? Something was very wrong. She knew that in her bones. But she could not quite remember what.

Her thoughts jumbled together. The more she

tried to concentrate, the worse it became until she gave up the struggle and snuggled against the warmth at her side.

Hmmm. She opened her eye again and peered upward. There was the handsome lieutenant she'd requested. Chiseled jawline, broad shoulders, and all. His hair was a bit rumpled but it would do. Despite the fog etching her vision, she was quite certain he was the most attractive seafarer she had ever had the pleasure to gaze upon. He frowned down at her. Obviously a serious sort. Probably career-oriented and no-nonsense. He would be a challenge to her skills despite the warmth of his embrace. So much the better.

The faint line of a scar rode his lower lip. A sabre fight? A duel at sea? Defending a maiden's honor? Perhaps she'd swoon when she elicited the story from him and gain his embrace that way. The plan had enough merit to warrant further contemplation.

Only, why was he already embracing her?

Did it matter? He was warm and apparently already in her thrall. If only she could remember the thrill of getting him there. She sighed, a ragged, raspy sound.

"We're almost there, hang on." His voice, deep and lovely, reverberated against her cheek as she started to drift away again.

Almost there. Had they reached port already? She wondered lazily where *there* was.

She forced her eyes open again and peered blearily forward. A large house loomed in front of them. Who would have built such a place so close to a harbor? Perhaps she was not on a sea voyage at all. Where had the lieutenant come from if she was not aboard ship? Where was Papa?

Lights burned in the tall windows of the house like a thousand tiny stars, welcoming her home.

Home.

Papa was gone long ago. Her home was gone, too. And Jonathan. And . . . and . . . she couldn't quite remember. So many losses. Nothing was dependable, not even her memories.

Another sigh rasped from her depths. My, how her chest ached. How strong and dependable the lieutenant's arms felt.

Her heart swelled. The burning in her throat tightened even as her mind swirled. The effort to hold her head up exhausted her. She closed her eyes and sank back against his solid warmth. The lights from the windows still danced inside her eyelids.

Somewhere in the recesses of her mind, she knew something about this house. Something important, but at the moment her thoughts spun out of her control. The lieutenant's boots rang against the steps taking them up onto the broad porch she had spied a moment before.

But if there were no ship, no sea voyage, the man holding her would not likely be a real lieutenant, would he?

"Open the door," he shouted loud enough to wake the dead as he came to a halt.

The dead. The phrase stabbed through her. Dead. Robert was dead.

Robert?

"Oh, the poor dear." A woman's voice followed the sound of a door opening.

"Who is that, Michael?" a second woman called. "Is she the reason you disappeared?"

"Does she belong to you?" A man's voice boomed now from farther inside the beautiful home. Not her man, this time. He still held her securely in his arms. Michael, they'd called him. Michael. The most wonderful of names.

Warmth and a slash of light poured from the open door along with the babble of too many questions for her to sort through.

"Hurry up now, don't dawdle," the first woman's voice quavered.

"We have to get out of the way first, or he'll never get in," a man inside gruffed.

"Of course. Come in, Michael, come in."

There was a rustle of movement. Like the leaves on the trees lining Milk Street. Perhaps that was it. She'd been listening to the leaves, then running in the rain. She'd collided with a man at the corner. Perhaps she'd hit her head and that is why it hurt so and why all her thoughts were fuzzy. Amelia could only think how appropriate it was that she was being carried across the threshold of her new home. Except this wasn't quite right, was it? She wanted to protest, to explain, but it all seemed too difficult.

Her mind spun again. The lights blazing in the interior of the house, so welcoming only moments before, now seemed much too bright. The dull thumping at her temples, eased by the crisp, cold air outside, returned with a vengeance as the warmth of the house swallowed her. She groaned aloud, but the sound came out as a pitiful little squeak of protest.

"Oh, my."

"Where did you find her, Michael dear?"

"And why bring her here?"

The two ladies and the stern gentleman trailed them, still peppering Michael with questions.

"She practically collapsed in my arms at the train station," her faux lieutenant huffed. Michael, wasn't that his name? Like the archangel. Where was he taking her?

"Festive, could you see if the doctor is about? This is one of his days in Warm Springs, is it not?" Michael didn't sound very angelic; his tone rang with command.

"Perhaps you'd care to enlighten us all as to who your visitor is."

She felt cushions beneath her and her forward progress stopped as Michael surrendered her to them. She missed the security of his arms as the motion spun on inside her head and they were no longer there to anchor her.

Fingers touched her forehead, cool and gentle. Something warm was being drawn over her.

"She claims to be Mrs. Robert Mitchell." Michael's voice again, so close and yet so far.

"Robert's wife?"

"This is Amelia Lawrence?"

"She appears a trifle younger than I had thought."

"You know her?" Her guardian angel seemed surprised.

"We . . . knew of her. She's prettier than I imagined."

"I told you she would be pretty, Clara."

"Hush, Cora, now is not the time."

Robert's wife. She was Robert's wife. No, his widow. Leaden memories of the few days since her marriage dropped on Amelia. The pain in her temples intensified. She'd never felt so ill. Surely she would not be far behind her husband in his journey to the afterlife.

Who were all these people? Relatives of Robert's? Here to greet the body and help her make arrangements? Had Carstairs or the undertaker thought to send a wire ahead of her journey? Her stomach swirled at the thought and her remaining energy seemed to leach away into the cushions beneath her. She didn't even have the strength to open her eyes and meet these unknown relatives or thank them for their kindness. If she could just rest. Just for a moment.

"But where is Robert?"

"There was . . . an unexpected complication . . . on his recent trip." Michael sounded far less assured.

"Was there an accident?"

"Is he all right?"

"This should explain. I picked it up from the post at the station just before I . . . met her."

Amelia winced at the sharp, crackling sound of papers being unfolded. Despite the warmth of the coverlet over her, she shivered. Gasps of dismay followed in varying tones as the wire's bald contents were read aloud, then repeated. Tears burned the backs of her eyes. For Robert. For his family. For herself. There would be so much to explain in the morning. But at the moment she could hold on no longer.

"Rest." Michael's command penetrated the haze.

Welcoming darkness closed in around her.

She awoke several more times amidst the haze. Always there were the voices, nowhere and everywhere, all at once. Lost in the light and dark surrounding her, she missed her angel, her valiant lieutenant.

"She's awake."

"Not really."

"Poor Robert—we really thought he would be so happy."

"Do you think she knows where she is?"

"To miss the funeral."

"It couldn't be helped."

"Drink this, dear. The doctor left it for you."

They offered her broth and some other concoction which tasted awful, but helped her throat. And then she would fade back into blessed darkness, chased by exhortations to rest.

When the fog finally cleared from Amelia's mind, she had no idea how long she had been ill, but was grateful to feel like herself again. Weak, but definitely herself. She would not be joining poor Robert in his final journey to the lake just yet, contrary to her fears that she would do just that. That was a good thing, despite the disloyalty behind that thought.

She studied her surroundings for a moment, noting the spacious bedroom with its walnut molding and tasteful, dark-blue walls. Ceiling-to-floor windows graced two adjacent walls. A pitcher and basin sat atop an ornately carved washstand in the corner. The need to splash some water on her face, to rinse her mouth, overwhelmed her. Surely she was rested enough to indulge such basic needs.

The four-poster bed she currently inhabited was sheltered by a lace canopy embroidered with dark-blue flowers, just the tiniest bit threadbare at the edges. Odd for a man of Robert's means, but probably a family heirloom. She would have to see about restoring it. She felt compelled to do whatever she could for Robert's home and family before she set about reclaiming her own life. Especially given the utterly inappropriate way she'd entered his home. It was the very least she could do for the man who had treated her as though she were the most exquisite thing he had ever encountered—from the moment they met until he passed from this world.

"I'm so sorry, Robert." She hadn't been much of a wife to him so far. She hoped she could do better by him now. And that would begin by making amends to his family and seeing to it that he had a proper funeral.

Thoughts of his funeral niggled at her until she sat up. What about Robert's funeral? The voices had said something about Robert's funeral. She needed to find out what was being done to honor him. She finger-combed the mass of hair tangled atop her head. She'd have to tidy herself first before she could accomplish any of her goals. And that meant making her way across the random-width planked floors to the washstand.

She took a deep breath and slid to the edge of the bed. Placing her feet carefully on the floor, she curled her toes from the cold, polished surface and steadied herself with one hand on the mattress. So far, so good. She stood, gathering one of the coverlets around her shoulders, when the door popped open before her.

"Good morning. Are you sure you should be up so soon after your fever broke?" The gentleman she had first seen at the train station in Chicago filled the doorway.

She stood in silence for a moment, transfixed by the easy smile tilting his lips, the comfortable way he angled himself against the doorjamb, and the fact that he made her more than conscious she had nothing on but a thin nightdress and a quilt. What on earth was he doing entering this bedroom as though he had every right? How was it possible for him to be here?

"Lieutenant." The title came of its own volition as her thoughts and memories mixed and his very presence made her uncertain. "Michael?"

He shrugged, but said nothing.

He'd helped her onto the train and been so kind. When they'd announced Warm Springs at last, she'd felt so very ill that seeing him on the platform had seemed a blessing. She remembered introducing herself, and then things had spun into blackness. How awful. There was something about a sea voyage and an angel jumbled in there. And strong arms. His strong arms. Is that why he felt free to enter this room without even knocking?

"I . . . I should get dressed before I receive visitors—"

She made a quick turn and took a step back toward the bed, lost her balance, and headed for the floor, only to find herself cradled once more against his chest. Held in his arms. The heat of his body seeped into hers, making her more conscious of the chill in the air and the state of her undress. He smelled of autumn leaves and rain on new grass. For a moment an unreasoning and wholly unbidden desire surged through her to stay right where she was for the foreseeable future.

Get hold of yourself, Amelia.

"This is getting to be a habit," he told her with another flash of that smile as he lifted her. He made her feel like she weighed next to nothing as he turned toward the bed. His rumpled dark hair glinted red in a wash of sunlight. She resisted the urge to smooth it into place.

"I can walk." Her voice sounded as unsteady as her legs had turned out to be.

"So I saw." He ignored her unspoken request. "But I think we'd both feel a bit better if you sat for a few moments before attempting it again. And I agree."

"You do?" She had lost all track of what he could possibly be agreeing to. The feel of his muscles flexing against her back and thighs despite his clothes, the quilt, and the thin fabric of her nightdress, pushed all other thoughts completely out of her head.

"You need to get dressed before you have the entire household in an uproar," he told her in a husky tone.

He bent and set her carefully on the bed, releasing her from the exquisite torment of his embrace. It didn't help. His face was so close to hers she could see the tiny flecks of blue in his steel-gray eyes, almost feel the thick fringe of their lashes sweeping against her cheek, and taste his breath on her tongue. She almost reached her finger up to trace the faint but familiar scar along one side of his lower lip. Impossible memories of a saber fight pricked her.

Her eyelids felt heavy. Her breathing quickened. The temptation to tilt her head for his kiss was nearly overwhelming. His fingers brushed the edge of the quilt as he pulled it tighter around her neck. Heat spiraled into her middle.

"Oh." Embarrassment singed her cheeks at the casual manner with which this stranger touched her, and at the wild thoughts rather than protests pulsing through her as he took such liberties.

Obviously she was not as much herself as she had assumed. Amelia Lawrence, the toast of Boston society, undone by a stranger's touch.

The easy smile curled his lips into a decidedly more pronounced upward curve. Was he deliberately provoking her? Trying to tease a reaction from her? Testing her? She struggled to ignore the deep disconcertion warming her face and the humor lighting his.

"You said something about the household." She tried diverting his attention—and her thoughts—from the madness he provoked. She'd thought him dashing in her delirium. He was far too galling for any such appellation. Too galling and too unkempt. Her fingers itched to smooth the disheveled crimp in his hair.

"That's right, you haven't really met the members, have you?" He straightened and rested his hands on his hips, either unaware of or unconcerned by the turmoil his presence in this bedchamber alone with her, his looming over her, caused. "Surely your husband told you all about us?"

No further details were forthcoming. Who was this man, this Michael? Why was he trying to fluster her?

She gritted her teeth, annoyed enough to slap him. He was entirely too comfortable, cavalier even, about her sensibilities and the respect due a recent widow.

She drew in a silent breath and let it out on a slow count to ten.

"No, I haven't met them." Her best polite disdain

shrouded her answer even as the disembodied voices from her illness played through her memory. "And what was discussed between my husband and me is private."

He slanted a disapproving eyebrow at her. Good— she hoped she had annoyed him in return.

"Well, there you are, Michael. I wondered where you had gotten off to, and here you've come ahead of me." One of the voices from her delirium preceded a genteel and elderly lady into the room. Michael practically sprang from the side of the bed.

"Oh, our sleeping beauty is awake at last. And sitting up." A diminutive woman with silver hair wound in a bun atop her head and dressed in a pewter-gray gown that might have been the height of fashion thirty years ago, bustled into the room with a light scent of lavender and a warm smile. A pale-blue woolen shawl covered her slender shoulders and brought out the lively color in eyes that sparkled with interest.

"Hello, my dear." The woman frowned and placed her hand on Amelia's forehead before nodding with satisfaction. "Not the least bit overhot despite the flush on your cheeks—good. You certainly look much better, too. We were all quite worried. Weren't we, Michael?"

"Not all our worries can possibly be resolved yet, Miss Cora," Michael answered cautiously. Amelia darted a glance up at him as he leaned casually against the bedpost, looking entirely too comfortable. His features carried the innocent air of a choirboy despite the dry edge to his tone.

"I-I am feeling much better, thank you," Amelia

managed, ignoring the hammering of her pulse brought on by the man in her bedroom. This poor woman must be scandalized, especially if she was a relation of Robert's. She was a new widow. There was decorum expected.

"Of course, but we'll take comfort in the small blessings." The woman patted Amelia's hand, apparently unaware of Michael's mixed message.

"You're feeling much better—that's wonderful," Cora continued. "In a day or two you may be ready to get up and sit in a chair. Then you can meet us all and get properly acquainted. I must tell Clara."

"Are you hungry, dear?" She reached over and plumped the pillows before settling them behind Amelia's back for support as she fussed without pausing long enough for Amelia to say anything. Not that any response seemed to be expected. "Oh, you must be. Days and days it's been. And you traveling all that way after poor Robert . . ."

Cora caught the last on a gasp and put a hand over her mouth. "Oh, my wayward tongue. You poor thing. You poor, poor dear. Don't think of it. You'll have a relapse and it will be all my fault. Rest now—I'll send Clara along with a tray and we'll get you fed and right as rain in the springtime. There's time enough for introductions and conversation once you've eaten and are really feeling up to snuff."

Her visitor turned toward the all-too-comfortable Michael, still leaning on the bedpost, and took his arm. "Come along, Michael. I believe Clara said something about more kindling and we'll need a hot stove to make tea.

"I'll be right back, dear," Cora offered over her

shoulder as she ushered him out of the room. Amelia was surprised that he went along so docilely. And without his own backward glance.

In a moment, she was alone again and breathless, as though she'd just run uphill. She'd never been so beset by any man before. Or irritated. What had been the purpose that brought him into this bedchamber in the first place? What had given him the idea he could take such liberties with her person? Her very skin felt branded by the touch of his fingers on the quilt edge, the flex of his muscles as he carried her. Was he just another Carstairs, albeit robed in a more attractive package?

Her illness must have taken far more out of her than she had realized if she found a man of such an obviously working-class background attractive. His manners, his dress, everything about him was far different from any of the usual gentlemen of her acquaintance. Her loss, and her illness, were the only explanations possible. She'd had no time to pull herself together and prepare to see anyone, let alone a man with blue-flecked eyes that looked as if they could pierce right through you.

"Amelia, get hold of yourself."

Desperation edged the command. She had enough worries without losing all control of herself and allowing her thoughts to dwell on someone who would be nothing but a memory a few weeks from now.

Who might be Robert's son, for all she knew.

"Oh, good heavens." What a horrible thought. She drew in several deep breaths and forced herself to calm down as she blew them out again.

She turned her thoughts to Cora. Whoever that little

lady was in this household, she was definitely used to dominating the conversation. She didn't seem old enough to be Robert's mother. A sister, maybe? An aunt?

Amelia sighed in frustration. She really was none the wiser for having encountered either visitor. The only thing she had learned, beyond the fact that she needed to offer Michael a wide berth in the future, was that she was most definitely in the right place.

This was Robert Mitchell's home. His grand estate. Or at least it had been.

Michael allowed Cora's prattling to drift over him as he escorted her down the steps. He'd learned early on that a strategically timed nod or a noncommittal hum were truly all Miss Cora Brown required in the way of conversational exchange. She far preferred carrying the lion's share of any dialogue. And that was fine with him.

His thoughts turned too easily to the young widow gracing Robert Mitchell's bedroom. Even recently ill, she was breathtaking. Soft enough to make a man's integrity turn to lust without a second thought, without any thought. All that lustrous dark hair against pale ivory skin. Ice-blue eyes, lush lips above the long column of her neck. The sight of her in nothing but a quilt and the thin folds of her nightdress had been unsettling to say the least. The feel of her in his arms nearly had him forsaking his honor to tumble her upon her dead husband's bed. He winced inwardly. He didn't have the freedom, or the time, to follow such inclinations, propriety be damned.

He shook his head.

"Oh, you don't think so?" Cora prodded him as they reached the landing below.

"Don't think so?" he repeated, biting back a groan. His thoughts had been so preoccupied with Robert's widow he'd lost all sense of Cora's conversation as they proceeded down the back hall to the kitchen.

"Why, that Robert's new wife will fit in here. Haven't you been listening, dear?"

"Yes, of course, Miss Cora. I'm sure she'll fit in just fine." Just as she had fit in his arms. All too well. "If she decides to stay."

"And why shouldn't she stay? It's not as if she has much to return to." Cora's cohort, Clara, wiped her hands on her apron as she paused in rolling out some biscuits.

"Of course she'll stay," Cora put in without giving Michael room to reply. "Why, we knew she would be the perfect addition, didn't we, Clara? She really needed a home. A family. Despite Robert's untimely demise, God rest his soul, there is no reason she can't find those here still."

"My sentiments exactly." Clara nodded for emphasis. "She's awake, then?"

"Yes, yes. Awake and ready to be fully recovered."

"Did you tell her about Robert? About the funeral?"

"Goodness, no. I thought we should all tell her together. First thing awake, with nary a moment to set herself to rights, just didn't seem the time to share such discomfiting news. Why, Michael had to steady her there in the bed, didn't you, dear?"

Steadying her had been the furthest thing from his mind. Pressing her back against the pillows and testing the limits of her softness had been the thought burning foremost in his head. But that certainly was not what Cora and Clara were waiting to hear. He offered them the truth.

"She was up and about when I got to the room. She slipped a little and I helped her back to bed."

"Ah." Cora and Clara echoed this together, their eyes round with that mixture of interest and concern only the two of them seemed able to achieve.

"Then it's as well you got there first." Cora smiled at him and patted his shoulder. "I'm certain she's hungry, Clara. We need to help her get her strength back."

"Yes, of course. I've got some soup on the stove. I'll set her up a nice tray."

"I'll help you, dear."

The two of them bustled about the kitchen like two hens, clucking softly together. Michael couldn't help but smile as he took the kindling bucket out the back door and set about refilling it. A few minutes wielding a hatchet would help him regain perspective. They'd pinned their hopes on Robert's widow. He only prayed she wouldn't disappoint them. At least now that Mrs. Mitchell was gaining her health back, he could return to the real reason for his presence in Warm Springs.

Too many days had been taken up with this matter already, between the need to appear to be in mourning to maintain his pose and the two chicks in the kitchen needing a strong back to assist with their charge's care. He'd come here with every intention of keeping to himself and finding out what he needed to know. Sometimes it was easier to plan to hold yourself aloof, to separate from life, than it was to actually carry that plan out.

That thought was even more unsettling as his kindling pile grew.

He planned to hold himself as aloof and separate as possible from the siren he'd just encountered upstairs. He couldn't question the impulse that had led an older man to choose such a woman as his wife, despite the brevity of their acquaintance. She was enough to whet any man's appetite. But he did question *her* motives.

What had prompted such a beautiful, and young, woman to marry a man of Robert Mitchell's age and circumstances? The veiled hints Cora and Clara had just mentioned regarding the widow's previous situation did little to alleviate his questions. Amelia Mitchell was a puzzle.

Just the thought of her set his blood simmering. Not a good thing, given his present circumstances. There was too much to be done. He did not have time for more puzzles. Puzzles that had no bearing on his work here.

"Damnation." He raked a hand through his hair and released the curse as loudly as he dared without upsetting the two elderly sisters inside the house.

Enough was enough. The kindling overflowed the bucket. Sweat dripped from his brow and he swiped it with the back of his hand. Cool and crisp, the air whirled in off Warm Springs Lake, offering a refreshing tang of cool water and autumn russet. Not for the first time, the irony of the name and the nearly year-round frigid temperature of the small body of water struck him.

Robert's eyes had twinkled so when he had explained that they'd named the lake, and the town purposefully, despite the temperature, nearly three decades before in an attempt to attract more visitors than nearby Cold Springs. The effort had failed, but the names remained. If only the trail that had brought him here did not prove as false.

Robert Mitchell had been a good friend, despite the relatively short length of their acquaintance. He would be missed. He had been a man to be trusted, just as the federal magistrate in Peoria had recommended. The only one here in Warm Springs who Michael had been willing to put any faith in, providing the means for him to stay here without raising suspicions. He owed it to Robert to see that his ready assistance had not been in vain. Another spur to his need to get the job done.

Michael sighed. This was getting him nowhere. Once Robert's will was read, or anyone took a good look at his family records, they would discover his deception and his investigation would be blown out of the water here. Warm or cold. He couldn't let that happen.

Michael tightened his lips and turned away from the house. He had things to do.

And only so much time to do them in.

Three

"Of course, of course, Cora. But let me at least introduce myself before we—"

The door edged open and an elderly lady entered the bedroom, accompanied by the one Amelia met earlier, Cora. Did no one in this family believe in knocking first before coming into a room? Amelia tried, and failed, to stifle the unkind thought before it fully formed. These people had taken her in and nursed her back to health without any question or recrimination over her hasty wedding, followed so quickly by Robert's death. Who was she to criticize?

The first woman through the door carried a tray laden with covered bowls, a basket, teacup, and what looked to be a teapot under a pink gingham cozy. A bouquet of delicious smells wafted in with her. Cora clutched a set of cutlery and a linen napkin as she trailed behind. They came to a halt together on the far side of the bed as though Amelia's presence in the room caught them off guard.

"Why, she's fully dressed," the woman with the tray exclaimed. She closed her lips tight and blinked as if she were deciding how to react to this unexpected development. Cora halted beside her and they both proceeded to drink in every aspect of Amelia's appearance.

The almost equally diminutive women were clearly sisters, judging from the roundness of their faces, the matching topknots of silver hair, and eyes and noses that were very nearly identical.

Amelia drew herself to her full height, ignoring the slight rumbling of her stomach in the ensuing hush as the two older women perused her, keen interest shining in their blue eyes. She wasn't quite sure what to say in the face of their inquisitive silence. How did one address one's newly married, newly deceased spouse's as-yet-unmet relatives? Should she do a slow pirouette so they could get a full view of her?

She was grateful she'd found her belongings in the solid walnut armoire that matched the bed and wash-stand in Robert Mitchell's room—matched in both elegance of line and the slight tinges of use marking them all. Perhaps Robert had liked to keep heirlooms and old family belongings around him. That would account for the frayed lace canopy and the matching fray of the curtains. Also, the wear and tear on the rugs on either side of the bed.

At least she had been careful to dress herself in her mourning outfit. That should meet with their approval. Someone had seen to cleaning and pressing her dress while she had been ill. The small tear in one sleeve from when she'd caught it on the railcar seat was mended so that if she hadn't known where it was, she never would have guessed at the damage. Which of these women should she thank? Probably both, since they had undoubtedly borne the brunt of her care while she'd been in her fevered state.

The tickle of a cough, lingering from her illness, nearly overwhelmed her. How long could they all stand in this awkward tableau? Although it had only really been a few seconds, at best, since the sisters had entered the room, the silence seemed interminable.

"Hello, my name is Amelia. Amelia Law . . . Mitchell." She held out her hand. Someone needed to take charge or they'd be frozen like this all day and she was sure there were many things that needed attending yet for Robert's funeral.

The taller of the two women glanced at Amelia's hand for a moment before a nudge from her companion urged her forward. She placed the tea tray on the nightstand.

"Hello, Mrs. Mitchell." She took Amelia's hand in her weathered one. "I am Clara and this is my sister, Cora. Misses Clara and Cora Brown, and we are so happy you are finally on the mend. You suffered quite a shock for one so young."

Clara Brown squeezed Amelia's fingers reassuringly and stepped back.

"Yes, dear." Her sister clasped both Amelia's hands in hers. "We were all so worried at your heart-wrenching introduction to our household. I'm glad we will get the chance to get to know you properly at last."

Cora glanced at Clara and then back to Amelia, her eyes twinkling warmth. "Although we feel as if we already know you. Traveling all the way from Boston just to make our dear Robert's final days happy ones."

"I am very pleased to meet you both."

They seemed so friendly, as if they already viewed her with more fondness than most of her former social circle back home. Yet they were strangers. She had never felt so awkward. Robert must have told them things about her from her letters. Well, of course he had. Marriage was a big occasion for most people. Not everyone slipped away at dawn leaving nothing behind for their family save a brief note. "I am sorry to have this opportunity under such tragic circumstances, though."

"I quite agree, dear. Such tragic circumstances," Cora nodded.

"Dear Robert, he was so pleased to be going off to Chicago to meet you," Clara supplied.

"And then to marry." Cora sighed. "It was like one of those sad old fairy tales. Meeting the man who should be your partner through life, only to lose him so quickly."

She clucked her tongue.

"Yes, Miss Brown. What should have been a dream turned into a nightmare," Amelia said.

Amelia meant her words in all sincerity. Her life had been nothing but horrific from the moment she'd realized Robert Mitchell was no longer breathing. She shuddered. They all paused for a moment of reflection.

"Since you're up and we're all home, we'd like to invite you downstairs to meet the rest of us, if you feel up to the task." This invitation came rather gently from Clara.

Amelia's heart twisted as a pang of anxiety went through her. *The rest of us?* Just how many family members were there? She vaguely recalled numerous voices surrounding her when her phantom lieutenant— Michael—had brought her from the train station.

She and Robert really hadn't discussed very much of his background during their brief courtship. He'd listened intently as she'd divulged far more of her short life's events than she'd thought possible for him to find interesting. Right down to the cat she'd adopted when she was three. She had assumed there would be plenty of time to learn his stories once they were wed.

She realized both of the Brown sisters were studying her intently, almost anxiously, again. "Of course I would be happy to meet the rest of my husband's family."

Cora and Clara exchanged a silent glance that seemed to communicate some unspoken piece of information.

"Yes, of course, the family." Clara paused for a moment.

"He would have thought of us that way," Cora chimed in. "Dear Robert. We shall miss him so."

"Come along, Cora." Clara took her sister's elbow. "We'll allow Amelia a few moments to prepare herself."

The Browns headed to the door. "Try to eat something, dear—you must keep up your strength," Cora called over her shoulder.

Clara paused and turned to face Amelia as she nodded her agreement. "A relapse would never do. We'll gather everyone in an hour or so in the large drawing room to the left at the bottom of the stairs. Come down when you're ready. No hurry."

"Of course." Amelia nodded, though neither one of them seemed to be concerned with her response. Clara was already steering her sister out the door in a quite determined fashion.

"But we haven't—"

"It doesn't matter."

"Well, of course it does—"

"We'll talk downstairs, Cora."

In a moment they had gone, leaving Amelia feeling decidedly overset by the whole encounter. She must have upset them both somehow. Were they dismayed by Robert's choice? She sighed. Her appetite had diminished, but was still clamoring. Better to meet and deal with them all on a full stomach than an empty one. She sat by the window and looked out at the trees surrounding the property.

Robert's estate was situated in a peaceful spot. Quiet. There were no houses nearby, and only a dirt lane meandering up to the gate. Living here would have been a definite adjustment for someone raised in the city like she had been. Her aunt and uncle's cottage in the Berkshires had several others in sight, but even there the stillness had nearly driven her mad at night. All that quiet and unending darkness in the country.

There was no sign of the lake Robert had described so vividly. Not from this room, anyway. She drank the hot tea and finished a muffin with barely a pause, leaving another in the basket and the soup untouched.

Hunger satisfied, there was no point in staying in the bedroom any longer than necessary. There were arrangements to be made and things to be taken care of for Robert. She owed it to him to see him properly buried next to his beloved first wife. She did know about her, his Betty. About how much he had loved her. And how happy they had been.

When he proposed, Robert had told her his dearest wish was that he could make Amelia as happy as his first wife had made him.

The dull ache in her middle returned.

She would miss Robert Mitchell. More than she had ever thought possible when she'd answered his ad in that paper she found on Milk Street.

Or perhaps more to the truth, she would miss the future they could have had together. For though she hadn't known him long enough or well enough to fall in love with him, he had managed to endear himself to her.

She paused and gave her appearance one last perusal in the mirror. Her normally pale reflection gleamed back at her even paler than usual as the black mourning gown highlighted her fairness, the icy blue of her eyes, and the faint circles beneath them from her illness.

Then she forced herself out the door.

The steps wound back and forth with a landing in between. Each window curtain was graced with the same faded elegance and slight fraying at the edges as those in her bedroom. Perhaps Robert had made no changes to the house since his wife's passing. She sighed as she ran her hand over the fine walnut paneling. She would have enjoyed redoing this home for him.

She reached the bottom of the steps with a decided feeling of melancholy. A hum of voices emanated from behind the drawn doors to her left. Just how many people was she about to face? She swallowed and straightened her spine, hoping the suspicious glances and family members who might think she had married Robert for his wealth might be kept to a minimum. All she wanted, all she hoped they would grant her, was a modicum of dignity and the means to return to Boston with that dignity still intact.

She lifted her hand to knock as the decibel level on the other side of the pocket doors rose slightly.

"You haven't told her yet?"

"But you haven't seen her, the poor dear. She's very pale and only just over that dreadful fever. She must have loved Robert deeply."

"But she should be told immediately. It isn't right to let her wait like this—"

Curiosity overcame good manners and Amelia pulled the drawing room doors apart. It would surely be better to face any concerns and suspicions in person, rather than to hear herself speculated about. She'd had enough of false friendships and whispered gossip to last her a lifetime.

A collection of astonished glances turned toward her.

Two men. Three women. The men were standing by the windows. The ladies were seated nearby.

"Good afternoon." Amelia managed a polite smile as she moved into the room with her head held high, years of being a scion coming to her aid. "I apologize for my rather dramatic entrance into your midst the other night."

Silence greeted her entry. All eyes remained fixed on her.

"Pray, do continue your conversation. It was not my intention to stop any discourse you were engaged in. Miss Brown, if you would be so kind as to introduce me to the rest of the family, I would—"

"Family?" The taller and older of the men interrupted her without the slightest attempt at an apology. His eyebrows, rather bushy and dense, rose to meet his hairline.

"I told you, Ethan," Clara Brown spoke up from the sofa she occupied with her sister, "she doesn't understand. Robert must not have told her."

"It would definitely appear so." He puffed out his white-whiskered cheeks with disapproval as he turned his glare on Clara Brown standing next to her sister. "Didn't Michael talk with her when they met?"

"No, there wasn't time. She was ill from her grief. She fainted in his arms. You were here . . ."

They were still discussing her as if she weren't even in the room. As if she had no place here and they meant to bring that point sharply home for her. The realization was like a slap. Heat tinged Amelia's cheeks and she fought to keep herself from going into a full flush. These people obviously didn't know who they were dealing with.

She lifted her chin, determined to take command of the room and the conversation. Her position as Robert's widow demanded at least a show of respect from his family no matter what they might think of her privately.

"Whatever there was no time to discuss before is irrelevant. There is now sufficient time to discuss any subject which is of concern to you." She arched a brow upward and turned her gaze toward the first of the two sisters she had at least met. "Miss Brown?"

"Of course, dear." Cora squeezed her sister's hand as though looking for silent support and then rose from the sofa and made her way to Amelia's side.

"I'd like to introduce us all to Amelia Lawrence Mitchell, Robert's new wife . . . er . . . widow."

A round of nods and murmured greetings rose from the room's occupants.

Cora drew Amelia's hand into hers. "Come, dear, and meet . . . Robert's family."

She pulled Amelia with her and approached the shorter of the two men. "This is Festival Miller. His parents were a bit whimsical, don't you know."

"Hello, ma'am." Festival Miller offered his hand in greeting. Far younger than the other man, Ethan, he seemed to be a bit shy as he stuck out his hand and spoke in a deep, slow voice.

"Hello, Festival." His grip was firm even if he could not quite meet her gaze.

"Folks just call me Festive, ma'am," he told her in all seriousness and looked up at her at last through the fringe of his lashes.

"Of course." She smiled at him as Cora drew her along.

"This is Ethan Turwilloughby. Ethan has been with us almost as long as Clara and me. Haven't you, Ethan?"

"Indeed." The bushy white brows rose up and down for a moment as he offered his hand to Amelia. "A pleasure to meet you, Mrs. Mitchell, despite the circumstances. I respected your husband. He was a good man. He deserved every chance at happiness."

"Thank you."

"You've already met Clara."

Clara smiled from the sofa and drew her shawl a little tighter around her arms. "We are truly happy you are well enough to join us at last, despite appearances to the contrary."

"It's good to see you again, Miss Brown." How was she going to keep them straight? The usual rule of referring to the elder sister by the last name and the younger one by her first name surely did not apply when the women were spinsters of such advanced years.

"We don't stand on much formality in this household, dear," Cora's commented. "We are all on a first-name basis. You should feel perfectly free to call me Cora and my sister Clara."

"And this is Eleanor Holmdale." Cora turned to the woman occupying a comfortable-looking cushioned rocker. This one had salt-and-pepper hair and dark brown eyes.

"She's a widow, too," Cora confided.

"My Jacob's been gone for almost five years now." Eleanor nodded politely and offered her hand in a manner reminiscent of the drawing rooms in Boston. Amelia returned the gesture, which seemed almost ludicrous given the immediate circumstances.

The circuit of the room accomplished, Amelia was seated at the marble-encased hearth opposite the doors. What an odd collection of relatives Robert had housed with him.

"Ethan, now that we are all introduced, perhaps you would be good enough to explain," Clara nudged.

"Yes, of course. If you would be kind enough to take your seats, I would gladly explain. Mrs. Mitchell looks confused enough already without us waiting any longer. And I'm quite certain, given the circumstances, Michael will not be bothered by our intrusion into this family matter."

Cora coaxed Amelia onto the settee between her and Clara. She couldn't help but notice the nervous glances still being cast her way. And the fact that no one seemed eager to meet her eyes.

"Mrs. Mitchell." Ethan drew back his jacket and

hooked his thumbs through the loops of his suspenders in what was surely an unconscious action. "We are pleased to welcome you to our humble home. Which is truly yours, now. The first thing you need to know is that it has been well over a week since Michael found you at the train station and carried you home."

She must have started at the news, because Cora and Clara each patted one of her shoulders in sympathy. A week? She had thought she'd been ill only for a day, two at most.

"Thank you." She glanced at each one of the sisters and struggled to pull herself back under control. "I wondered how long I had been ill. Please go on."

Mr. Turwilloughby pursed his lips together for a long moment, his brows knotting like a hedgerow over his dark eyes.

"As you may realize, that was the length of time required for us to attend to Robert. I am sorry to inform you that we have buried your husband, madame. His wishes were closely heeded as he left a detailed accounting of his desire to be buried next to his first wife, Betty. We assumed you would concur with his dictates."

"Of course." Amelia nodded again as the numbness that had dropped on her so precipitously right after Robert's death assailed her again. What a poor wife she had made him. She had not even been able to present herself at his funeral.

Oh, Robert, I am sorry.

"Don't worry, dear, it was a lovely ceremony," Cora sympathized. "Robert would have been pleased."

"Indeed. It is what we do in life that matters," Clara added. "Robert would not begrudge your recovery."

It is what we do in life that matters. Somehow that sentiment only made her feel worse. A prickle of tears gathered at the corners of her eyes. For Robert, or for herself? What had she done to truly make any difference in Robert Mitchell's life? Mariah's words about how happy Robert had been on their wedding day and the look she remembered in his soft brown eyes were the only things she could cling to.

"I played his favorite hymn on my fiddle," Festive offered awkwardly. "I could play it for you later, if you'd like."

"Thank you. I'd like that very much." She pushed to her feet and paced to the window. Outside, waning sunlight skipped over Robert's lake, visible at last, muting the color of the water to a soft gray and blending the edges toward the horizon into inky blue and purple. The sight snagged her throat and brought tears to her eyes. It was exactly as Robert had described it. How he must have loved this place and this house to be able to make her picture this very scene so vividly.

She drew in a deep breath and let it flow out of her, taking some of her doubt and pain along with it. There was nothing more for her to do. She turned back to Robert's family and found them all looking at her anxiously.

"Thank you for taking such good care of me. And for caring enough to try and assuage my guilt over having missed my own husband's funeral. Since there is no more I can do for Robert, I will not be staying long. Whom should I address about the estate?"

"The estate?" Clara drew in a sharp breath

"Oh, dear." Cora gripped her hands together.

"Mrs. Mitchell, I'm not sure we understand," Ethan spoke up. "What is it you wish to address?"

Amelia put her hands together and assumed her primmest posture.

"Robert was very dear to me, despite the briefness of our time together. I do not wish to intrude on the grief of those who knew and loved him much better than I. I shall make my way back to my own home and grieve within the bosom of my family."

Heaven forgive the lie. She couldn't picture gaining any help and sympathy from her mother or her new husband. Especially not after the way in which she had left their house so abruptly. But there was no need to burden these kind people with the mess she had made or the bridges she had burned.

"It was my hope that whoever was in charge of the estate would take pity on me as Robert's widow and advance me enough money for passage back to Boston. I used all my reserves to pay for our fares to Warm Springs."

"Oh, my."

"Oh, dear," the Brown sisters chorused.

"She's not gonna stay?" Festive looked at Ethan as if for guidance as to what was going on. Amelia knew exactly how he felt.

"My dear, I sincerely doubt there is any money to advance." Ethan Turwilloughby looked truly perplexed. "And it would seem there is no one for you to speak with, save yourself."

The finality in his tone made her stomach tighten with dread. "I don't understand."

"Robert never changed his will in all the years since

Betty passed away. He left his Grand Estate in your keeping."

Something in Mr. Turwilloughby's tone underlined the words *Grand Estate* as they had never been before.

"His grand estate?"

"Why, our home, dear. This house." Clara spread her hands.

Her stomach clenched a little tighter. "I don't understand."

"Robert's will directed that his belongings be given directly into the keeping of his beloved wife. You are his beloved wife. Therefore, all that was his, is now yours."

Amelia's head spun. She pressed a hand over her mouth as the implications struck her. She was definitely not as recovered as she had supposed. All they were trying to tell her made no sense. Something in the tone of Mr. Turwilloughby's announcement told her there was more yet to come. Had she truly inherited Robert Mitchell's wealth and belongings? What was she to do with it all? How would she manage?

"I don't want Robert's estate." The words came out in a whisper.

"Oh, we so hoped you wouldn't feel that way. The old Grand Estate may not be in the very best condition, but young Michael has been working on it ever since he arrived," Cora rushed to fill the awkward silence following her reaction.

"Michael is Robert's nephew. On Betty's side, of course," Clara explained. "He's the only one of us you've yet to truly meet. Unless you include his retrieving you from the rail station."

"Here he is now," Eleanor Holmdale observed.

"And we're full-up, too. As we hadn't been in some time. That made Robert so happy. He liked nothing better than to know his house was full of boarders," Cora prattled on. "And after the time we had last year, Michael and Robert had such plans. They spent a great deal of time together this past month or so, didn't you, dear?"

Robert's nephew stomped into the drawing room with his brows twisted together in what was surely a perpetual frown. And no wonder if he had just lost a part of his inheritance to a stranger.

Mud caked his boots and his shirtsleeves were rolled up to reveal corded forearms, arms Amelia knew far too well. Arms she had a feeling she would need again as the true import of what had just been revealed filtered through. Reality hit Amelia. Robert Mitchell's *Grand Estate* was a boarding house.

Blackness swept upward, accompanied by a wave of nausea.

"She's not going to last, Clara."

"Catch her, Ethan."

"Hurry, Michael."

When Amelia opened her eyes again it was full dark outside and she was back in the large bedroom upstairs. The frayed edges of the lace curtains mocked her from above as the oil lamp someone had kindly left lit flickered over them. She was in a boarding house.

She drew in a deep breath and blew it out slowly. "Dear heaven, what now?"

"Feeling better?"

Michael, the nephew, sat in a chair next to the bed. "It was suggested that I sit with you until you awoke. Family and whatnot." He slanted her a wry smile.

"Family." Amelia pushed herself to a sitting position. "Are you . . . family?"

His lips twisted at the question and his brows tightened ever so slightly. Then, after a moment, "Yes, I suppose I am in a roundabout sort of way. I am Michael Thompson . . . Betty Mitchell's nephew."

"Oh."

Yes. She remembered now. Downstairs, amid the swirl of other unpleasant information, had been the fact that Michael was related to Robert's first wife. Her temples began to throb, dull and distant. But worst of all had been the realization that this charming old house was not in genteel shabbiness due to Robert's grief over Betty. It was not simply that he was a man and therefore incapable of paying attention to the things a woman noticed without conscious thought.

He had boarders.

Boarders!

And now they were hers. Robert's legacy.

The dull ache intensified and she could have wept in frustration and pity for her own set of circumstances. After the reaction she had given her mother about marrying beneath her station and binding herself to a merchant, her own situation was inconceivable. Poor Robert. There was no cache of money. Just a group of people he thought of as family. How had he managed to take her to dinner and show her such a wonderful time in Chicago?

Heat poured into her cheeks along with surely what was all the remorse in the world.

She had treated that poor man as though he should have the funds available to satisfy her every whim, as if he could raise her to her former station in life. And he had responded by offering her all he had. Was there no end to the ills she had managed to perpetrate?

"This just cannot be happening."

For a moment she was tempted to just close her eyes and wish the whole awful situation away. Perhaps if she slept long enough it would turn out to be only a nightmare and she would find herself safely back in charge of Aunt Sophie and Uncle John's disgraceful offsprings. She shuddered again, uncertain at this second which would be worse.

"*What* can't be happening?"

She started, so caught up in her own thoughts she'd forgotten Michael Thompson was still perched awkwardly on the edge of the chair he'd drawn near the bed.

"I'm sorry, I spoke my thoughts aloud. Truly, I am not myself."

"Granted." His gaze narrowed. "And just who are you, Amelia Lawrence Mitchell, late of Boston?"

"I beg your pardon?" And she probably should, despite the effrontery of his direct question. She was the interloper. She was the one who did not belong. She shoved the knit coverlet aside.

"A small attempt at humor." He looked at her intently. "Are you too hot? Has your fever returned? I'll send for the doctor."

"No." She swung her feet over the bedside. "No, I don't think that will be necessary. I need to get myself fully acclimated to my circumstances."

He said nothing to this.

"Who would be the best person to help me with that?"

"With what?"

"My circumstances. It would appear that I am now the . . . owner . . . of this establishment. Surely there are some sort of books I should be looking at. Some type of accounting I should be aware of."

"Money you should be looking for?" He rocked his chair back on two legs and propped his booted feet on the edge of her bed. Both objects squeaked in protest. At least he had scraped the mud off his soles.

Heat filled her cheeks at his accusatory tone and the cavalier intimacy of his boots on her bed. She lifted her chin a notch and struggled to ignore them.

"Yes, but not only money. I need to be made aware of the entire situation before I can make any intelligent decisions. I have allowed myself to be too much in the dark. To make assumptions. I cannot afford such foolishness any longer."

Michael Thompson lifted a brow at her. Silence was his only answer for some time.

The steely gray of his eyes pierced her and made her want to tell him everything burning in her mind. It took every ounce of self-possession at her command to keep from rambling on in the face of the silent contemplation on his features. Whatever he was thinking didn't matter to her. Couldn't possibly matter. Yet the urge to squirm beneath his unspoken inquisition was strong.

"You have a point," he said at last. "I don't know what assumptions you've made in the past or whether they have anything at all to do with Robert Mitchell. But I agree that no one can be expected to function in an unknown environment without all the facts at hand."

He dropped the chair back to the floor with a bump and pushed to his feet at the same time she did.

The motion brought them closer together. He was very tall and he smelled of fresh-cut oak and pine. The memory of his arms about her as he had carried her into the house, and again this morning when she had nearly lost her footing, returned in vivid detail. Heat touched her cheeks again.

"Thank you." The words quavered on her lips, low and intimate. She couldn't honestly say whether she was thanking him for upholding her position or for carrying her home to Robert's house.

He nodded, apparently suffering none of the turmoil surging in her at their closeness. She clenched her hands together and refused to allow herself to back away from him, despite the temptation to do just that.

"Mr. Salzburg is the solicitor in town. He is the one who apprised us of the language in Robert's will. I'm quite certain he has been waiting to speak with you. I'll find him first thing and tell him you are ready to see him tomorrow."

"Thank you." This time she offered her gratitude in a more even tone.

"I'll see you in the morning." He bent and retrieved the knit coverlet from the heap it had landed in on the floor when she got up. He put it on the bed behind her. "Try and rest. And eat the cheese and bread on the tray. I promised Clara I would stay until you finished the last crumb. There's milk in the pitcher."

He turned to leave.

"Do you do that often?" she asked.

"Do what?" He turned back, the frown settling on his brow again.

"Make promises you have no intention of keeping?"

The frown deepened. "Not when it matters."

"Well, it matters very much to me that I promised to honor Robert. I intend to do just that by taking care of his home and his family just as he would have wished. At least, to the best of my ability."

He stood and looked at her for a long moment. Then he nodded. "Good night, Mrs. Mitchell."

Michael Thompson turned and stepped out of the circle of lamplight. A few seconds later she was alone in the room. Her room.

To the best of my ability? Who was she kidding?

Four

"All right, Thompson. Let's have your report. I hope you've made significant progress."

The brawny man sitting in Marshal Bill Fallon's chair leaned forward with both arms resting on the desk and narrowed his eyes into a glare definitely intended to intimidate subordinates.

"Where's Fallon?" Having grown up clerking in his father's law offices, Deputy U.S. Marshal Michael Thompson was not easily intimidated. Wealthy in his own right, W. G. Thompson's clientele included some of the most powerful men in Illinois.

"On assignment."

The man making himself right at home in the cramped Springfield federal courthouse office that housed the district's marshals service raised one eyebrow as he appeared to size up Michael. After a minute he relaxed his shoulders and his glare softened. He stuck his hand out over the stacks of paper bundled together on the desk. "Name's Ben Taylor."

The Marshal Ben Taylor? Benjamin Franklin Taylor's reputation was legendary in the service. Will had regaled Michael with long accounts of the older man's exploits which he'd in turn shared with his classmates at Harvard Law. They'd all envied Marshal Taylor's ingenuity and bravery.

"It's a pleasure to make your acquaintance, sir." Michael pumped the outstretched hand. "My brother told me quite a bit about your career."

"Only believe half of what you see and less of what you hear. Especially if it's colorful or scandalous." A smile edged up behind the man's bushy mustache despite the warning in his gruff tone. "And most stories worth repeating are usually one or both of those. Have a seat."

Michael settled on one of the wood chairs Taylor indicated across from the desk and rested his hat on the worn knee of his stained work pants. He scrubbed his hand along his unshaved chin. After getting a cryptic summons from Fallon, he'd hopped the midnight freight, arriving in Springfield without even a change of shirt or a shaving kit. Choosing not to seek those items out, he'd headed straight to his boss's office.

"You sure don't dress like you're the son of one of Chicago's most powerful men." The veteran marshal gave him a thorough once-over, not bothering to hide his displeasure over the deputy's unkempt appearance. He shook his head. "As long as I'm playing nursery maid to Fallon's charges, you'll report to me. I expect you to dress like you were coming to court, not a barn raising. You never know when a commissioner or judge might walk in."

"Yes, sir." Michael nodded. Not only was the man correct, but any explanation he might offer would sound like a weak excuse at this point.

"Good." Taylor eased back in his chair a little. "I believe in plain speaking. I read your service record.

And your brother's. I don't give an owl's beak how many court commissioners or federal judges your old man knows, sorry as I may be that your brother bit it on the job. I'm interested in results. Period."

He steepled his fingers and favored Michael with another cockeyed look. "Even with that time you took off to sip champagne with the folks recently, you've been in Warm Springs for the past month without gathering any further information. That's a damn paltry showing for your time there."

Now was the time for explanations. Michael wouldn't let anyone halt his investigation. Not when he was so sure he was closing in on the last of the gang who'd murdered his brother. "There have been complications—"

"Yes—yes." Taylor's wave cut him off. "The commissioner told me about his friend's untimely death. Sheer foolishness, if you ask me, a man of his years taking such a young wife. Bound to lead to disaster."

Disaster indeed. Amelia Mitchell's mass of black silk hair, her haunting ice-blue eyes, and her lips that fairly begged for regular and thorough kissing sprang far too readily to mind.

"It's because of the little widow that I summoned you here."

Michael's attention snapped back to his superior, who was shuffling aside one of the stacks of papers before him. "If you're concerned about my status, I can assure you she has accepted my position in her late husband's household without question, sir."

She might be uncomfortable about his presence, but she had not ordered him out.

"Although that is gratifying to affirm," Taylor paused in his pursuit of whatever file he was seeking, "especially given my concerns over your qualifications, it is not why the Widow Mitchell is of interest to the U.S. Marshal Service."

Michael's concern deepened. "What about Ame . . . er . . . Mrs. Mitchell has drawn your attention, sir?"

"Fallon has been assigned to a protection detail for Senator Douglas. At the senator's request. Seems those debates he engaged in with Mr. Lincoln last year elicited quite a bit of attention throughout the entire Union."

What could Amelia have to do with the senate election? "I had the pleasure of hearing both Mr. Douglas and Mr. Lincoln when they were in Jonesboro last September. There was quite a crowd there. Both men made good points."

Taylor snorted as he lifted another stack of papers and frowned. "Damn fool waste, if you ask me. Too many gawkers, too little control. They could just as easily write things down and deliver them to the voters by post."

Taylor dropped the papers and fixed Michael with his cockeyed stare. "Thing is, no one asks me. No one ever asks the marshals. It's just our job to keep 'em safe. Seems a group of abolitionists down Kansas way think the nation would be better off without Mr. Douglas, now he's won reelection and is looking to the presidency. Stopped just short of actual death threats. But they're none too happy, particularly with the speculation that Douglas might run next year."

"So Bill's off to see to the senator's safety?" Michael still did not see the connection to Mitchell's widow.

Taylor nodded and patted his waistcoat pockets. "Bill's stuck with the senator until he returns to

Washington at the New Year. Can't have the next president assassinated in his prime, you know."

"What does this have to do with Mrs. Mitchell?" Michael swallowed hard against the sinking feeling in his gut. He'd wondered what could have made a woman of Amelia Lawrence Mitchell's obvious breeding travel across the country to marry a stranger. Especially a stranger like Robert Mitchell, with little to offer her beyond his honor and a ragtag collection of strays in his ramshackle home.

"Your hostess arrived in Chicago by train in the company of Regina and Paul Johnson from Rochester, New York. Mr. Johnson is actually a compatriot of that radical, John Brown. They are currently in residence at their elder daughter's home in McLean, meeting with Illinois abolitionists who feel Douglas did not go far enough in his defense of states' rights."

"So you think Amelia . . . Mitchell could be part of a plot to murder Senator Douglas?" Michael could not credit this assumption, no matter his own suspicions over the young widow's hasty move to Illinois.

"She hails from Boston, does she not?" Taylor pronounced this last as if it put paid to any further discussion. "Ahhh, here it is. This was the first. Others have arrived almost weekly and they get much more ugly."

Michael took the folded papers the marshal pulled from his jacket's inner pocket. First he read the postmark on the envelope. The packet had been mailed from Boston. The crumpled letter warned the senator to . . . *beware the furor you encourage lest it bring ruin on your house.*

"Still," he handed the letter back to Taylor, "this hardly makes a connection to Mrs. Mitchell."

"Quite right, Thompson." Taylor shrugged. "But you are to keep a close eye on the woman. Befriend her. Know who she meets with. Who she corresponds with. Chat her up, flatter her, flirt with her—that sort of thing. Should help you fill in the time since your other investigation appears to be going nowhere fast."

Befriend the widow? Normally, with a woman as beautiful as Amelia Mitchell, he would have had few qualms about an innocent flirtation no matter how pointless he thought the pursuit would prove. But for some reason the idea of deliberately deceiving the woman who already haunted him did not sit well. Especially when he doubted he had the strength of will to keep any flirtation with her innocent.

"Now, how about you fill me in on your progress in the apprehension of the remaining scoundrel who shot your brother and got away with that $50,000 of the government's payroll."

An hour later, Michael headed back to the Springfield train station, his mind spinning with the information he'd just gathered from Ben Taylor and humming with possibilities that had nothing to do with his real reason for being in Warm Springs. He raked a hand through his hair.

He doubted Amelia Lawrence Mitchell had anything to do with any political plans or possible assassination attempts. Someone in Boston might be mailing the threats, but it wouldn't be her. His gut told him that. She could probably plan a damn decent soiree without too much thought, but political intrigue? He leaned his head back against the car wall and let the train's rhythmic motion soothe some of the tension out of him. He was certain to have plenty of opportunity to watch her in the next few weeks.

He'd felt honor bound to see her to Mitchell's attorney's so she could fully face her circumstances. The summons to Springfield had almost prevented him from fulfilling that commitment. Luckily, he'd learned that the lawyer was out of town himself until the next day. He'd scribbled a message for Festive to deliver in the morning and hopped his train to Springfield. Now he chafed at the delay. How far had his brief note of explanation and disappearance sunk him in her graces? Especially in light of her softly worded question last night.

Do you often make promises you have no intention of keeping?

A day's delay would make no difference in what old Salzburg had to say. He could only hope the attorney would at least be able to bring that point home to her. Time would change none of the facts. There was no money.

Despite her assertion to the contrary, he had a strong gut feeling money was exactly what she had been expecting from her precipitous union. Her manner and her speech marked her as someone who would be only too comfortable cavorting in the same social mediums Eugenia loved to indulge in. Taylor was right in that assessment. Amelia was entirely out of place in the Grand Estate of Warm Springs, Illinois. Very out of place.

Visions of Amelia Mitchell in black on the Chicago platform, of her fainting in his arms and fancying him as a dashing lieutenant or some kind of angel in her fevered state, of standing in her nightdress and quilt with her hair tumbling over her shoulders and her bed behind her, revolved through his dreams as the train sped through the Illinois countryside.

He arrived back in Warm Springs well after dark, not feeling the least refreshed for having slept. He entered through the back door of the quiet household into the pantry and the Grand Estate's roomy kitchen.

As usual, Clara Brown had left a plate for him warming on the banked stove. After pulling off his boots and leaving them on the mat in the back pantry, he ate the meat and roasted potatoes and the baked apple as much to express his gratitude for Clara's thoughtfulness as from hunger. Whatever became of the suppers he never touched on the nights he had not come home? He scraped the remains of tonight's meal into the slop bucket and washed his plate and cutlery.

A lawman on a quest had little control over his hours. Especially when no one knew he was a lawman. Clara Brown might not know or understand what he was doing, but she was steadfast in seeing to his welfare without question, whatever his activities or however odd the hours he kept might seem. The rest of the occupants of the Grand Estate had followed her and Robert's examples. The big question plaguing him was if Amelia would prove as understanding and unquestioning as the people she now shared this house with.

Over the weeks since his arrival, he had narrowed his list of suspects to two men, but it had taken a great deal of checking and cross-checking to get this far. He was sure he was close, Marshal Ben Taylor's skepticism notwithstanding. He couldn't afford to let anyone or anything interfere with his original warrant. So how was he going to manage keeping a close eye on the pretty widow, gaining her confidence and learning her secrets, yet keeping her at arm's length?

Michael sighed and ran a hand over the back of his neck as he climbed the back stairs to his room, his mind turning over the possibilities Taylor had presented, and the probability of his having any success in his dealings with Amelia Mitchell. He padded down the hall, past the room she occupied even now, glad the room was dark and silent and he would not have to face her until morning.

He awoke early the next day after a restive night, his dreams a continuation of those on the train. He grabbed a cup of Cora's coffee and strode out behind the house to the Grand Estate's barn after she informed him that dear Amelia would be ready to go with him to Mr. Salzburg's as soon as he brought the wagon around.

He surveyed the rickety building with a shake of his head. He'd made some early progress on this hopeless project when he first arrived, "hired" by his uncle to do repair work on the place in exchange for room and board. The number of loose planks then had made it seem more like a building that was *once* a barn, rather than a working structure. His amateur efforts at least made it serviceable, if far from pretty. He hadn't gone to Harvard Law School to study carpentry—that much was evident. He hitched the one carriage horse left to the wagon that served as a conveyance for the household.

Robert Mitchell had been a very good man, just not

a wealthy one. He had been a man interested in justice and willing to do his part, even if it meant
inventing and harboring a nephew for his dear departed wife in order to conceal a United States
Marshal tracking the last of his brother's killers.

The true crux of the matter that had pursued him
through the night was the juxtaposition of his two
jobs here as a marshal. He was in Robert's debt for
the man's unswerving determination to follow
through on his promise, and by that promise en-
abling Michael to fulfill his own to his father, and to
his brother.

That meant Michael was indebted to the people
Robert cared about and had left behind. Including
his widow. If she were embroiled in a radical abolitionist plot, could he turn her in?

It bothered him more than he wanted to admit that
Amelia might have married Robert under some false
assumption, or worse, for some nefarious reason that
might even bring harm to the odd assortment of
friends and boarders Robert had collected beneath
his roof.

He pulled the wagon around front with a mixture
of guilt and impatience. How could he demand to
know Amelia Mitchell's deepest secrets and yet keep
his own? How could he risk his original mission in this
area by offending the woman who held his continued
welcome in this house in her slender fingers? But if
she were guilty of some plot . . .

The door opened at the top of the steps and *dear
Amelia* came out. Pale and lovely, covered in black, she
stepped onto the porch that wrapped the front and
side of the house. Somehow the color seemed dark

and mysterious on her, instead of evoking the sad melancholia it was supposed to.

She swept down the short flight of steps toward him and he found himself fascinated by the picture she presented. The sway of her skirts, the placement of her hand on the banister, the haunted look in her eyes—she was an odd mixture of grace and anxiety, refinement and fear. But fear of what?

He swung himself to the ground to meet her as a fresh breeze whipped over the lake and sifted dark tendrils of black hair loose from her sedate coiffure, despite her bonnet. She grasped his hand as her skirts tossed.

"Good morning." He leaned toward her and she glanced up, meeting his gaze at last.

Her mouth was parted, full and soft, and her cool blue eyes grew wide and uncertain. The extra day of rest his trip to Springfield had necessitated before he could take her to meet Salizburg had done her good. She was very lovely indeed. The flare of anxiety in her eyes reminded him of Katie. Somewhere deep inside him this woman had ignited a desire to protect her from the very beginning, when he had first seen her in Chicago. Despite his growing suspicions about her motives, he couldn't seem to dislodge the idea that she needed sheltering, cherishing. He fought the urge to pull her into his arms and tell her everything would be all right.

"Good morning." She moistened her lips when the greeting came out raspy.

He watched the tip of her tongue, all too aware of the sudden tightening in his groin and a desire to taste those moist, sweet lips beneath his own. Did she have any idea of the effect she was having on him?

"Are you ready?" she asked.

It took him a moment to realize she was speaking of their departure and not his base, need-induced confusion. The urge to kick himself soundly followed quick on the heels of his unwelcome desire. How could he have stood lusting after Robert Mitchell's widow in the full light of day? He didn't even want to glance at any of the Grand Estate's many windows to see if any of the inmates were watching.

He could only too easily picture the avid interest and speculation playing across Cora and Clara's well-meaning faces.

"Yes." He bit the word far too sharply, grasped Amelia by the waist, and placed her on the wagon seat, unsure whether he was more angry with her for attracting him so strongly or with himself for his reaction to the feel of her slender waist in his hands.

She sat with the prim decorum of a young lady at home in a proper carriage. He climbed up onto the seat beside her and urged the one horse left in her possession to a trot. Better to get this over with as quickly as possible.

Horace Salzburg was the town solicitor and had been in Warm Springs nearly as long as Robert and Betty. He handled their legal business affairs—he handled everyone's legal business affairs. He'd been married once, even had a son who had left town years before, never to be heard from again, and had loved the law alone once his wife passed away.

They accomplished the ride to Salzburg's home and office in relative silence. Several townspeople paused in their errands to greet him as they passed, all really craning their necks to get a glimpse of Robert Mitchell's pretty young widow.

"How lovely," Amelia exclaimed as they rounded the bend in the road at the far end of town.

"Wait until you see the inside." Michael had to smile. Salzburg had a lovely home, modeled after the grand southern mansions of his native Virginia, with a wide portico and tall Georgian columns. The attorney had been able to provide the best for his wife. With her passing, Robert said the house had no longer mattered to him.

Michael pulled the wagon to a halt and jumped to his feet.

"Don't go anywhere now, Becky." He patted the horse, who blinked at him with large black eyes, and circled the wagon to reach for Amelia. He braced himself. Her waist fit his hands so perfectly and she smelled of tart apples with a hint of cinnamon.

He set her on her feet and released her.

"This way." He led the way across the portico's wide slate tiles to the heavy walnut front door inlaid with thick glass. He raised the polished brass knocker and let it fall once.

"Come." Salzburg's sharp greeting rang out from the depths of the house.

Michael opened the door and walked into the relative gloom, gesturing for Amelia to follow him. He turned to watch her face as she entered. Her eyes widened and she pressed a hand to her mouth. The interior of Salzburg's home was wall-to-wall, floor-to-ceiling books, papers, ledgers, boxes, and files. Getting from one room to another was accomplished through a series of rabbit warren-like alleyways, which changed on a regular basis, according to the work currently holding Horace's attention.

"Oh, my." The anxiety in her eyes had sharpened as she viewed the disarray. "Are you certain this man is a competent attorney?"

"Robert had faith in him." Michael watched her as her eyebrows rose and she paled at the magnitude of overflowing paperwork, newspapers from across the country, and massive tomes.

She took a deep breath and turned back to him with an expression of resolute determination. "Where do you suppose he is?"

Michael tilted his head back and called toward the ceiling to enable his voice to be heard over the piles. "Mr. Salzburg? It's Michael Thompson and Mrs. Mitchell."

"Of course it is." The rather snappish reply came without hesitation. "Meet me in my study."

"Where do suppose that is?" Amelia was busy trying to keep her skirts from brushing the various dust-laden piles around them.

"When Robert brought me here, it was in this direction." Michael pointed to their left. "But I must warn you there may be detours along the way."

"You lead."

"As you wish."

True to his warning, they ran into two changes to the pathway he'd trod the week before when he'd come to see Salzburg after hearing that Dr. Walker was interested in buying property in the area. At one point he was quite certain they had passed the study altogether and were on their way out the back door when the path turned and led them directly to their destination.

"Ah, there you are, at last." Satisfaction laced their host's version of a greeting.

"Michael." He shook Michael's hand and turned to peruse Amelia. "And this must be Robert's bride."

"Yes." Pink washed her cheeks as Salzburg continued to study her, but, as she had done two nights before when Michael had kept his silence, she did not squirm beneath the solicitor's soundless appraisal.

"A pleasure to meet you, Mrs. Mitchell," Salzburg offered at last, extending his hand with firm formality. "Robert was a good friend of mine. His Betty and my Elvira had been great friends throughout their lives. I'm sorry your chance at finding happiness with him ended so abruptly."

"Thank you."

"Now, come, sit." He gestured toward two chairs free of stacked papers and awaiting their arrival.

Amelia took her seat gingerly, managing to keep her skirts as close to her as possible while keeping her attention fixed on the attorney. Michael hid a smile as he took the seat next to her.

"Now, Mrs. Mitchell, I understand from the note young Michael sent me that you have some questions. I will be happy to go over the provisions of Robert's will with you."

"Please, Mr. Salzburg." She reached out and placed one slender, black-gloved hand on the solicitor's firm knuckles. "Since you were a friend of my late husband's, call me Amelia."

"Thank you, my dear." He patted her fingers.

"Amelia. A lovely name. Now, I have Robert's will right here."

He drew out the long piece of vellum he had originally uncovered for Michael a few days previously.

"According to Robert's wishes, the care of his boarding house, the Grand Estate, along with any other items he possessed at the time of his death, were bequeathed in total to his beloved wife."

"That's what I had been told, Mr. Salzburg—"

"Horace, please."

"Thank you, Horace. But I also believe this will was written before his first wife, Betty, passed away."

"Yes, that's true, Amelia. But it in no way invalidates the will."

"Even if there are other relatives available? Relations of long standing?" Amelia was staring intently at the hands she had folded primly in her lap.

So that is what was troubling her. Michael leaned forward. Robert's young wife was concerned that his nephew might step forward to challenge her claim.

Salzburg glanced over at Michael. The old solicitor was the one person Robert had suggested Michael take into his confidence about his true identity. He had done that when the need presented itself and blessed his host for his foresight.

"I understand your concern, Amelia." This time it was Horace who covered her hands and gave them a reassuring squeeze. "Let me reassure you, Robert came to visit me before going to Chicago to meet you. I knew his plans. We discussed this will among other things. He did not want anything changed. So you see, he knew if anything happened to him, his wife, *you*, would inherit his household. That is what he wanted."

Her brows knitted and she turned a troubled gaze to her escort. "Michael, are you sure there's nothing—"

"I do not plan to challenge Robert's will, Amelia. The estate is yours, free and clear. My relation to Robert technically ceased with my aunt's death."

"Well, there are several matters that need attention." Salzburg shifted in his chair and the papers beneath him crackled faintly. "The Grand Estate is not in the best repair. There are debts owed against it and taxes due in the not-too-distant future. As the new owner, Amelia, you will need to settle those debts as well as see to repairing what you can. Robert's finances have suffered several reversals in the past years. Unpaid loans and losses in business ventures."

Amelia swallowed as the solicitor's words echoed through her head.

Debts owed? Taxes? Losses?

She shuddered at the thought. The words were all-too-familiar. She and her mother had suffered through enormous embarrassment and struggle after her brother absconded with what little wealth they had and left them to face the debts and obligations he had abandoned. Would she now be faced with the same choices her mother had? Marrying any man with funds in order to cover her indebtedness? The fact that her mother claimed to be happy with her choice did not matter.

She closed her eyes and pressed a hand over her mouth.

Michael's hand touched her shoulder and she looked at him.

"I had so hoped there would be enough to see me back to Boston. I . . . I . . ."

What more could she say? *I understand now why Jonathan ran away rather than face his responsibilities because I'm tempted to do the same thing? I don't care about the debts left by my husband? I don't care about those people in the boarding house who nursed me back to health and obviously meant something to Robert? A man I barely knew?*

The man who thought she had a good heart.

The self-pitying tears that had welled behind her eyes refused to come. She had brought Robert home because he was her husband. She had given her word to honor him. She would see what she could do to help his Grand Estate and the boarders living there who had made him happy. She might not succeed, but she would try.

She drew in a deep breath and blew it out slowly.

"Very well, Horace." The solicitor's gaze had never wavered from her face. "Thank you for your candor. Would it be possible to procure an accounting of matters to do with the Grand Estate or whatever funds there might yet be available?"

His eyebrows twitched just the tiniest bit and a flicker of approval showed in his eyes. "I'm quite certain that can be made available to you in very short order. I'll send them along by way of my assistant later today."

There was an assistant hidden in these piles? The look she caught on Michael's face betrayed similar astonishment at the notion.

Horace Salzburg reached for her hand, his grip firm and steady. "Robert made a wise choice. Never doubt that."

His words tightened her throat as warmth crept over her skin. She would never have imagined that the approval and acceptance of a man whose home was a rabbit warren of legal papers and books would affect her so. But his belief that Robert had done the right thing in marrying her made her want to weep.

"Thank you."

She felt like a sham as she and Michael stood to leave. Yes, she was trying desperately to do the right thing. To honor the husband she'd had for barely a day. But somehow she'd made these people believe she was . . . she was . . . something she was not.

"Thank you, Salzburg."

"Anytime, Michael. You know my door is open should you require any assistance."

She paid little heed as they made their retreat through the precarious hallways of papers and books. Her throat was tight and her mind was awhirl with the information just given her. Robert Mitchell had known if anything happened to him the Grand Estate would fall to her. He had known as they said their vows in the little anteroom in the courthouse.

Surely that meant this is what he wanted.

Tension throbbed between her brows and she wanted nothing more than to get home and rest. A few moments to think.

With a start she realized she thought of home as the tall manse that was the Grand Estate. Home was now a boarding house. The thought choked a laugh from her as she reached the front door of Horace Salzburg's home.

"You find something in this business amusing?" The censure in Michael's voice was barely contained.

"No." She waited for him to open the door for her. "Nothing is funny. Ironic, perhaps."

"Really?"

"Yes." She swept past him out into the cool air and bright sunshine.

"Anything you would care to share with me?" His hands circled her waist and he prepared to lift her onto the wagon seat.

His hands were warm, reassuring. So strong and capable. Utterly unlike hers. For just a moment, the thought of all the things she could share with this drifter, with Robert's nephew, sifted through her mind. The memory of wanting him to kiss her in her bedroom. The feel of his arms.

Her guardian angel.

She shook off the urge to lean against him and reached for the seat edge.

"I own a boarding house." She fought back the urge to laugh again as he climbed up beside her.

And I am in Illinois with no prospects of getting back to Boston. And I'm not sure what to do next.

"Indeed it would appear so." He shook the reins and clicked to the horse. Her horse.

I own a boarding house.

She had finally said the words aloud. Now they echoed in her mind.

What did one do with a boarding house?

She hadn't a clue beyond the fact that the people living in one paid some kind of . . . fee . . . for the privilege of living there. Perhaps the accounting Horace Salzburg supplied would provide some direction.

"How long have you been here?"

Michael started at her question and turned his

steel-gray gaze in her direction. He never answered a question without perusing the person asking, she realized. How odd. For a ne'er-do-well drifter, he had amazing self-possession.

"You mean at the Grand Estate?"

"Yes, and in Warm Springs."

He thought about that for a moment before answering. "A few months. Why do you ask?"

"Well, you are one of my . . . boarders . . . are you not?"

He smiled that lopsided smile he gave when he didn't quite agree with her. "Well, yes, I suppose you could say that, in a manner of speaking."

"In a manner of speaking?"

"Yes. My . . . arrangement . . . with my uncle was a simple one. I stay at the Estate and in return for my room and board I provide repairs and do odd jobs around the house."

"Oh." She hadn't considered that there might be arrangements with anyone other than a financial one. She had been wondering what the fee was that her boarders paid and what that entitled them to. But then, as Michael was a relative, perhaps that explained it.

"Will that be a problem?"

"A problem?" she echoed, caught up in her own considerations and not sure what he meant.

"Yes, will there be a problem continuing that arrangement now that the house belongs to you?"

She considered the discomfort he had managed to put her through in the short span of time she'd known him against the need to do what repairs she could around the house. "Is your time spoken for in any other way?"

"My time?"

"Yes." She bit her lip and considered how best to put the question about his tendency to disappear or to keep odd hours. Cora had told her it was so and his disappearance yesterday was a timely example.

"You seem to be somewhat . . . unsettled . . . Mr. Thompson. As I understand from Cora and Clara, there is little you actually do other than help around the house. If such is the case, does that mean you are fully at my disposal for whatever I need you to do?"

"You mean, is that the arrangement I had with Robert?"

"Your Uncle Robert," she corrected, suddenly aware that he never addressed his uncle with the respect due him.

"Uncle Robert," he repeated without any particular inflection as those steel-gray eyes held hers. "If that is your question, then yes, within reason, my time is at your disposal."

She wasn't sure she liked the addition of *within reason* and she was certain she wouldn't like him disappearing and reappearing at will, but knowing assistance would be at her disposal would help enormously as she tried to come to grips with what to do.

"Then your previous arrangement is acceptable to me."

"Good. Welcome to the family, Auntie Amelia." He turned his attention back to the horse and the progress they were making through town, but she could have sworn there was a ghost of a smile curling the corner of his lips. She wasn't quite sure if she should be outraged or pleased with his teasing.

Five

Amelia watched Michael lead Becky and the wagon back toward the barn, then looked up at the enormous house before her with it's gabled roof and boxed windows. The Grand Estate. *Her* Grand Estate.

A bubble of despairing hysteria caught in her throat. It could have been a one-room shack or a medieval European castle, for all the ideas she had of how she was to keep any place running on a practical level.

Her years at her mother's elbow had prepared her for nothing beyond organizing the guest lists and menus for various social affairs. She knew which fabric and color were appropriate to wear for each occasion, depending on the season. She had a keen eye for color and line, using the same often to flay those who lacked that skill for lapses in judgement regarding the detail or cut of their gowns. She knew that one day it would be her responsibility to oversee the housekeeper and consult with the cook in the ordering of her husband's household. But in the absence of myriad maids, footmen, and grooms to actually lay out and accomplish the tasks set forth by the mistress of the house, she was lost.

She was weary beyond words as she climbed the

back steps and turned the knob of the oak-and-glass door that opened onto the back pantry leading to the kitchen. At least, she thought it led to the kitchen. She didn't even have a clear picture of how many rooms her new home contained. A drawing room, study, dining room, and kitchen with various butteries and pantries or storage areas downstairs. At least six rooms upstairs and the attic space occupied in part by Michael. How many was that, and who was responsible for keeping them all in order?

It was one thing to look at a room and suggest that it needed tidying or rearranging. But how often did one need to dust or sweep a room? What was used to bring the gleam out in wood? Had Robert been as lost as she when his first wife's death left him saddled with all the responsibilities for so many people? The frayed lace canopy in her bedchamber, threadbare rugs, and sun-spotted curtains throughout the house seemed far more understandable, given that perspective. Especially if Robert's finances were as reduced as Mr. Salzburg indicated.

It was like staring down a long, dark hallway. However was she going to manage it all?

"I don't know. I just don't know."

"Don't know what, dear?"

She hadn't realized she'd spoken aloud, nor even that she'd actually entered the kitchen, until Cora Brown addressed her. She took one look at the older woman's kindly face and her sympathetic expression and promptly burst into tears.

"There, there, dear. You sit right down here and have yourself a good cry." Cora put her arm around Amelia's waist and guided her to a chair by the table.

"It's not good to keep everything bottled up inside. Do you have a handkerchief?"

Amelia nodded as she collapsed more than sat, embarrassed beyond measure at her unladylike outburst, which only spurred her horrifying sobs to new heights.

Cora patted her shoulder for a few moments. "I'll go fetch Clara. She'll know what to do. She's been dreadfully worried about how you would react when Robert's loss finally hit you."

Robert? Robert. Oh, not Robert. She was an awful wife, crying for herself. An utterly horrible person. Her lofty goals of upholding Robert Mitchell's memory and his life were buried beneath the overwhelming mountain of responsibilities she was so ill-prepared to face.

Cora stepped to the swing door in the kitchen and called for her sister in an urgent tone, obviously bewildered by what to do with the quivering mass of self-pity before her.

"What is all the fuss, Cora?" Clara came through the door a moment later.

"Oh. Oh, my," was all she managed after that.

The tears kept flowing despite Amelia's best efforts to stop them because she knew they were selfish tears, shed for herself, not for the loss of her husband as these women who had known him, lived with him, assumed.

"I'll make a nice pot of chamomile tea, shall I?" Clara bustled to the cupboard and retrieved a cannister. "Chamomile is very soothing for frayed nerves."

"That's just the thing, sister." Clara moved back to Amelia's side and patted her shoulder again. "You have your cry and a nice cup of tea—then you'll see, things will look much better, dear."

Amelia shook her head and swabbed at the tears. "I don't see how. I just don't see how."

Her protest was little more than a pathetic squeak. She had no patience for girls who dissolved into watering pots. Even when Jonathan had first fled Boston as the scandal broke, she had refused to allow anyone to know how distressed she was by the dire circumstances he had left Mama and her to face alone. Alone and penniless.

Mama had aged right before Amelia's eyes from the strain a year ago. Gray was sprinkled in her hair and lines added to her face with every loss as they sold off pieces of their life to pay for Jonathan's sins. Mama's recent marriage had at least restored the bloom to her cheeks and put a new light in her eyes. Even Amelia had been forced to admit her new stepfather, no matter his lowly origins or utter unsuitability for polite society, appeared to have made her mother happier than she'd seen her in years.

"Now what, dear?" Cora's soft question brought her thoughts back to the situation she faced now.

She took a deep breath and blew her nose before answering. At least the tears had stopped, but she was quite certain her complexion was blotched and she looked a mess. "However am I going to manage running a boarding house? How am I, how are we, going to make a go of this?"

"Why, we'll go on as we always have. Helping one another, dear." Cora patted her again.

"You'll see." Clara took the kettle from the stove and poured boiling water into the teapot she'd prepared. Amelia tried to pay attention in case anyone expected her to fix tea in the future. "Cooperation goes a long way in smoothing out life's little troubles."

"But how does a household like this run? Who does the cooking or the cleaning? If it's all up to me, we're doomed to starve or live in squalor."

The sisters exchanged glances.

"We'll work together, just as we always have." Clara reiterated their earlier explanation, which told Amelia nothing.

"Like family, dear," Cora added.

That was still no help for Amelia. Her skills with family relationships were limited at best.

"Listen, dear." Cora pulled another chair close and sat down. "There was a time when Robert and Betty were quite prosperous. He knew so many people across the state through his investments and business dealings. Calling this house the Grand Estate started out as a joke between the two of them when they were having the house built."

"When our house was lost in a fire, they took us in with no questions." Clara came to stand on the other side of the table after putting a cozy over the teapot to let it steep. "As time and some of his ventures failed, we started to pay something toward board. Each of us here at the Estate has a similar story. The Mitchells took us in for various reasons and made us into the family they never managed to have."

"After Betty died, the light just sort of went out of Robert for a long while." Cora continued, "When he had to let the cook go, Clara and I took over the kitchen."

"Eleanor helps with the mending and keeping the upper hall clean," Clara supplied. "Ethan was a college professor and is quite a whiz at fixing small things. Festive does the heavy lifting and tends the horse and fireplaces when Michael is not here."

"And we each clean our own rooms," Cora added. "The linens are sent to a woman in town once a week for laundry. And we take turns caring for the downstairs. So you see, dear, a little cooperation and everything is quite pleasant."

Amelia was too overwhelmed to speak. They made it sound so effortless. It could not possibly be that easy. She was not having that kind of year. She pushed at a stray lock of hair that brushed her temple. Her hands still trembled from her outburst.

"Why, you're shaking. Why don't you go on up to your room and lie down." Clara took the cozy off the pot. "One of us will carry up your tea. After a rest, things will seem clearer."

Amelia shook her head. After meeting everyone and when Robert's nephew had not been available to take her to the attorney's, she'd spent the better part of yesterday ensconced in her bedroom. "I can not hide from this situation any longer. I want to be available when the papers Mr. Salzburg promised me are delivered."

"Well, why don't you wait in the drawing room, dear."

"The rocking chairs by the windows are especially pleasant this time of day. You can put your feet up on the chair and sip your tea until you're feeling more the thing."

A tempting suggestion. Especially since she had no idea how long it would take for Horace to assemble the paperwork for her, nor what surprises awaited her within them.

"I think I will do that." She pulled off her gloves and untied her bonnet. A few minutes looking out the windows at the lake might help her pull her scattered thoughts into better order and allow her to see the way through this mess that the Browns were trying so valiantly to point out to her.

Despite the tea and the scenic view, rest eluded her at first. She closed her eyes and memories washed over her. Robert Mitchell and his warm brown eyes. Mariah and her no-nonsense reassurances. Carstairs and his leering suggestions. The household awaiting any changes she might decide to make. And Michael Thompson's compelling gray gaze that seemed to measure her with every step she took. Odd to have such command in a man who settled for life as a drifter.

She finally fell asleep for a few dreamless and comforting moments, until Clara brought her a second cup of tea along with a thick envelope.

"Thank you, Clara." Amelia straightened in the chair and accepted the tea. The few moments of sleep had refreshed her more than she had expected.

"This came from Horace Salzburg. Michael seemed to think you would want to see it straightaway."

Amelia wasn't sure whether to be grateful or not that the disheveled state of his home had not prevented the attorney from fulfilling her request for her husband's papers so promptly. She guessed only an examination of the contents would tell.

She accepted the envelope, thicker than she had supposed, and braced herself to open it. "Thank you again."

"You may not feel so grateful when you see the boxes awaiting you in Robert's study."

"Boxes?"

Clara nodded. "Also from Mr. Salzburg. Michael put them in the study for you. Apparently the envelope is the most recent or urgent material."

Boxes? How long would it take her to wade through everything? Before her fears could spiral out of control, Cora appeared in the doorway.

"There you are, Clara—our afternoon is here." Cora stopped as her gaze caught Amelia's. "Hello, dear, are you feeling better?

"I knew you would if you could rest for just a moment." Cora did not bother to wait for Amelia's answer as she rushed on. "So much to do in such a short span and all of us to get used to. Do come along, Clara—they are waiting. We'll have to reschedule."

"If you don't mind my asking, Cora, who is waiting and what do you have to reschedule?"

"Our afternoon appointment, dear," Cora answered.

"Cora and I teach piano." Clara brushed her hands down her skirts and smoothed imaginary wisps of hair back into place. She pursed her lips for a moment before continuing. "It is our source of income. Small, but adequate when added to an investment our father left us."

She gestured to the large piano opposite the hearth and then looked at her sister. "Robert kindly allowed us to use his when ours was lost in the fire. I'm afraid we hadn't considered—"

"Oh, no, dear, we didn't. And here you are, so comfortable, just as you should be in your own home . . ."

"Will it be all right for us to continue?" Concern furrowed Clara's brow and echoed on her sister's.

Amelia smiled at them both. "Certainly."

"Well, that's good," Cora exclaimed. "You see? I told you she wouldn't mind."

"We'll just cancel for today, so you can stay just as you are while you read whatever it is Mr. Salzburg sent you." Clara turned to leave.

"No, no." Amelia rose from the chair. "I'll move to the study since that is where the bulk of the material has been placed. Keep your appointments."

She left them as they tried to thank her, and managed to smile encouragingly at the two young girls standing in the foyer awaiting their lessons as she passed them on the way to Robert's study. Cora and Clara taught piano. What else didn't she know about the inhabitants of the Grand Estate?

Opening the study door, Amelia stepped around the pile of boxes by the desk and sat on the small settee by the windows to take advantage of the light. She took a deep breath and tore open Mr. Salzburg's envelope. Inside were Robert's will and several ledger sheets.

She scanned the figures and breathed a small sigh of relief. There was a small balance left in Robert's bank account. They were not entirely destitute. She blew out another sigh tinged with sadness as gratitude swelled inside her.

She was immensely thankful that while Robert had struggled to offer her a grand time in Chicago and win her heart, he had not completely drained his resources. He had depleted them significantly, but he had not bankrupted himself. She hadn't realized until this moment just how strongly she had convinced herself that the monies he spent in Chicago had contributed to his death. And that had added weight to the guilt already mantling her shoulders.

Poor Robert. Thank God such was not the case. And, she would at least have a place to begin.

That digested, she moved on to the next sheet of paper as piano notes sounded in the distance, hesitant, but not without charm. This sheet detailed the arrangements made with all of Robert's boarders, including how long they had been in residence and little notes about how and why Robert had taken them on.

Festival Miller was alone in the world. He had been injured as a child, a severe blow to the head. This had left him somewhat slow-paced and limited his capacities. Robert had given Festival a home through an arrangement with his father before his death. He received a reduction in rent based on the chores he did for the Estate. She frowned over that one, even as she understood the impetus behind it.

Cora and Clara, the Brown sisters, had come to Warm Springs, drawn by the name, while they were still quite young. They'd sung in the church choir with Betty Mitchell and managed the rent on a modest home through an investment made by their father long years ago, which still paid them a small quarterly stipend, supplemented by teaching piano lessons to anyone who showed an interest, just as Clara had explained.

Their rent was lowered, too, as they took over the duties of the cook. The distant piano repeated the same musical phrase over and over as if to underscore the lesson. Due to the timing of their stipend, the Browns sometimes needed to pay their rent on a quarterly basis as well.

She frowned again. Reduced rent? And rent in return for services. Unease twisted in her belly. A balanced exchange she blessed on one hand and regretted just a little when she saw the effect on the Estate's annual income as opposed to its outflow.

She read on.

Ethan Turwilloughby was a retired professor who tinkered in the local livery and paid a full rent, every month. Precisely on time. The tension in her stomach eased a notch. Robert noted his admiration for this man for his character and his ability to face things head-on. He apparently reminded Robert of a younger version of Horace Salzburg. Interesting comparison.

Eleanor Holmdale was a more recent addition to the hodgepodge family inhabiting the boarding house. Her husband had died a little over three years ago. She paid her rent on time as well. She took in sewing to supplement her income and was known to have a fine hand.

The notation at the bottom in connection with Michael seemed almost an afterthought. Repairs and household help in return for room and board. That was all there was. No little side information about Robert's feelings for his wife's nephew or how long Michael intended to stay.

She lowered the sheets of paper and rested her head against the back of the settee, allowing her gaze to drift out over the room where Robert must have spent many hours.

Her mind swam with figures and information about the people living in the house and now depending on her to keep everything in balance.

The last sheet of paper dealt with the debts and obligations yet owed to the town of Warm Springs and against the Grand Estate. It was a daunting list. Taxes, pledges of assistance, repairs—some of which had already been contracted, some completed—obligations which now fell to her.

She couldn't deal with it all. There was too much to take in at one sitting. There was only one piece of information that really mattered.

"There is more owed than there are monies to pay."

Oh, Robert, what am I to do?

No wonder they had all looked at her as though she'd grown a third head when she asked to speak to someone about funds to return to Boston. There was barely enough money to last out the winter, let alone spare any for a flighty society chit who thought of no one besides herself.

"Did you think it would be otherwise?" Michael Thompson's question invaded her derisive self-pity.

She lifted her head to find him standing over her in that irritating, self-possessed way he had.

"I beg your pardon?" Although she doubted she'd misheard him.

"Your life? Your marriage? Your inheritance?"

What should she answer? *There was always hope the situation might not be as bad as I feared.* Prim, but relatively honest. Only to be perfectly honest, why should she answer this man who was wholly dependent on her for the roof over his head and the food on his plate? Anger stung on the heels of that thought.

She pushed to her feet. Momentum brought her toe-to-toe with him. For a moment, all her training in propriety demanded she retreat, that she put a respectable space between them. The rush of anger pushed that away, too. What on earth had propriety ever brought her but grief? What had her *life* brought her but grief?

She lifted her chin and looked him straight in the eye. If anyone needed to retreat, it was he. "What difference can it possibly make to you what I expected?"

He raised an eyebrow. An insignificant reaction that only added fuel to the indignant fire burning within her. Fury raged in her heart.

"What difference does it make to anyone what I expected?" She was exploding again, only this time it was irrational anger, not tears, suffusing her. "The only important thing is that this household is now my responsibility. I haven't the faintest idea what to do or where to begin. And you have the gall to ask me if my life is what I expected it to be?"

His eyes narrowed and he leaned toward her as though he hoped to intimidate her into silence with his physical presence.

"You might wish to lower your voice." Answering anger laced his tone.

Good. She hoped she provoked him every bit as much as he irked her. He was a drifter. A man without responsibilities. What did he know about what she was trying to come to terms with?

"Lower my voice?" Outrage raised it another notch as the lonely pain inside her screamed for release. Flat, discordant notes from the piano grated over her nerves. "You have no right to tell me what to do or how to behave. You have no right to—"

In an instant his mouth covered hers, cutting her off in mid-tirade as his fingers gripped her shoulders and pulled her closer. Shock held her immobile as his lips invaded her mind, her soul.

His mouth was warm and firm against her own, all too real and demanding. And then his tongue tickled her lower lip. A flood tide of longing raced through her veins in hot, unexpected need. She moaned. Fire of a wholly different sort licked her as his tongue darted inside to touch hers. So intimate. So provocative.

His arms slid around her and tightened, pulling her closer still, pressing her to his chest. The contact inflamed her further. Her fingers locked at his collar, clinging as he kissed her as no one else had ever dared.

Certainly not the hesitant, hopeful suitors from the world she'd left behind in Boston.

Not even her husband.

Dear heaven. Her husband. She was a new widow, her husband dead less than a month.

Shame, scalding and yet icy-cold, doused her to her toes.

She broke away from him, her breathing ragged and uneven, revealing the turmoil this arrogant stranger, this drifter, wrought so easily inside her.

"How dare you?" The words trembled from her lips, still smoldering from the pressure of his mouth, so knowledgeable and commanding against hers. "How dare you touch your uncle's wife in such a manner?"

She raised a hand to slap him, determined to vent all the tumult seething inside her.

His hand caught hers before she could deliver the blow. His fingers laced hers, gentle but firm as he lifted a brow. Appreciation for their unforgivable encounter glittered in his eyes.

"You needn't offer me any mock outrage. You needed to lower your voice before those on the other side of this door became the recipients of your misplaced abuse. I used the most expedient means available. And you enjoyed that kiss just as much as I did."

"Mock outrage? Expedient?" Turmoil churned within her. A man had kissed her and she had indeed liked it. More than that. She had wanted it to go on and on. And somehow he had known all the guilty secrets in her heart. Shame washed her again. When she had thrown propriety to the wind to upbraid him, she had never intended to watch it sail out of her grasp forever.

"You find kissing a woman an expedient means to limit speech?" The question was as ragged as her feelings. "You, sir, are a cad."

She lifted her other hand to attack him and had that one trapped as well. He drew both behind her, imprisoning her once more in his embrace.

"Perhaps you're right, princess." His breath stirred the hair at her temples. "I am a cad. But then I am a ne'er-do-well, as you were only too happy to point out to me this morning."

Had she struck his pride with her questions earlier? In light of his actions just now that was nowhere near what he deserved.

"Release me," she demanded, struggling vainly to ignore the roiling emotions inside her.

"Only if you promise to behave yourself." His gall drew her gaze back to his. He had the audacity to deliver that lopsided smile of his, the one that undid her insides and made her want him in the first place.

"Oh." She struggled against him and he tightened his hold still further, imprinting the strength of his body against hers despite her many layers of decorous mourning black.

What good could she possibly do here? She couldn't even manage to honor her husband's memory.

Tears burned the backs of her eyes and she ceased her struggles. Failure tore at her. Perhaps she was more like her brother Jonathan than she wanted to admit. Michael's hand cupped her chin and turned her face up toward his. His gaze marked her lips and her breathing tightened within her. He was going to kiss her again and, heaven help her, she wanted him to.

She needed him to. *Robert, I'm sorry.*

"Please let me go." A single tear escaped and scorched a hot trail down her cheek.

He brushed it with his thumb. Consternation knit his brows together. For a timeless moment nothing passed between them but their own quickened breathing.

"I'm sorry." When his words finally came, they were so soft she almost didn't hear them. Then his lips brushed her temple and he released her. Long strides took him from the room without a backward glance.

There was no excuse for his behavior, Michael thought as he strode quickly to the door. He left without looking back at her. His mind all too readily supplied the image of her looking torn and confused about the surrender she had offered in his arms.

What had he been thinking?

Intending?

He growled, wishing he could take back the last ten minutes. He was behaving as if Robert really was his uncle and she was a harpy who had married the old man merely for his money. Only Michael knew Robert had precious little actual coin in the world.

What had brought Amelia Lawrence to marry Robert Mitchell? Could she really be a radical abolitionist ready to foment revolution and assassination? She'd likely never let him get close enough to find out now. What had he been thinking, practically attacking her that way?

He hadn't been thinking at all, no matter what Ben Taylor had told him to do. Woo her, flirt with her, find out what he could. He had done nothing but react to her proximity.

The need inside him to follow his impulse had grown all too easily since he first saw her, until he'd seized the moment and chosen to silence her in what was surely the most inappropriate manner. He *was* a cad.

The taste of her lips still lingered on his. Despite her widowed status, she was an innocent. Unskilled, but filled with untapped passion. He knew that just as keenly as he knew he would be aching for the rest of the day with unfulfilled lust. And he had been ready to remedy that situation right there in Robert's study, despite knowing it would end his quest as surely as if he'd announced his true vocation.

Despite that single damning tear streaking her cheek and her genuine sorrow touching his heart, he had still been ready to kiss her senseless and find the release he needed in the depths of her softness.

Hell and be damned to the consequences.

Even now he would be lucky if he did not find himself tossed out on his reprobate's ear, his reason for staying in the area blown.

He groaned again and headed for the yard.

He could taste snow in the air, an almost ever-present occurrence once the weather truly turned cold. They would need extra kindling to keep the fires going. And even if they didn't, he needed to excise the tension from his body in the only acceptable way open to him. He hefted the axe and put himself to work.

He returned to the house late enough to avoid the other occupants of the Grand Estate and took his dinner plate straight up to the attic. The night proved to be every bit as frustrating as he had pictured it to be. Between his failure to resolve the task that had brought him here and his inability to stop thinking about the beautiful Widow Mitchell, he was driving himself mad.

He also couldn't stop regretting the broken note in Amelia's voice when she had begged him to release her. That had undone him more than anything else. He'd always thought of himself as an honorable man. Perhaps his masquerade as a drifter and a no-account had spilled over into his real life and changed him into the lowlife she believed him to be.

With a curse he pushed from the tangle of bedsheets that had become more prison than haven in the past couple of hours. A derisive smile twisted his lips as he pulled on a pair of trousers. What would Cora and Clara think if he went outside now and started chopping more kindling? Cora's eyes had already gone wide enough at the pile he'd produced earlier in the evening. Perhaps Becky needed an extra portion of feed to stave off the cold.

He glanced out the window.

Snow fell in soft, tiny flakes, dusting the world outside in white and gray. He sighed and raked a hand through his hair. Perhaps he wasn't up to frostbite and snow in the middle of the night after all.

The kitchen would have to do instead. A hot cup of tea might relax him. Or perhaps, more to the point, a healthy portion of whiskey. Although Robert had not been a drinking man, Ethan kept a flask hidden in the depths of the pantry. He shrugged into a shirt and padded barefoot down the steps, leaving his disquiet behind in the darkened attic.

Moonlight glinted on the new-fallen snow, shimmering fresh, cool light throughout the house and giving him a clear view down the steps. There would be no need to so much as light a lantern and take any chance of disturbing anyone.

He reached the bottom of the steps and turned down the hallway toward the kitchen. He pushed open the door, passed through the kitchen, and made his way to the pantry. He lit one match to help him in his search. Ah, there it was. The single flame licked the slender whiskey bottle.

He pulled the bottle off the shelf, and took a healthy plug. The whiskey burned a welcome path down his throat. Rough and ready. Not something that would have graced his father's and Eugenia's table, but more than adequate for his purpose, to erase one pale and lovely widow from his thoughts long enough to get some sleep.

He pushed the pantry door open and froze as the very thing he sought to avoid confronted him.

Bathed in pale moonlight, she looked like an angel, a vision in a loose white gown with dark hair tumbling over her shoulders. Very like the first morning of her recovery when he'd still been her fevered state's lieutenant, her angel, not the vagabond she thought him now. At least this gown was nice thick flannel protecting her from the cold and from his eager gaze.

Her pale cheeks in the moonlight were lit with a radiance that made his mouth water as she attempted to stir up some flames in the stove with some of his kindling.

And very unsuccessfully at that.

For a moment he was caught between the temptation to just stand and watch her and the need to put as much distance as possible between the two of them before he continued to be the cad she thought him to be. Each movement she made held the unconscious grace that defined her even as the fabric of her gown dipped and swayed around her. Yet her frustration seemed to be growing with each failed attempt to coax heat from the stove.

He took pity on them both. "It helps if you stoke the fire first."

"Oh." She straightened and knocked into the kettle on the stove with a clatter. Water sloshed over the side. Her gaze moved over him in one swift assessment, noting his unfastened shirt and the whiskey bottle still in his fist. He was tempted to close the buttons and release the whiskey—anything to erase the sudden flare of fear on her face. But perhaps it would be better for her to fear him and keep her distance.

"I . . . I didn't know anyone else was about. What are you doing up?" She hugged her arms about her as though suddenly conscious of the gown, the late hour, and everything that had passed between them earlier.

"Probably the same thing you are doing." He walked toward her and she retreated the tiniest bit before lifting her chin and arching a fine brow upward. He could almost read her decision to stand her ground on her features.

"I doubt that—I am attempting to make tea." She made the whole enterprise sound like some lofty calling.

"So it would seem." He bent and perused the cold stove and spilt water. "Like I said, it helps to feed the fire first. Here, hold this."

He thrust the whiskey flask unceremoniously into her hands, opened the stove front, and stoked what was left of the fire to life, adding more of the kindling his frustration had produced. He smiled at the thought.

"There—that should do it." He maneuvered a few levers on the stove and flames flickered beneath the kettle.

"Thank you." She was holding the whiskey as though it were a dead cat—with two fingers and a moue of distaste. He took it back from her. "I've never had to . . . well, thank you."

What had she never had to do? Light a stove? Make her own tea? Drink whiskey from an open bottle?

Any one of those was fully evident. He was quite certain his stepmother had never heated her own tea water, either.

She turned toward the cupboards and after a few moments had successfully located a canister of tea and the pot. He was impressed despite himself. She was not one to give up easily, his little widow. She struggled with the tea tin; its tight fit didn't seem to want to give beneath her prying fingers. He watched her work at it, caught despite himself as her gown edged down one shoulder.

Somehow he had never imagined it might be quite so interesting to watch a woman attempt the process of making tea. Particularly one who smelled of new fall apples, crisp and tangy, and looked like she belonged at a ball or soiree despite her state of dishabille.

Finally she glanced up and caught the look on his face. She ceased her struggles instantly, blew out a quick breath, and swiped her long hair over her shoulders with an impatient toss.

She thrust the tin toward him. "Perhaps you are more familiar with this contraption."

"Are you asking me to open it, princess?"

Six

That determined little chin edged upward as he couldn't resist goading her. This was exactly what had gotten him into trouble this afternoon when he'd prodded her in the study. He really liked the way she didn't back down when challenged. Was there anything about her, anything at all, that he could manage to resist?

Her brows rose and for a moment he thought she would argue with him as she had earlier that day. He found himself anticipating that reaction and the sparkle it would add to her eyes. He really should never have entered the kitchen.

She blew out a quick breath, disappointing him as she held her temper.

"Yes." One quick nod as her lips tightened.

He pried the tea tin open with a push from his thumbs. The aromatic leaves rustled in the can, like pieces of the puzzle he was still struggling to put together. The dusty edges of his life. Was it any wonder he was as susceptible to this woman as he was? Was this the same reaction Robert had experienced?

His brother had once written after a grueling exam week to say adversity that did not break the spirit would serve to make it stronger. Amelia reminded Michael of those words as she faced her new life.

"Thank you." She accepted the tin back and turned away, an unfortunate motion that presented the graceful length of her back to him. He wished he hadn't drunk that whiskey. All it seemed to do was weaken his abilities to withstand temptation still further. He also wished he'd had the gall to finish the bottle and damn them both.

Her hair fell forward as she worked. The back of her neck offered him a tempting blend of innocence and soft sensuality. The gown dipped in the back. He could see the movement of her shoulder blades as she measured the tea.

All soft, tempting skin under a single layer of flannel.

The urge to move closer and pull her into his arms grew stronger by the moment. He clenched his fists. The effect she had on him was potent and unrelenting as it sifted its way through his self-respect, his good intentions. For a man who prided himself on his ability to reason and react correctly in any given situation, he was discovering a tremendous weakness where Amelia Mitchell was concerned.

"You needn't stay." Her voice was quiet and just the tiniest bit off-key. Was she aware of what he was thinking? "I am quite certain I can manage from here."

She was right. He ought to leave. He knew that as surely as he knew his own name. Why, then, was he planting a hip against the stalwart kitchen table and crossing his arms as though he intended to stay for a while?

"I'm certain you can manage just about anything if you try hard enough, princess."

She turned to face him. "Why do you keep calling me that?"

"It fits." He shrugged and let his gaze wander the length of her as he reached for the whiskey bottle again.

She shook her head, sending dark hair cascading over her shoulders. Tempting him to do what she requested and leave. At once.

"Perhaps I was at one time, but I have long since ceased to be anyone's princess." Longing threaded that sentence for what once had been.

Then she sighed. "Besides, I somehow doubt you mean it as a compliment."

He smiled again. She was very astute, attuned to the nuances of social interaction from years in a drawing room full of capricious society darlings. Did a quiet boarding house kitchen in the dead of night unnerve her enough to force honesty to the surface? Would he learn more about her this way than through seduction?

"Whose princess were you?"

She snapped the lid on the tea canister as the kettle behind her began to whisper. She shot him an appraising look. Who was gauging whom more accurately?

"Does it matter?"

"I'd like to know." He shrugged a pretense of casual interest. Surprise caught him in the gut. He wanted to know far more than Ben Taylor's justifications for investigating her allowed.

He gripped the whiskey flask tighter. It really was time to execute a strategic retreat before he did something he would regret in the morning.

She smiled and shook her head. "There are things I'd rather not tell you. I'd rather not tell anyone. My life is far different now. But then, you know that already."

Her smile drifted away and her gaze slid from him as she realized her words were a direct link back to their heated exchange earlier, to his unorthodox method of silencing her. He couldn't help wondering if she was still awake in the middle of the night because of the warmth of that kiss.

Guilt asserted itself again. She might not have married Robert Mitchell for reasons of undying love—in fact, he was ready to bet that had not been the reason at all. She might be adept at social courtesies and public facades, but she lacked the basic ingredients to be truly deceptive. In any event, she could not hide the struggle trying to live with Robert's death had thrust on her.

"Amelia—"

"Thank you again for helping me with the fire. And the canister," she interrupted. "As I said earlier, I'm quite certain I can handle things from here. I'd hate to think I was keeping you from your bed."

Truer words had never been spoken.

"You're not." He denied them anyway.

"Oh. Well, that's good." She placed her hands together. "Really, Mr. Thompson, I find I am not comfortable alone with you at this late hour. Neither of us is even remotely attired properly for mixed company."

Her gaze flicked away from him for a minute and then back. "I should have left the kitchen as soon as I knew you were here. But since this is my home and I am your landlord, I think it would be very good of you to respect what I am asking and take your leave. Even if you do not respect me."

Such a prim and proper little speech, delivered in a firm tone. Yet beneath it he sensed that she was holding her breath and wondering if he would obey her.

"Very well, Mrs. Mitchell. It is certainly not my desire to be responsible for making you uncomfortable in any way." He bowed slightly and took another step toward her.

She shook her head. "There are times when you do not seem to be a drifter."

"Really?" He arched a brow at her. "And what do I seem?"

"I don't know." Her brow crinkled as she considered her answer. "A misplaced gentleman perhaps?"

All too close to the truth. She was no dummy, his little widow.

"Appearances can be deceiving." He leaned toward her as the tea kettle began to whistle in earnest.

Her gaze strayed over his mouth as he came closer.

He reached behind her and grasped the handle, pulling the protesting kettle to safety.

"Amelia."

She hadn't moved. "Yes."

"Your kettle is ready." He told her. He needed to apologize for his earlier behavior and for the guilty thoughts even now gathering in his mind. He needed to offer her the respect she deserved as Robert's widow. He could already taste the full resilience of her mouth beneath his.

"Yes." She tipped her chin just the slightest bit.

It was all the encouragement he needed.

"Hell."

He closed the remaining distance between them and tasted her waiting lips. She was every bit as soft and passionate as he remembered.

He deliberately kept his hands off her, allowing only his mouth to show her what he felt. Each worshipful pressure was his apology. If he touched her now, if he allowed himself the warm feel of her skin, he would lose the internal battle he'd been fighting since he'd first seen her bathed in the cool, snow-drenched moonlight. He would make love to her regardless of his unspoken promises, to her and to himself.

She moaned very softly as her mouth opened beneath his. He dipped his tongue inside to taste her in long, slow strokes. She was heaven, responsive and sweet. She was hell and damnation rolled into one tempting package as she returned each slow stroke with one of her own. Desire pounded, hot and demanding, in his veins. He would need more than whiskey to get her out of his blood.

He pulled away from her as everything in him screamed to possess her.

"Good night, princess." The words rasped from him, low and husky.

Her fingers brushed her lips as her gaze tangled with his. There were no tears shimmering there this time. It was the one thing that would make the coming night of torment worthwhile.

He turned away from her and headed for the door.

"Michael?" He gritted his teeth at the sound of his name on her lips. The soft entreaty. It made him want to throw his good intentions out the window and follow through on his true desires.

"Yes." He barely managed the word.

"Thank you."

He nodded his head, having lost all capacity for speech as her gratitude took him off guard.

Robert's widow was very astute, indeed. If women were allowed into the U.S. Marshal Service, she would no doubt make a fine investigator.

She had understood the unspoken things he'd been trying to tell her. That was something he wasn't ready to deal with. That would make her so much more irresistible and undeniable. There was something between them that had sparked all too quickly in the train station in Chicago. Some invisible link that didn't care for propriety, honor, or obligation. That was why he felt in his bones that she already belonged to him. She was his. There was no need for ceremony and announcements to the world.

He cursed inwardly and forced himself out the door. The whiskey had been no help. It was still going to be a very long night.

Amelia watched the door swing shut behind Michael as the feelings unleashed by his tender and ardent kiss swirled on inside her.

This kiss had been every bit as forbidden and deeply passionate as the first they'd shared. There had been no excuse for it. And no excuse for her own part in it. She was worldly enough to know the tilt of her head had encouraged him to break through whatever restraints he had placed on himself.

Heat burned in her cheeks and lingered on her lips. It had been wrong. There was no denying the scandal broth she was deliberately brewing. And yet, kissing Michael just now hadn't felt like the wrong thing at all. It had felt like the first right thing she'd done since she'd arrived in Warm Springs and awoken at the Grand Estate.

Which, of course, didn't make any sense whatsoever.

She rubbed a hand across her brow and poured hot water over the tea she'd come downstairs to make in the first place. Warm and sweet, the aroma drifted up from the pot.

How could anything that just passed between her and Michael Thompson, drifter, ne'er-do-well, and man of mystery, be right?

She shook her head.

There wasn't anything about such an exchange that could be right.

But then, what was true and correct about her entire situation since she had run headlong into that newspaper cart back on Milk Street?

Had that truly only happened a few short months ago?

Somehow it seemed like that incident had happened to someone else. In another lifetime. She let the tea steep for a few moments as she turned her gaze out the kitchen window. It was darker than dark outside, save for the bright reflection of the moonlight on the snow. No street lamps or reflections from windows down the lane. No sounds of passing vehicles or people going about their occupations or entertainments. Would she ever get used to the idea of being far away from people? Any people at all, let alone the family and friends she had left behind.

She couldn't help wondering how Lenore and Tori were dealing with any problems on their chosen journeys. Would either of them even believe what had become of their friend? Could she? They'd dreamed of changing their destinies, hopefully her friends were faring better than she.

She blew out a sigh and added sugar to her cup then poured tea into it. Enough. She couldn't dwell perpetually on the life that used to be, that never would be again. This was her life now.

But for how long?

The future seemed as dark and forbidding as the depths of the night outside. There was no telling what lay beyond the outer edges of the buildings in the yard. Just as there was no way to know what lay in her future.

One thing she knew was that she couldn't go on torturing herself over the decisions she'd made—the choices that had brought her to Robert Mitchell's Grand Estate.

She was here now. And that was truly all that mattered. Michael Thompson. Taxes. Investments. All the things threatening her with a night full of worries would sort themselves out eventually.

She wrapped her hands around the warm teacup and turned away from the cold snow-shrouded scene in the backyard. She was here now and this was her future. These people needed her, even if they hadn't yet realized it.

The thought made her smile in spite of herself.

They needed her.

She took a sip from the cup and nearly choked on the leaves swimming at the top. So much for making her own tea.

Her tenants might need her, and it was apparent that she needed them.

Morning came all too soon.

Amelia's eyes popped open even before the sun had fully risen. She'd had just about enough dreams of stolen kisses. Her feet curled away from the floorboards. For a moment she was caught between the urge to snuggle back into the depths of the big bed and stay that way for a few more hours—and the equally strong and surprising urge to take charge of her life.

True, she tried that once already with less than successful results, but anything else seemed the wrong way to approach her newfound responsibilities.

We'll go on as we always have. Helping one another. Cora's words of encouragement came back to comfort her.

What kind of example would she be setting for these people who so revered Robert?

She forced herself out of the bed and hurried to wash and dress. She donned her one mourning gown again and admitted to herself that it just would not do. Not for the daunting task of learning to actually keep house. The few other gowns she had couldn't possibly help. None of them were suitable. Perhaps it was time to pay an official visit to Eleanor Holmdale and engage her services.

She drew her hair up and bundled it into a chignon, perused herself once in the mirror, and sailed out of the room, gathering her determination as she went.

She brushed her hand lightly over the paneling as she made her way down the steps. She liked the staircase. And she could all too easily imagine Betty Mitchell had liked it, too. The curved banister felt good beneath her fingers, and the intricate carvings at the landing benches showed care. Each one offered a lovely view of the lake, snow-dusted and frozen in the murky, early morning light.

She reached the bottom with her determination in high gear. There were already sounds coming from the kitchen—so much for her certainty that she would be the first awake. But when she entered, there was no one there. Perhaps she had only imagined the sounds. Yet . . . She glanced out the back to find footsteps etched in the delicate dusting of snow leading away from the house. Someone had braved the cold and the snow at this early hour.

But who?

Judging from the size of the footsteps and the spacing between each footfall, it was a woman. Cora? Clara? What would draw one of them outside at such an hour? And if it was important enough for such a trek, perhaps they needed assistance.

"Nonsense," she shushed her unwarranted fears. And tried to concentrate on what she had observed while Michael built up the fire last night. That would be a useful task even if she had no idea what to do next. Making tea was out of the question.

Her gaze strayed once again to the footprints outside. Amelia bit her lip for a moment and then shook her head as her curiosity got the better of her. She couldn't allow whoever it was to wander off alone in the snow-dusted cold.

What if something happened? What if something was wrong? She couldn't just stay inside and keep herself warm when someone was out alone in the cold.

She retrieved her black cloak and bonnet quickly from a peg in the hallway and made her way out into the cold without further delay. Picking her way carefully along the row of footprints, she ventured out past the barn and along a row of trees and still the trail moved onward.

She hurried her pace, her breath coming as great unladylike puffs of steam in the cold air. She shook her head, not bothering to slow down. Mama would be disturbed by the picture she presented, chasing after one of her boarders, but what difference did it make out here? Absolutely none.

She walked for what seemed like a long time. Beyond the last stand of trees lay an open meadow and in the distance beyond it, a small farmhouse.

And there in the meadow stood a lone figure.

Amelia hurried up to join Eleanor Holmdale, swathed in an overcoat and woolen scarf.

The woman's gaze passed over her; a small frown creased her brow.

"Hullo, Amelia. Did I disturb you, going out so early this morning?"

"No, you didn't." Amelia shook her head. "I was just surprised to realize there was anyone else about. And I had no idea why . . ."

Mama also would not approve of baseless curiosity, but she couldn't help herself. She'd come all this way. "Is . . . is everything all right, Eleanor?"

"Of course, why shouldn't it be?" The woman had a bearing and elegance of manner that Mama would have approved of, that much Amelia knew. Gracious in her answer, but revealing nothing more than she intended.

"Well . . ." Puffs of white punctuated each word they spoke. The cold nipped at Amelia now that she had stopped moving. She tried to suppress any shivers.

"It seemed an odd time to go walking and we are far from the house. I was . . . worried about you."

"Really? How kind of you." The elderly woman brushed a smile over Amelia and looked across the meadow at the house in the distance. Was there someone there they were going to visit?

"You haven't grown accustomed to the varieties of your new household yet, have you? That's to be expected." She started walking and signaled for Amelia to join her. "However, if you intend to make a habit of going out on such cold mornings, you'll have to dress much more warmly."

"This is all I have, at the moment."

"Really?" Eleanor quirked an elegant brow. "We can address that more quickly than other aspects of your wardrobe.

"Not," she hastened to add, "that your dress is not perfectly adequate for your current needs. But I imagine you might like a change or two and much of what you brought with you must be unsuitable for a winter spent in mourning, especially situated in the country as we are."

They continued across the field in silence for a few minutes. "I do believe I disconcerted Robert when he first realized what I was doing. I should have thought to tell you ahead of time."

"Tell me what?"

"This is what I do. Rain or shine, no matter the season. Snow just makes it more of a challenge. Not that this counts as much of a snow. Wait until January."

"But . . . what are you doing?" Amelia was breathless from anticipation.

"Something my husband and I started many, many

years ago." Eleanor smiled as she lifted the small pouch at her side and loosened the bindings at the top. "Feeding the deer."

Real warmth lit Eleanor's face for the first time since Amelia had met her. For a moment, a dreamy cast softened Eleanor's otherwise controlled and proper gaze. "We used to do this every morning. Together."

She sighed and reached into the pouch, extracting small bits of dried corn with her bare hand. "It is especially difficult for them to find food at this time of year. And the corn is good for them."

As she sprinkled the ground, she sang softly under her breath. An old tune about love and togetherness and the sorrow of love lost.

"We'll have to hurry." Eleanor finished and wiped her hands on the cloth pouch, then pulled on her gloves. She reached for Amelia's hand. "Come along. They won't come out if we are too close. And, of course, they will try to smell you long before they show themselves."

"Smell me?" Amelia couldn't keep the horrified tone out of her voice, though she was quite certain the woman meant no offense.

Eleanor chuckled. "Of course. Now hurry."

For an older woman, she had quite a bit of strength in the grip she placed on Amelia's hand. Must be from the sewing. Eleanor drew Amelia back across the meadow. Puffs of breath steamed from them both as they reached the meadow's edge. Eleanor stopped.

Amelia's toes were cold and damp. She should have put boots on instead of going out in her soft kid house shoes. In truth, she should have been more sensible in her determination to find out who and what her missing tenant was up to. Now there were two of them gone from the house without explanation.

"What—"

"Shhh." Eleanor held a finger to her lips and her eyes sparkled. "Just watch."

Silence echoed across the meadow, heavy with waiting in the early light. Amelia held her tongue as she waited and wondered what on earth could be so interesting about feeding deer.

Then at the edge of the meadow opposite their position, movement showed.

Eleanor squeezed her hand. "There is the buck."

A single deer stepped forward and tensed, sniffing the air. Smelling for them, perhaps?

"Watch him," Eleanor whispered. "The others will wait for his signal before coming any closer."

The single deer, the buck, turned his head slightly to the left. Dark eyes flickered toward them. He was lovely; *handsome* was too plain a word for so majestic a bearing and stance. A smooth grayish brown, his coat was sleek and short. Nobility defined even the tiniest movement from the arch of his neck to the flick of his tail.

For the span of several heartbeats he stood still as stone. He could have been a statue, save for the small puffs of white breath that disturbed the air in front of him.

Then he moved forward with sublime dignity. Several smaller deer edged quietly out of the woodland's edge behind him.

"He has accepted your presence on your first visit. That is a high compliment," Eleanor whispered.

Warmth flooded Amelia, followed quickly by

amazement. She'd been thrilled to think these animals had accepted her. As thrilled as she might have been a few months ago by a special invitation to an exclusive party. She had hoped for change when she'd had her fateful encounter on Milk Street and she had certainly achieved that.

The buck and the first does were joined by a host of other graceful, brown-gray, sleek-bodied animals that just seemed to melt out of the trees. One moment they were not there and the next they were. They moved as one harmonious unit until they had reached the corn scattered in such loving disarray, and began to eat.

"Come, we'll leave them now." Eleanor squeezed Amelia's hand as her whisper disturbed the morning air.

They picked their way carefully back to the edge of the trees before Eleanor spoke again.

"Thank you for coming after me, Amelia. That was very thoughtful of you."

"You're quite welcome. Thank you for sharing your morning routine with me."

Eleanor laughed. "You are quite welcome in return. It is the first time I've had company since my dear husband passed away."

She sighed and looked over at her house. "Dear Jacob. He enjoyed this even more than I do. It was his passion to watch them. He sketched them quite often. The deer, the turkey, rabbits, and hawks."

A shimmer of tears gathered at the corner of her eyes. "He had talent, my Jacob. Though he was a modest man and a farmer at heart."

"You had a farm, then?"

"Oh, yes." Eleanor smiled to herself for a moment. "Did you notice the farmhouse in the distance?"

"Yes."

"That is mine. Mine and Jacob's."

"Is?" Amelia couldn't help the prod. She talked as if she still owned the farm.

"Yes." Eleanor slanted her a look. "Does that surprise you? I suppose it does. You are wondering why I live at the Grand Estate when I have a perfectly serviceable home nearby?"

"Yes." Heat tinged Amelia's cheeks. She was prying horribly, but Eleanor didn't seem to mind.

"The farm was Jacob's dream. He loved it. That's why I cannot part with it. And I cannot bring myself to leave Warm Springs. Can you imagine? I never thought I would hear myself say those words. But it's true. This is where I spent my life and where I married my Jacob." She laughed again, though melancholy edged the sound.

"You see, my dear, I came to Warm Springs with dreams that were far different from Jacob's. I wanted him to be an artist. To make something of himself and take us both into an entirely different life." She turned a glance toward Amelia. "I believe that your life before you met Robert was . . . different as well."

For a moment Amelia was stung by the observation. Was it so terribly obvious that she was out of place here and that she had been raised with an expectation of gracious living?

"Yes." She acknowledged the comment quietly.

"It's all right. You needn't share anything with me that you are not comfortable telling. I sense in you the girl I once was. That gives us a kinship beyond the others. They are good people, though, all of them. And that is why I came to live at Robert Mitchell's Grand Estate."

She stopped. "Other than the terrific irony of the name—it is the perfect place for me. I have company—and my memories, whenever I choose."

Amelia pictured the Grand Estate as it had been this morning, snow-washed and rising high in the early morning sun. It was a lovely old building.

"You run along before the others are worried. I'm going home for breakfast today and so should you."

"Home?" That's how she'd termed the Grand Estate yesterday.

"It just might turn out to be the perfect place for you as well." Eleanor squeezed her hand, and set off back to her farm the way they had just come.

And Amelia continued on to the Grand Estate.

The perfect place? Only time would tell.

Seven

"You don't mind if I come in, do you, Mrs. Mitchell?" The man on the front porch clutched a large package wrapped in brown paper as he tipped his hat. "I'm Otis MacNamara, owner of MacNamara's Emporium. I need to leave these items for Mrs. Holmdale."

"She's not here at the moment. Perhaps I could take them for you?" Amelia reached for the package after wiping her hands on her apron. "I'll see she gets this as soon as she returns."

"I couldn't ask you to carry this. It's quite heavy." The tall, slender man peered at her through his spectacles. "I know you are only recently recovered from the initial shock of your husband's demise. I'll just bring this in and leave it for Mrs. Holmdale on the hall table, along with a note and my directions. This is a rush job."

He looked Amelia up and down for a moment. A faint bead of sweat gathered on the upper fringe of his light mustache as he awaited her answer.

The worn gray skirt and overlarge white blouse she had donned this morning, at Clara and Cora's urging when they learned of her plans to dust and organize the study while they attended the Ladies Mission Society meeting at the church, had seemed appropriate enough at the time. Now, she wished she had kept to her strict mourning. Except for her mourning outfit, most of her remaining clothes were either frilly tea dresses or evening gowns. Not for the first time, she felt a bubble of hysterical laughter building at her foolish naivete in thinking that was all she'd need for her new husband's Grand Estate.

"Besides," Mr. MacNamara leaned forward slightly as he pressed his entreaty, "I have a matter I must discuss with you regarding your late husband."

"Robert?" Had they been friends, her husband and this man? How ridiculous. To take even a portion of Cora's chatter to heart would confirm that her husband had been the best of friends with nearly half the population of the entire state of Illinois. "You said you were the owner of MacNamara's Emporium. You're Festive's employer, are you not?"

MacNamara nodded. "Yes. It was made clear to me that Festival Miller came with the store and goods when I bought out the former owners last spring. He's minding the counter for me even now, so I can not be long."

He looked down the lane toward the curve to town for a moment as if seeking reassurance that all was well, then turned back to the doorway.

Amelia was alone in the house. Ethan had headed to his workshop at the livery at the same time Festive had left for work. The Brown sisters would be gone through luncheon. Eleanor was off for one of her walks and Michael had disappeared before breakfast. She was reluctant to entertain a stranger on her own. But then, even the people she lived with were strangers.

"Normally," Mr. MacNamara dropped his tone, "I

would have sent this along by way of Festive, but I did want the opportunity to speak to you in person on a confidential matter. And as I said, this is a rush job for some of the rail workers."

Although still reluctant, Amelia finally nodded and opened the door to admit her visitor. Alone or not, what harm could there be in allowing the Emporium owner in to deliver a package? He was Festive's employer and he paid Eleanor for her work altering his ready-to-wear clothing, too. Eleanor needed the money and in turn would pay her for room and board. She really could not afford to offend Otis MacNamara. Besides, he looked harmless enough.

"Please come in." She stepped back to let him pass. "I'm afraid I was not expecting any callers."

"No need to explain, Mrs. Mitchell." He plopped his bundle down on the table and pulled out a handkerchief to swipe his face. "I entirely understand that you are not yet up to entertaining.

"If I might trouble you for the means to write that note to Mrs. Holmdale." He placed his hat on the table and looked at her hopefully after pushing his spectacles back up his nose and smoothing his hair back on his temples.

"Of course." Amelia closed the door with a lingering tug of reluctance and gestured toward the open study door. "There's paper and ink in my husband's desk. I was just in there working on organizing some of his books."

"Thank you. You are indeed as kind as Festive described." McNamara stepped back to let her usher him into the room.

"And even more beautiful," he added in that lower

tone he obviously felt conveyed intimacy in what now seemed an entirely too narrow hall.

A cold shiver streaked down Amelia's spine as she passed him. She was being ridiculous. Just because this weasely-looking man paid her a compliment. There had been a time when half the men on Beacon Hill would have said as much and she'd paid them no heed. His remark should have flattered her, given the dark circles still lingering under her eyes from her recent illness, not to mention the lines caused by her new set of worries.

"I think you'll find what you require over here." She moved to the far side of the massive mahogany desk she had just finished polishing when the front doorbell rang. She felt more comfortable with as much distance and furniture as possible between herself and her guest. A guest who appeared to have his gaze fixed on her bosom, although she prayed it was just the impression the thick lenses of his spectacles gave, rather than the truth.

He mopped his upper lip again and pocketed his handkerchief. "It's been unusually warm this past week or so, given the time of year. Could I trouble you further and ask you for a glass of water?"

Trouble? Amelia was grateful for the excuse to escape him long enough to compose her wayward reactions.

"I'll be right back," she excused herself and practically fled the room as Otis MacNamara set about scribbling his note without even looking up.

She was letting her imagination run rampant over her better judgement. Really. It was outside of enough that she had allowed, let alone enjoyed, Michael

Thompson's heated kisses far more than was proper under any circumstances. She must not let her swift changes in marital status make her suspect every man who made her acquaintance of having lascivious thoughts.

"Stop being ridiculous, Amelia," she scolded herself as she pushed open the door to the kitchen.

After dipping a tall glass full from the covered crock in the back pantry, she put several lemon sugar cookies on a plate. She did not want the first person from Warm Springs she met outside of Horace Salzburg or Robert's eclectic household to think she was a less than gracious hostess. That would never do.

If she knew anything about people, it was how much they loved to talk about one another. There was enough fodder in Robert's hasty marriage, his sudden demise, and her own dramatic entrance into town without her adding new fuel to the gossip fires. After hunting a tray, she turned to leave the kitchen and very nearly collided with her guest. Despite herself, she let out a little squeak of alarm.

"I beg your pardon, Mrs. Mitchell. I did not mean to startle you. I thought you said something to me I did not quite catch as you departed the study." Otis MacNamara's face appeared flushed with his embarrassment.

"No, no." She could feel heat spreading across her own cheeks. Her mother had chided her quite often as a child for talking to herself. If she wasn't careful, she'd be labeled as some sort of eccentric or lunatic. "I was just reminding myself where I could find the glassware. Everything here is still strange to me."

"Well, you appear to have fulfilled my simple request not only with great efficiency, but also with a touch of graciousness. Those cookies look delicious." He pushed his spectacles back up his nose and peered at her intently as if cookies were the last thing on his mind.

What was wrong with her? Surely this man was not like the hotel manager in Chicago, who considered a widow easy prey. She was his neighbor. His customer.

"Clara . . . Miss Brown left these from the batch she baked for the Mission Society meeting." She added a napkin to the tray, fighting to ignore the fact that her neighbor's gaze was now fixed on the too-short hem of her cast-off skirt and the small expanse of ankle and calf exposed above her demi-boots. She'd have to hunt for longer hand-me-downs as soon as he left.

"Perhaps we should return to the study so we can discuss that matter of business you mentioned earlier. You said it was confidential and I am quite sure one of my boarders will be home any minute."

She prayed that was true. She hated this feeling of utter vulnerability.

"Ahh, yes. Our business." Otis MacNamara smoothed his thinning hair as he appeared to collect his thoughts. "Could I carry the tray for you? I know you are only just recovering from an illness."

"I can manage." She squared her shoulders. She was a Lawrence of Boston. No matter her reduced circumstance or cast-off garb, she was not going to be intimidated by a local shopkeeper. "Thank you anyway. If you would get the door, perhaps?"

He stood to one side and held the door for her. With a few quick steps they were back inside the sun-lit study. She set the tray on an end table on one side of the sofa and took a seat in a wing-back chair on the opposite side of the tufted velvet settee.

"Please have a seat, sir. And help yourself to the cookies before you impart whatever information you hold regarding my husband's business." The cool edge she'd put into her invitation should serve to keep any errant overtures from Otis MacNamara at bay even before he might think of them.

And if she was too late to influence his thoughts, she could at least forestall any action. With her back to the window, she was pretty sure her guest would be hard-pressed to continue staring at her. Which might or might not be a good thing, she second-guessed herself, as he settled next to a decidedly worn spot on the burgundy fabric. She did not want all and sundry to know just how strained her finances were before she'd had time to consider all the options that might be available to her.

"What is it you wish to discuss with me, Mr. MacNamara?" Now that she'd seized control of this interview, she intended to keep it.

He took a sip of the water he had requested and cleared his throat while he reached into his waistcoat pocket. Unfolding the creased paper he withdrew, he tendered it toward her as he edged closer to her side of the settee.

"After going through the former owners' accounts and adding up the chits your late husband signed since I took over, this is the figure I am submitting to his estate for payment."

She accepted the paper he proffered and her heart sank. Looking at the figures scrawled there, she knew there was no way she was going to be able to pay such a large sum. Not at once, and most likely not in full until there was a drastic change in the handling of finances around here.

"Oh, my." She hated that her fingers trembled a bit as she handed him back his bill. She dug them into the arms of the chair.

"It is somewhat staggering, I know." Mr. MacNamara fairly oozed sympathy as he edged even closer and pocketed the paper. "But I did not come to press you for payment today."

What was the proper length of time to elapse before pressing for a deceased person's debts? The random question floated through her thoughts as Otis MacNamara leaned closer. Somehow she had missed that portion in Mama's lesson's in deportment.

"Once you are over your initial grief . . ." He'd lowered his voice to his intimate tone again. She positively loathed the sound. "I'm quite certain we can reach . . . equitable terms."

She should have left him standing on the front porch. Equitable terms indeed. But then again, she had a household to feed and his store was the only one in town. Add to those facts the debt owed him, and she was in a quandary over how best to react. She couldn't lead him on, but she couldn't afford to offend him, either. She chewed her lips as she chewed through her limited options

"What sort of terms, Mr. MacNamara?" Naivete had led her to open the door to this odious man. Perhaps she could use it to dodge him for the interim.

"Pray, call me Otis, my dear Mrs. Mitchell." He took her hand in his. "I can see you are overset by all of this. That was the furthest thing from my intentions in bringing such matters up at this time."

She almost snorted.

"Why thank you . . . Otis," she stammered instead. Naivete was all well and good. Now if she could just figure out some way to pry her fingers loose from his.

"You really are so young to have to face the burden of running a household this size all on your own." He gripped her so tightly she almost winced. Beads of moisture gathered on the top fringe of his thin mustache once again.

He took a deep breath and tilted his head to meet her gaze with his own eyes wide behind the thick lenses of his spectacles.

When he'd entered law enforcement, Michael had never imagined how much of his time would be spent surreptitiously eavesdropping on the unsuspecting. Or, more accurately, on those he suspected. Still, he felt more than a little foolish skulking on the porch, listening at the study window.

What game was Robert's young widow up to, anyway? Even a green girl like Katie knew better than to be caught alone with a man. He tried not to dwell on the searing fire he'd felt in the brief kisses he'd shared with Amelia Mitchell, bespeaking a woman who was far from naive.

"You really are so young to have to face the burden of running a household this size all on your own . . ."

The words were barely slipping from Otis MacNamara's tongue on the other side of the glass before Michael was moving to intervene. He'd heard enough.

Festive had waved him down to show him his new apron and tell him how he'd been entrusted with minding the store while his employer ran an errand that included urgent business with Mrs. Mitchell. Urgent, his badge.

Until Michael nailed down which of the two individuals he had his eye on as the guilty party in his brother's murder, he felt duty-bound to make sure both men cut a wide swath around the pretty young widow, no matter Marshal Taylor's suspicions regarding her own activities. And no matter Amelia's own questionable intentions with this private tea party. She obviously had no sense of propriety regarding her recent widowhood.

"Hullo, Auntie," he called from the foyer, hoping to both prick Amelia's conscience and provoke a rise in her. She'd clearly been displeased the last time he'd called her by their pseudo-familial connection.

He slung his jacket over one arm and carried the satchel of Ethan's tools he'd retrieved from under the porch step and strode into the study, feigning surprise. There sat the recently wed and widowed Mrs. Robert Mitchell in cozy proximity to her gentleman caller, holding his hand as if they were the most intimate acquaintances.

"I hope I'm not interrupting." Although who Robert Mitchell's widow took up with, or how soon, was really none of his business, Michael would gladly have strangled her, especially when he glimpsed the panic shimmering in the gaze she turned on him. Was he spoiling her plan or offering her a timely rescue? "I didn't realize you were entertaining a caller."

He retrieved a cookie from the tray and plopped

himself down on the opposite end of the sofa. He let the satchel of tools fall to the floor with a satisfying clank, stretched his legs out to get comfortable, and took a bite of cookie.

"Otis . . . Mr. MacNamara dropped off some work for Mrs. Holmdale."

Amelia stammered as if she were guilty of some trespass beyond the stupidity of inviting a man into her home when she was alone. Not to mention allowing a virtual stranger to clutch her hand like that. What could she be up to? Looking for a successor for Robert already? Again, the kisses they'd shared, the feel of her in his arms, scorched him. He realized both the other occupants of the study were looking at him expectantly. Had she asked him what he was doing here? Why were they still holding hands?

"You asked me to replace the counterweight in the window sashes," he deliberately lied. Her reaction would go a long way toward telling him if the panic he'd seen was spurred by relief at his arrival or by having been caught. "'Winter will be here soon enough and we want everything to be tight and warm,' I believe you said."

She finally pulled herself free of the shop owner's grasp and clasped her hands in front of her on her lap, looking for all the world like a prim and proper young lady.

"Thank you for responding to my request so promptly, Michael. If you continue to do so, I'm sure we'll get along famously."

She smiled almost too sweetly, despite knowing she'd never said anything about the windows and probably had no idea what a counterweight was, to boot. But at least she was going along with his story. So he was rescuing her. Relief poured through him. Could she possibly be as innocent as she seemed?

"Mr. MacNamara was just expressing his concern over my handling the burdens of running this household on my own." She turned her attention back to her guest. "But as you can see, sir, my husband's family is more than prepared to assist me."

"My aunt has no worries with me here to see to her every need." If he laughed at the expression on Otis MacNamara's face, he'd ruin this whole farce. He took another bite of cookie.

"Quite right. That's what family's for. You are to be commended for standing by her." The shopkeeper cast an assessing gaze between his hostess and her nephew-by-marriage as his complexion paled by several degrees, obviously measuring the claim being staked by Amelia's nephew-by-marriage. Good. Michael had wanted to make the warning he issued quite clear without completely calling Amelia's reputation into question or causing her any trouble once he'd completed his assignment and left town.

Now, all he had to do was send the fellow packing. "I want to commend you, too, Otis, for allowing Festive to handle the store while you came out here to see to Mrs. Mitchell's welfare. That's a great deal of trust you're showing in him."

Michael rather enjoyed the buildup to the point that he was certain would send the other man scurrying out the door. "When I walked by, the Weatherbys were handing him their winter supply list. I'm sure he'll do just fine with it, if they give him plenty of time."

"The Weatherbys?" True to expectation, MacNamara stiffened with surprise and smoothed his
thinning hair back from his temples. "Oh, my. According to my records they usually make this trip the
last week of November."

"Well, they were at your establishment not more
than a half-hour ago." Michael reached for a second
cookie, even as he turned his attention to Amelia,
hoping his description of the family would needle
MacNamara further. ". . . I think at last count there
were close to eighteen children altogether."

"Nineteen." Otis rose to the bait—and his feet.
"Gerald Weatherby's wife had a new baby just last
month. Another boy, I believe."

"That would make his sixth." Michael nodded.
"Why, the shoes they'd need to order alone must net
a tidy profit. I'm sure Festive has them all set up by
now, though."

"I'd best go supervise, in any case." Otis finally
stepped around Michael's outstretched feet. A moment later, the front door opened and shut.

Michael waited until he heard the crunch of the
shopkeeper's boots on the stone drive before he
turned his attention to the woman in the chair. She
had the gall to look both relieved and vexed which ignited his indignation further.

"Thank you—"

"Don't." He cut off her gratitude by standing
abruptly. He wanted to close the small distance between them. He wanted to grab her by the shoulders
and shake some sense into her. But the last time he'd
touched her in anger had lead them both in the opposite direction.

He paced over to the desk instead, then turned back to face her. "What were you thinking, entertaining a man alone in an empty house?"

Walking into the room to see her sitting with a man—not just any man, but a suspect in several heinous crimes, at that—who was clutching her hand and practically drooling all over her had struck him to the core. A core it disturbed him greatly to discover.

She stiffened her spine ramrod-straight. Spots of bright red burned on her cheeks as she held her peace for what seemed an interminable amount of time.

"He had a bill," she said finally, as if that explained everything.

"Then you should have accepted whatever he had to deliver at the door and arranged to discuss the matter at a later time in his place of business. Yesterday you were sharing kisses with me, today you are holding a local merchant's hand. Have you no sense of propriety or the respect due your recently departed husband?"

If ice could spit fire he would have turned to ashes on the spot from the heat of anger in her gaze. She rose from her seat, looking every inch the regal princess he had dubbed her despite the oddly sized hand-me-downs she was wearing. She clenched her hands at her side and thrust her chin out.

"I have the sense to determine the extent of the obligations left me by my husband. The means and manner in which I conduct my business is none of yours, no matter our very tenuous family connection or the fact that we have shared a kiss or two."

Eight

Amelia had never been so angry in all her days. She'd called Michael Thompson a cad just yesterday and then racked herself with guilt over her behavior. Right at this minute, she very sincerely repented every ounce of the regret she'd wasted on this man. And she'd just been silently blessing him for his timely rescue!

Now, he was practically accusing her of playing fast and loose with Otis MacNamara. At the top of his lungs, no less. And after the way he'd kissed her last night in the kitchen, she'd actually dared to hope they could be friends. *Friends.*

Michael stood there in his shirtsleeves and suspenders, glaring at her as if it was his right, his responsibility, to manage her affairs. To manage *her.*

She was tempted to turn on her heel and walk out the door. What he was implying, what he was shouting, did not really deserve an answer. But this was her study, her house, and she had no more intention of retreating from this room than she did shrinking from the pile of problems and responsibilities that kept heaping up in front of her.

Michael closed his eyes and took a deep breath. He emptied his lungs slowly, his jawline relaxing as the air escaped. Then his eyelids snapped up and he looked at her with considerably less emotion evident in his eyes. His lips, however, were still set in a grim line that did not bode well.

"You're right," he said in a tone that voiced just the opposite. "Your business is indeed your own. It would appear I owe you yet another apology."

His last apology had nearly melted her bones. If he took a step toward her, she would flee the room after all. She could not fathom the swift changes in his moods. The light glinted off his dark hair, bringing out red highlights in its crimped mass. What was it her mother had said about her stepfather, a man with bright red hair? She couldn't quite recall and the sound of the front door opening drove the fleeting memory away.

"Hello, dears," Cora Brown called from the foyer.

"We decided to excuse ourselves from the Mission Society luncheon and come home to keep you company, Amelia." Clara's voice followed close behind.

"The oddest thing just happened. Festive's employer, Mr. MacNamara, rushed by us at the gate with barely a greeting."

Both Misses Brown appeared in the study door with looks of concern etched on their faces as they stripped off their gloves.

"All the ladies of the Society are anxious to make your acquaintance, dear."

"They hope you will join us for Sunday services."

"You, too, of course, Michael."

When neither party in the study answered them, they paused and just looked at Michael and Amelia.

"Is everything all right?"

"We thought we heard raised voices."

This time it was Amelia who took a deep breath as she tried to hide her anger. "Everything is fine. Please do not concern yourselves. It was nice of you to come home early."

"But the shouting?" Clara looked inquisitively between Michael and Amelia.

"A lapse in manners. I have already apologized to my aunt." Michael ducked his head and smiled ruefully at the sisters, looking for all the world like a little boy caught in a misdeed. Surely he knew how much she detested his reference to their tenuous familial connection.

"Now, I will beg your forgiveness if you were overset by the volume I used to make my point," he continued, with the hint of mischief now absent in his tone.

"Point—"

"Family matters, Cora. We shouldn't interfere." Clara halted her sister's inquiry with a touch to her shoulder. "Let's hang our coats up and put the kettle on. We'll leave these two to settle their business amicably while we make lunch."

"I believe we have settled all that we need to, haven't we?" Amelia looked to Michael for affirmation. She really wasn't up to a full-blown confrontation and if he was willing to make peace, so be it. He raised a brow and nodded once.

"Did you get your dusting and straightening accomplished, dear?" Cora asked.

She shook her head. "I did not get very far before Mr. MacNamara called with a bundle for Eleanor. And now Michael is going to work on the windows."

"You'll have plenty of time to finish later, dear."

Cora beamed. "The windows rattle in here dreadfully when the wind whips in from the lake."

"I'm sure tightening the windows will make the room warmer, too," Clara added.

"That being the case," Amelia wasn't looking on this as so much a retreat as a graceful exit, "I would very much like to accompany you to the kitchen. If you don't mind?"

"Mind? Why, we'd love to have your company, dear. Come along." Cora was already removing her hat.

"Quite right." Clara gestured for her to follow them. "It's usually best to leave a man to do his repair work on his own. We'll let you know when luncheon is ready, Michael."

His thank-you was muffled as he bent over to retrieve his tool satchel.

"You can make the tea," Clara told Amelia as she helped the older woman take off her outer garment.

Images from last night's near-disaster flitted through her, chased by delicious ripples from the kiss she'd shared so inappropriately with Robert's nephew. She'd left the kitchen, undrinkable tea and all, almost on his heels. No wonder he'd been concerned when he'd seen her with her hand in Otis MacNamara's. Her actions were scandalous, no matter what excuse could be offered.

"I certainly love to drink tea, and I can pour out at a gathering with a certain flair," she confided. "But I have yet to master the actual making of it. Perhaps you would be kind enough to show me your method?"

"Never learned to make tea? Fancy that." Cora clucked as she hung her coat in the cedar-lined closet under the steps and took Clara's from Amelia.

"What was your mother thinking?" Clara placed their hats and gloves on the shelf and then turned with a start as if she realized what she said. "I beg your pardon. I never meant to criticize your dear mama, of course. She certainly did a fine job of raising you."

"Perhaps." Amelia shrugged. "No offense was taken. My mother was not the most practical of women. I'm not sure Mama even knew the way to the kitchen in our old home. She always summoned the cook to her study to go over the menus or accounts."

"Was there no one else in your family to show you the basics at least, dear?" Cora sounded somewhat scandalized.

Amelia shook her head. After several misadventures in the cook's province, her uncle's family had quickly learned that their poor-relation was hopeless with kitchen matters.

"Oh, no," she confirmed with a giggle. "My Aunt Sophie actually forbade me even to approach a kettle after several disasters."

"Well, don't you worry." Clara slipped a reassuring arm around Amelia's waist. "I promised you cooking lessons and cooking lessons you shall have. You'll not only be boiling water, you'll be ready to produce all sorts of festive dishes by the holidays. Don't fret."

"You can spend as much time in the kitchen with us as you like, dear," Cora chimed in. "We do not have any pupils coming today. We can prepare a feast."

Since the study, with its stacks of materials regarding her husband's investments awaiting her, had been invaded, Amelia could not think of any objection to this plan. In fact, it felt rather nice to be wanted. If an afternoon in the kitchen would also help her to avoid the excesses of emotion Michael Thompson provoked in her, so much the better.

By the time she saw Michael again, Amelia was exhausted. She had dutifully gone to fetch him when the luncheon Clara had prepared was ready, but the study was deserted. He must have accomplished his repairs in short order because when she checked the windows, they didn't rattle. She could have safely gone back to the daunting task of trying to untangle Robert's finances, but at that point she was having too good a time with the two ladies.

Instead, she spent the afternoon in her kitchen being introduced to the staple goods stored there and looking through recipe cards while discussing the various aspects of yeast and soda or sourdough cultures. When the household gathered for their common meal that evening she had not only made the pot of tea, but she had rolled out a batch of biscuits and basted a chicken for the first time.

Clara cut the chicken into pieces, but she insisted Amelia carry the platter into the dining room. Everyone was assembled around a spacious oval table with a buttercream-yellow damask tablecloth and twin tri-branch silver candelabra. Beeswax candles added light to the oil lamps glowing from wall sconces over an imposing sideboard. Amelia had set the table herself and it looked quite nice—almost inviting, in an informal way. She felt ridiculously pleased.

"Look what our Amelia did today," Cora exclaimed as she preceded her to the table, carrying a bowl of stewed tomatoes and the basket of biscuits.

"It smells delicious," Ethan declared as she set the rose-painted china on the table end and took the seat

Clara had indicated was hers at the near end. "It was good of you to join us this evening."

This was her first meal in the Estate's dining room. Up until now she'd been taking her evening meals on a tray in her room and going straight to bed, still battling the exhaustion from her illness and her unease over her unexpected responsibilities. She took her napkin and placed it on her lap, trying to smile as each of her tenants welcomed her and asked about each other's day. It was not drawing room talk; the warmth of familiarity and mutual respect filled the room. Even Michael seemed to be willing to forego their earlier tension as he joined in the general conversation.

"I'm powerful hungry," Festive declared as he reached for a biscuit. "I loaded two wagons full for the Weatherbys this afternoon. And they're coming back Friday for the rest."

"Wait until the blessing is said, young man." Eleanor touched his wrist gently. He blushed and ducked his head, folding his hands in his lap.

"No need to blush, Festive dear," Cora said as she took her seat after returning from the kitchen with the gravy boat. "It's always nice to see a young man with an appetite. And it's been a long time since our whole household has gathered for a meal."

"But we should display our manners as we welcome Amelia to our first shared meal." Eleanor smiled at Festive, softening the censure in her words. "We must not lead her to think we were all raised in the backwoods."

"I grew up right down the street from the church, missus." Festive looked so serious as he turned to reassure Amelia directly. No one at the table even cracked a smile. "Nowhere near the woods. My daddy ran the feed store. I surely am glad you are here."

"Quite right. Tonight is the first of what we hope to be many more pleasant evenings." Ethan raised his water glass in salute.

Amelia looked down the table at the assemblage. Ethan had brushed his white whiskers and changed into a formal evening waistcoat and jacket upon his return from his workshop. With the touch of gray at his temples, Festive hardly looked young until you studied the warm friendliness and open innocence that always seemed to mark his gaze. He, too, had washed and changed before coming to dinner, his hair still damp from recent combing.

Eleanor sat between these two contrasting men. Her shoulders were squared, her back straight in a burgundy watered-taffeta gown as she sat with unconscious elegance even as she gave a discreet cough into her napkin and replaced it on her lap. She was a lady, but she did not put on airs nor hide the fact that she used the sewing she did for others to supplement her income. Amelia made a note to pay more attention to how her quietest tenant conducted herself; perhaps she could use some of the same attitude to help her cope with this new position thrust on her.

She was grateful she'd taken the time to change, choosing a midnight blue walking dress that had always been her favorite despite the simplicity of its cut and the fact that her mother would have been scandalized to find her wearing a day dress in the evening, no matter how informal the meal. At least, the mother who had raised her would have severely chastised such a lapse. Would the woman who claimed to have forsaken social convention for happiness recognize the expediency of utilizing what was available in a small wardrobe? Something to think about later.

On the other side of the table, the Brown sisters flanked Michael, who looked for all the world as if he had no idea how to conduct himself in company. He was still in shirtsleeves and suspenders and his hair looked in need of both a good combing and a heavy pomade to tame its unruly waves. Yet, despite his rough appearance, there was something about him that radiated the exact opposite. He had the coiled grace and strength of the tiger she had seen long ago in an exhibit of rare animals her father had taken her to see on Boston Commons. Something about him bespoke him as more than a mere drifter, far more.

"Perhaps you will do the honors this evening, Michael, and say the blessing." Clara sat last, putting a bowl of mashed potatoes and one of bubbled apples down first. "You do not join us often enough."

Amelia realized with a start that Michael had been studying her with almost the same intensity she had fixed on him. She lowered her eyes and fought to keep the heat from her cheeks.

"We thank you this night for your bounty . . ." He bowed his head and began dutifully.

Everyone else at the table followed suit, but Amelia looked up at her most enigmatic dinner companion, caught by the contrasts in the man who had strolled to her rescue so casually this morning, only to turn on her so ferociously a dozen heartbeats later. The same man who kissed her with white-hot anger one time, and with tender apology the next, but had evoked the same shattering response. Who was Michael Thompson, and what was he doing here? Now that Robert was gone, how long would he stay? So many questions. So many other things that required her attention.

". . . and extend your grace to our families either here or with you."

"Amen," they said collectively.

Amelia smiled, remembering the first time she met every one, thinking they were all Robert's family. It occurred to her as the dishes of food she'd helped prepare were passed, that as odd as this gathering might appear, this was a family.

Her family now. The thought warmed her.

The entire dinner party participated in the clean-up after the meal. The kitchen and dining room were tidied in short order and the group reassembled in the drawing room. Minus Michael, who'd muttered something about checking on Becky the horse and put on his jacket right after he'd dumped the slop bucket for Clara.

"What would you like to do this evening, Amelia?" Ethan asked her as he passed around a small tray with dainty glasses of sherry.

"What do you usually do once dinner is over?" she inquired and took a sip, grateful for the soothing warmth of the heavy wine. She was ready for anything, as long as it included sitting.

She'd never realized how much time it had taken the servants to prepare, serve, and clear away the meals at home. To make her life in Boston so effortless. Even the small tasks she'd felt mightily put upon to have to perform for Aunt Sophie paled in comparison to the array of chores necessary to keep a household of this size in good order, day after day. It was exhausting just trying to think of it all.

"We do any number of things, depending on the weather or our current interests," Eleanor answered first. She had already taken out her sewing basket and positioned herself by a lamp to begin tackling the hemming job Otis MacNamara left for her. She coughed and cleared her throat before continuing. "We read or sew, do puzzles and the like."

"We don't live in each other's pockets, but we do try to share some common pursuits at least a few nights a week," said Clara. "Robert usually gathered us together on Wednesdays and Sundays for 'family time' as he called it."

"Mr. Salzburg comes over lots of times after church," Festive noted. "Michael almost never comes."

"Dear Eleanor taught us all how to play whist when she first came. We are quite addicted," Cora trilled.

"Very often the Brown sisters will play for us," Ethan supplied.

"Sometimes I play my fiddle, too," Festive spoke up again from the hearth as he put another log on the blaze he'd coaxed.

"Or the professor will treat us to a reading from Mr. Shakespeare's plays," Clara added.

Amelia looked wistfully around the room with its boxed window seats, comfortable chairs and sofas. A quiet evening passed pleasantly with people she was beginning to regard as friends seemed very appealing. But she was more than a friend to these people. She was their landlord and if she did not figure out where things stood financially, they might all be left without a roof over their heads before too many more such evenings could come to pass.

The back door slammed in the distance. Would Michael join them this night? That thought made up her mind. She was definitely not up to a night of dissecting his motives or being analyzed by him, let alone any verbal sparring or being taken to task for her earlier behavior. The fact that he had spared her during dinner did not allay the certainty that he had more to say regarding the conduct of his uncle's widow. The work she had put off earlier in the study gained in appeal by leaps and bounds.

"As enticing as all those pastimes seem, I really should excuse myself and retire to go through more of Robert's accounts."

"You mustn't leave us, dear," Cora exclaimed. "Not when—"

"When we've planned some musical entertainment just for you," Clara spoke up. "Besides, you can't possibly make heads or tails of such things when we've kept you so busy all afternoon. You'll make much more progress in the morning, you'll see."

She took Cora's sherry and set it next to hers on a tall, marble-topped side table. "Come along, sister."

"Festive, dear." Cora promptly rose from the settee. "We'll just play a tune or two while you fetch your fiddle. Then you can join us. I'm sure Amelia will be amazed when she hears you play."

"Please, say you will stay and join us this evening. Our country pleasures may seem simple for a city sophisticate but they pass the time very agreeably," Ethan said, joining in the entreaties.

"Festive is truly a gifted violin player. A natural,"

Eleanor added. She cleared her throat and took a sip of sherry.

"I would love to hear you play," Amelia agreed, a little concerned over the roughness creeping into Eleanor's genteel tones. Perhaps later Cora could make her a honey-and-lemon posset like the ones she had made for Amelia during her own recent illness.

Seeing the broad smile spread across Festive's childish face with her acquiescence, and adding in the eager anticipation of the rest of her new family, confirmed that she had made the right choice. Especially when Michael so seldom actually joined in the entertainments.

"Wonderful." Cora practically clapped her hands with delight. "Hurry along, Festive."

He nodded and ambled out of the room, completely unconcerned with his lack of speed. The Browns launched into a lively air, which they performed sitting side by side at the piano. The sweet notes filled the air. When Amelia closed her eyes she could almost picture herself back in Boston. At one of her circle of friends' homes, before everything had changed. A prickle of moisture teased the corners of her eyes.

"That Gaveau pianoforte is ideally suited to the works of Mozart, don't you think?" Ethan sat next to her on the sofa.

Amelia opened her eyes and blinked away her tears of homesickness. As lovely as the music was, she hadn't been listening so much as being transported by the notes. How self-centered. "I beg your pardon?"

"Mozart composed his works on a Viennese piano, much lighter in construction than those of English origin. This instrument is from a well-known Paris manufacturer. Their cases are light enough to match those used by Mozart and bring out the best in his compositions," he explained.

The depth of Ethan's knowledge astounded Amelia. Earlier he'd called her a city sophisticate, yet here she was, feeling sorry for herself while he was the one with the background and discernment to truly enjoy the music the sisters were just now bringing to an end.

"That was truly lovely." Eleanor set aside her sewing to clap.

Cora and Clara looked so pleased when they turned around to receive the applause from the household.

"I'm glad you insisted I join you tonight." Only then did Amelia realize Michael was leaning against the door frame. "Seldom have I heard one of Amadeus Mozart's concertos sound so sweet."

What kind of drifter recognized the works of one of the master composers? There really *was* more to Michael Thompson than met the eye.

"Well, there you are, Michael dear." Cora beamed at him as she rose from the piano bench. "And Festive right behind you. Wonderful! We are all here."

Festive ducked his head and scooted past Michael when he realized all eyes were on him as he reappeared with his violin and bow clutched in his hand.

Michael straightened from his casual posture as Cora advanced to take his arm in hers. "And now that we are all here, is there something in particular that prompted tonight's invitation?"

His tone was light, indulgent, and gentle as it almost always seemed when he was speaking to any of the women in the house. Any of the women save her. Amelia could not stop the envious pang that shot through her to knot in her belly. Not that she wanted his attention, mind.

"That special entertainment you mentioned?" he concluded.

"Dancing, of course," Cora exclaimed. The knot in the pit of Amelia's stomach tightened.

"We've been teaching Festive so he might make a little extra money at weddings and socials," Clara explained.

"But I have this rush job for the Emporium," Eleanor spoke up. "And a tickle in my throat that forbids overexertion."

"And my rheumatism is acting up. I can not keep up to the pace." Ethan poured himself another glass of sherry. It was practically a conspiracy. The last place Amelia wanted to be was in Michael Thompson's arms.

"So that leaves you and dear Amelia."

"Amelia and . . . me?" Michael began. He looked as disconcerted as she felt.

"To partner for the dance," Clara explained. "So Festive can see how his playing affects those on the dance floor."

"Oh, I don't think—"

"Robert would not want you to forego all pleasures," Clara stopped Amelia's protest before it was fully formed. "Especially if you will be helping another in the process. You will both be honoring him if you assist us."

"Please, missus?" Festive had gone to stand by the piano. "Dottie Stokes is getting married this February when her sweetheart gets back from a trip to Paris,

France, and her mama already asked me to play if I can learn enough tunes."

Michael quirked a brow at her and offered a lop-sided grin. "How can we refuse?"

If he was willing, she would not cower. It was only a dance, after all. Even if had been some time, she'd danced with more men than she could count since her come-out. And before, when she was young and her parents were entertaining, Papa had always managed to steal a dance with her in the nursery. She was a natural, he'd said.

"Very well." She smiled at Festive. "What is tonight's lesson?"

"Miss Brown said we needed to work on my waltz." He settled his instrument under his chin.

Not a waltz. She could have handled a reel or other country dance. The waltz was so, well, intimate.

"Clara plays pianoforte and I help the lad keep time," Cora explained. "Festive usually picks up a tune and remembers it after playing it through only once. You'll see, dear. This will be great fun."

"Are you ready?" Michael bowed over her hand and escorted her to the center of the room with surprising grace.

She faced him and thought of the last time they had been this close. The kiss he had shared with her in the darkened kitchen stirred anew in her thoughts. In truth, it had not strayed far from them all day. A fact that made her just a trifle unnerved. She took a deep breath and inhaled the scent and warmth of him that had haunted her as well—fresh oak and pine, the openness of all outdoors, so different from anything she had known in Boston.

The back of her fingers slid under Michael's palm until their thumbs locked. She'd never held a man's hand like this, without gloves. The rough pads of his fingers and the warmth of his skin against hers sent small shocks of sensation coursing up her arm. A contrast of sinful delight and dire warning. She placed her other hand on his shoulder as he brought his up to the small of her back. The music began and for the moment Amelia indulged herself with the power of the melody to sweep her to other times, other places as they whirled around the room.

But the only place her thoughts remained fixed was in the kitchen last night when he'd taken pity on her foundering to make a simple pot of tea. She closed her eyes and was lost in the swirling pattern of the waltz and the whirl of impressions from the night before. After initial friction between them, he'd surprised her by drawing close and tasting her lips with soft, gentle strokes. She'd surprised herself with her reaction. He was every bit as strong and passionate as she could have dreamed. As she should not have imagined.

Though they branded her now, he'd kept his hands off of her then, not touching her or drawing her to him, allowing only his mouth to show her what he felt. Each worshipful pressure seemed an apology for the anger that had spilled between them even earlier that day. Her apology as much as his.

If he'd touched her then, if she'd found herself in his arms, holding his hand as she was now, she felt quite certain she would have lost herself completely, lost all sense of who she was beyond being his.

He guided her now in the dance with almost the

same mix of coiled strength and purpose as she had felt in his kiss. She remembered moaning very softly as her mouth opened beneath his. He'd almost growled in response, then dipped his tongue inside to taste her in long, slow strokes. She'd been in heaven. For the first time in her life, desire had pounded hot and demanding in her veins. As it did at this very moment, despite their surroundings and the company in the room.

Last night he'd pulled away from her as everything in her screamed for more. This night she could not wait for the dance to end.

The music stopped. Michael's hand remained in place, impossibly scorching her spine through her gown and corset. She was afraid to raise her eyes to meet his. Afraid he might be feeling what he had reawakened in her. Afraid of her reaction if that were true.

"How breathtaking," Cora spoke first in the suddenly quiet room. "The dancing was delightful, as was the music, Festive dear."

"You are certainly well matched as dance partners," Ethan observed.

"Yes, you dance as if you have been doing so all your lives," Eleanor agreed. "And I believe Dorothy Stokes will be delighted if you play that piece after her wedding, young man."

Festive blushed with the praise. Amelia's own cheeks felt heated, as much from her torrid memories as the exertion of the waltz.

When Michael finally released her to sketch a small bow, she stepped back, more than a little overwhelmed by the intensity of her reaction to him.

"Thank you for the dance, Amelia. You are a natural at it." There was that heat she had been wary of seeing, glittering in the depths of Michael's gaze. Heat she recognized and prayed he did not see mirrored in her own.

"Thank you all." She looked around the room at all the smiling faces. "This has been delightful, but I fear I must retire now. Good evening."

"Thank you, Michael." She whispered the last words she'd said to him for the second night in a row.

Without waiting any longer, she turned and fled.

Nine

After a restless night, tossing and turning in her bed, trying and failing to deny the unwanted and utterly inappropriate desires seething inside her, then a morning spent in Robert's study with a dismaying look at the amount of money her late husband had once possessed but had lent out and lost, Amelia could not stand the thought of staying indoors any longer.

She also was not ready to spend time with any of her tenants. Not after the spectacle she'd made of herself last night: mooning over a man's kisses in front of them all and then fleeing the room more like a green girl than the woman responsible for keeping a roof over all their heads.

She'd taken a cup of coffee and a cinnamon roll and disappeared to the study as soon as she'd gotten dressed.

Her tenants were at least scattered about their business for the time being. Despite her feathery cough, Eleanor had gone straight off to her farm after breakfast, just as Ethan and Festive left for work. Michael was gone at first light, or so Clara related. He'd laid the fire in the kitchen and gone to finish some task or other, she supposed.

Cora and Clara had left for the Emporium to do their weekly shopping an hour earlier. Amelia could only hope that Otis MacNamara would see it was in his best interest to extend her further credit. If she could not feed her guests, they would not stay with her and she would never be able to pay her bill.

She was alone in the echoing emptiness of the Grand Estate with nothing but her thoughts, her questions, and her guilt.

She needed to clear both her head and her rebellious heart and for that her old nursery maid had always recommended a brisk walk down Charles Street and two or three turns around the Common, depending on the magnitude of the upset to be worked off. But the Common was a long way away. A walk around her property's perimeter would have to do. Besides, she'd yet to find her way to Robert's grave by the lake and she wanted to pay her respects.

So with a warm cloak wrapped around her and the map she discovered of the acreage that surrounded the Grand Estate, she was just closing the front door when the doctor pulled up in his small surrey.

"Hello, Mrs. Mitchell," he called. "Do you remember me?"

"Of course. Hello, Dr. Walker. It's good to actually see you."

She had a vague memory of his deep, comforting voice and gentle hands. Cora had told her quite a bit about Josiah Walker, the closest medical practitioner in the area outside of the midwife. That he was a former army surgeon and a bachelor, she recalled. That he was so young and far more darkly handsome than any doctor should be, she did not remember Cora mentioning.

She stepped off the porch and advanced toward his horse and gig. "Is there something I can help you with?"

"No, not really. When time permits, I try to call on my patients and see how their recovery is progressing. I know you have been up and about for a few days now. I want to assure myself you are not overdoing."

He swung down from his seat and paused to tether his horse to the hitching post. He had long, powerful-looking legs and broad shoulders that stretched the fabric of his tailored jacket as he tended his horse. He dusted his gloved hands together and turned back to her.

"I can see you appear to be in fine fettle, though."

"I am feeling much better." She smiled as she realized that his accent held a familiar clip and cadence. No wonder she had found his voice soothing in her fevered state. "Thanks to you, I've been told."

"Miss Cora and Miss Clara bore the brunt of your care. I offered advice and a few medicinals." He doffed his hat and made a deep bow. "You have a most extraordinary smile, if I may be so bold."

"You're from New England, are you not, Doctor Walker?" It felt very good to hear an accent from home, bold or not.

"Guilty as charged." He answered her smile with a broad one of his own. "Miss Brown told me you were brought up in Boston. I'm a Connecticut man myself. From New Haven."

"Oh, one of the New Haven Walkers?" She'd heard of the family. They were well respected throughout New England for their philanthropy, especially in education and medicine. She was grateful now for some of the presentations her friend Tori had made at their charity socials. Tori would often hold up the good works of others as examples for them all to aspire to. When she wrote she would have to tell her.

"I'm a mere cousin," he said, waving the importance of his family connections aside. "But you are stepping out. To town perhaps? I could give you a ride."

"That's very kind, but I discovered this map among my husband's ledgers." She held up the folded paper. "I thought I'd take advantage of the sun this morning to conduct a tour of the property."

He squinted up at the sky and took a deep breath. "It is a glorious day. Almost balmy. I wonder how many more we can expect before winter sets in?"

"I have no experience of the seasons here in Illinois." Although the sun was bright and the air not cold enough to see her breath, *balmy* was hardly the word she would have used for the chill nip carried by the breeze.

Still, it was pleasant to have a conversation with a true gentleman, one who did not appear to be wrapped in mystery or judging her every action. "But I can not stand being cooped up inside for long, so I hope the snow the other night does not foretell a harsh winter ahead."

He laughed. It was a rich sound that echoed across the front yard. "Hardly the response I expected from a fellow Yankee, even a debutante. Would you allow me to accompany you on your walk?"

"Certainly." Debutante, huh? His easy revelation confirmed her supposition that Robert Mitchell's young widow was the object of more than one conversation in the community. Attending services on

Sunday should prove interesting indeed. "If you have the time?"

"I had an appointment with Mr. Salzburg, but he has been called to Springfield on urgent business so I have the entire morning free."

With his eyebrows raised high, he looked from side to side quickly. "Barring a medical emergency, that is."

The drop in his voice laced with mock urgency set her to giggling. It felt good to shrug aside her cares, if only for a few moments. "I believe I would enjoy your company."

She ignored the pangs of guilt that shot from deep within her. Hadn't Clara assured her just last night that Robert would not have begrudged his widow a modicum of pleasure? What could be more pleasant than a stroll through the country with a dashing ex-soldier? Surely she would incur little tongue-wagging for such a walk if that soldier was also the town physician.

"Delightful." He beamed at her. "Just let me see to my horse."

Dr. Walker pulled a blanket out from under the seat and threw it over the sorrel mare. He moved with the precision of a cavalry officer and she appreciated the economy of motion that marked him as a man who knew what he wanted and where he was going. If there was truth in what Eleanor had told her about his looking to buy land and settle here, she couldn't help but wonder what such a man was doing in the heart of rural Illinois.

A year ago, she would have accepted without thought the attentions of a gentleman of his obvious breeding and education. She would have boasted to her friends of his manners and good looks, his connections and status, and his good taste in seeking out her company. Today, there was a horrified part of her that not only wondered how her husband's nephew would look dressed in tailored clothes such as the doctor wore, with polished boots and a neatly brushed bowler, but also wondered if there was more to Josiah Walker than met the eye. More she needed to be wary of.

He turned to her with his broad, dazzling grin and humor-laced green eyes and held out his arm. "Shall we go?"

She placed her hand in the crook of his elbow and they set off toward the ramshackle lean-to that passed as a barn.

"Are you sure you're warm enough?" Dr. Walker asked as they rounded the corner of the house and the breeze whistling up from the lake had him grabbing his hat and jamming it tighter on his head.

So much for balmy. Amelia was glad her bonnet was tied instead of pinned on, and that the cloak Eleanor had insisted on giving her earlier in the week was padded with enough quilted layers inside to make it as warm as the fur-lined one she had sold to make the trip out here.

They stopped for a moment at the top of the knoll where the barn stood. Leafless trees creaked as they swayed below them. Warm Springs Lake shimmered in the distance. Amelia took a deep breath of the bracing air, her air, tasting the freshness and savoring the knowledge for the first time that most of what she could see belonged to her. That she might belong to it.

Was Eleanor Holmdale right? Could the Grand Estate turn out to be the perfect place for a displaced Bostonian?

"What do you miss?"

Dr. Walker's question startled her from her reverie. "Miss?"

"From Boston. The Common? Shopping on Milk Street? The Faneuil Hall cricket? Your cook's Indian pudding on Thanksgiving Day?"

"That's a grasshopper weathervane atop the Hall," she corrected with a giggle. "And how could anyone miss great lumps of cornmeal mixed with molasses just because they disguise what it is by passing it off as Indian fare and a tradition? Our cook's specialties were her apple-and-pecan stuffing and cranberry-orange relish."

"Sounds like home."

"Is there anything in particular *you* miss?" she asked.

"Indian pudding."

He winked when she looked at him with dismay over her faux pas. "My great-aunt, a tiny, wizened tyrant, brought it to our house every Thanksgiving and made sure we each got a large serving and ate every bite. I liked the hard sauce she put on it, but the mealy texture . . ."

He shuddered with such horror, she laughed out loud.

"You have a delightful laugh, Mrs. Mitchell," he said with a smile. "You should do it more often."

"It feels good to laugh again." There had been so little to even chuckle over in the past year since her brother absconded with funds from a business partnership and set her life on the path to ruin. "Is this part of your treatment methods, Doctor?"

"I've found that laughter and good humor go a long way in aiding a patient's recovery." He nodded. "Especially one who has had to bear so much else in so short a time. I don't believe I ever expressed my sincere condolences on your loss. I did not know your husband well, but I do know that everyone I have met has had only good things to say about him."

"Thank you," she said and looked around her again. Robert Mitchell had been a good man who loved his home and his town. He'd placed a great deal of trust in her, based on only a few letters. Despite the daunting problems that faced her in trying to maintain his legacy, she had a great deal to be thankful for. Which gave her an idea.

"Dr. Walker, would you happen to be free next Thursday evening?"

"I have no plans, although I never know when I might be called out. What did you have in mind?"

"I'm not sure what the custom is here, but at home it will be Thanksgiving. Would you like to join my household for dinner? I promise I will not allow anyone to make Indian pudding."

"How could I refuse such a charming invitation?" He patted her hand, still held tight in the crook of his arm. It was a comfortable gesture, eliciting none of the dangerous sparks the mere suggestion of contact with Michael showered through her.

Chatting about inconsequential things with the doctor anchored Amelia in familiar patterns, even as they did their best to follow the map of her unfamiliar lands.

After making their way down the grassy expanse behind the barn and its small corral, they came to a path and a large meadow complete with shiny new barbed wire fencing.

"Whew," Dr. Walker whistled. "That's a lot of fencing. Especially for an empty field."

Amelia silently agreed, although she had no idea what really constituted a large pasture as opposed to a smaller one. Perhaps it had to do with the proportion of open land left once the fencing was put up?

"I wonder how much this is costing me." That was her real worry. How much had this added to her bill at the Emporium? And if she had no idea what Robert planned for this part of his land, was it all a waste? He must have discussed his ideas with Michael. She would have to ask him tonight at supper—if he came home for supper, that is.

I wonder how much this is costing me.

Money. Money. Money. Michael swore all that woman thought or talked about was money. How could he allow someone that shallow to dominate his thoughts so completely? He'd sunk the last post and tightened the last strand of wire, then sat down to rest for not more than five minutes and here she was, talking about money.

He opened his eyes and scrambled to his feet. What was Amelia doing out here? And who was she talking to?

He peered through the shrubbery, trying to locate her and spied her black bonnet first.

Damnation.

There she stood, inspecting his work all right, in the company of Josiah Walker, the smooth-looking doctor who had only moved to the Warm Springs/Cold Springs area last summer.

Was Amelia some kind of magnet for the men he most wanted to keep at a distance? She was a fetching magnet, that much was sure. The late autumn gusts had blown some color into her cheeks and teased several strands of her black silk hair loose in the process. They danced across her cheeks, practically begging to be smoothed back into place. Her blue-green cloak complimented her coloring in a way he would have thought calculated, had he not known it was one of Eleanor Holmdale's castoffs.

The doctor had his arm twined intimately with Amelia's as he leaned down to listen to her conversation as if nothing in the world were more important than whatever complaint she was chirping to him.

Michael fought an irrational urge to leap from the bushes and pull the two of them apart. He'd have to settle for a calculated interruption. He was not about to let a near-sleepless night spent haunted by one wayward widow's appeal spoil months of investigation.

"Good morning, Auntie." He stepped forward from the shadows of the treeline. "Dr. Walker. What brings you both out here?"

Amelia turned around with a look of complete shock. Or was that guilt at having been found alone in the company of a stranger for the second day in a row? It would almost be funny if he were not so furious.

"Why, Michael," she said in that breathless, surprised tone he'd found so irresistibly sexy the other night in the kitchen. She extricated her hand from Walker's arm. "The doctor and I were just admiring your handiwork."

"Indeed." Walker nodded his assent tersely. Did her voice have the same effect on the good doctor? "This project must have taken you some time, Thompson."

"Yup." They had no idea. He'd actually spent two days over at the Weatherbys' spread last month getting pointers on how to set fence posts and tighten the wires. Between that and the pamphlet he'd picked up in Springfield during his biweekly visit to the courthouse, he thought he'd done a fair job, all things—especially his inexperience—considered.

But patting himself on the back got him no closer to uncovering the purpose for Amelia and the doctor's current expedition.

"Is there something I can do for you, Aunt Amelia? Or did you trek all the way out here simply to examine your fence?"

"Yes." She shot him a piercing look, even as she surprised him with the terse honesty of her reply. How had she even known about this project? There were no outstanding bills for the fencing materials since he had paid for them himself to compensate Robert for his assistance.

"Mrs. Mitchell and I were just wondering what her husband had in mind for this bit of property." Walker tried to diffuse the tension, but his interest only served to further irritate Michael. Instead of being annoyed with Amelia, he should focus on the reasons Walker had for accompanying the widow.

Amelia turned her head to look at the pasture again, obviously upset with Michael for needling her in front of the doctor. Even with her lips pressed firmly together, her profile—with her smooth cheeks, pert chin, and elegant neck—was the sort that must have moved her Boston swains to poetry.

What was it about Amelia Mitchell that reached deep inside him and almost made him want to join their ranks? Not one of the spoiled debutantes his stepmother had cast in his path had ever affected him the way this one did.

Had the doctor been smitten while he tended her during her illness? The memory of her clad in a thin nightdress and quilt swam up to taunt Michael until he shoved it aside. Going down that path would only lead to strangling Walker, or worse.

"Robert mentioned horses when he laid out the perimeter with me last month." Michael offered as much of the truth as he could to Amelia. "Festive has a way with animals and I believe Robert hoped to give him gainful employment away from the Emporium."

"Thank you, that's exactly what I needed to hear." The sincerity in her voice was matched by the look she turned back to him. "We did not mean to interrupt you. It's just that the paperwork in Robert's study is a trifle overwhelming. I was hoping an actual look at the Estate would help me sort out what I am facing here."

"When I arrived to check on her recovery, Mrs. Mitchell was kind enough to ask me to bear her company," Walker supplied. "It's been good chatting with you, Thompson. Sorry if we've impeded your work. Shall we be off again?"

Michael was not about to let her amble off with one of his chief suspects unaccompanied, no matter how charming or handsome the packaging; if he was right, Walker could very well be a killer. "I was just finishing.

I could show you where Robert hoped to raise a barn next spring, if you like?"

"How thought—"

"A good suggestion, but I just noticed where the sun is," Walker interrupted. "I'm afraid I can not continue any farther, after all."

He pulled out a large gold pocket watch. "I am due back in Cold Springs by midafternoon. I have an appointment to look at a property. If you are ready, I will gladly escort you back to the house, Mrs. Mitchell."

Like a prickle on the back of his neck he could not scratch, Walker's proprietary tone sent unexplained danger signals racing up Michael's spine. He'd heard too many war stories from veteran marshals not to pay attention to this feeling.

Too often marshals and deputy marshals were led into situations with only their guts and that prickle of warning to guide them. Horace Salzburg had mentioned the new doctor's great interest in properties in the Spring Lakes district. Warm or Cold Springs, it didn't seem to matter. According to Horace, Walker seemed to spend nearly as much time examining abandoned homesteads as he did patients. He'd seemed content in Amelia's company right up to Michael's offer to join them—why the change of direction?

"Can you find your way back yourself?" Amelia asked the doctor. The two men's gazes connected for the first time in anything other than cold appraisal.

"I believe so," Walker said.

Michael certainly hoped so, considering the house was in plain sight at the top of the rise just behind Amelia's shoulder. The prickle intensified as he held the doctor's gaze a moment longer. Was Walker re-

luctant to share the widow's attention or did he truly
have an appointment? He'd have to visit Cold Springs
himself.

"Then if you don't mind, I would like to go on to the
lake. We'll look forward to seeing you next Thursday,"
Amelia said.

The lake? That was her destination? Then it
dawned on Michael. She had yet to visit her husband's
grave. Michael could have kicked himself for a fool.
Such a visit was not only natural, but well overdue, delayed by her illness. He should have brought her
there himself when she first recovered. Cold Springs
could wait.

"I don't mind." Walker released her hands at last.
"I, too, am looking forward to next Thursday. Until
then, good day."

"Good-bye, Dr. Walker." The smile she turned up
at him sent a streak of jealousy roaring through
Michael. What did Thursday have to do with anything?

Walker nodded at Michael and turned to retrace
the path to the barn and house.

"There's an easier path on the other side of these
trees," Michael said as he offered her his arm.

She reached out, hesitated, and pulled her hand
back. "Thank you, I can manage."

"Suit yourself." He shrugged, trying not to feel
slighted when she'd been hanging all over the doctor
not too many minutes earlier. If she wanted to go her
own way, if she were stung by one of her admirers
later on, let it be on her head. Brave talk. He could no
more let her continue on a dangerous path than he
could have let his sister Katie.

After a few steps he swung back to face her. He needed to at least try to warn her of the shaky ground she trod. He would only be in Warm Springs a few more weeks—then she would be on her own. "You need to have a bit more caution."

"I believe I can manage to avoid stepping in any rabbit burrows, if that's what you mean." She halted only a few inches away from him, close enough for the breeze to send a puff of fresh apples and cinnamon—her scent forevermore—slamming into him.

"No, I mean this habit of yours for finding the company of men, men you've only just met, so fascinating. Gentlemen will think you're an easy mark."

"An easy mark?" She frowned at him, the ice-blue chips in her eyes growing cold and hard again. Would she lump the kisses they had shared in with Walker and MacNamara's attentions?

"Entertaining Otis MacNamara while alone in the house might present one set of scandalous problems, but traipsing off with a stranger, even if he is a doctor, opens you to even more danger than a little scandal."

She nodded slowly, her eyes never wavering from his. "You were a stranger when I first saw you at the train station in Chicago. Would you say I am safe from scandal with you?"

Hell, no. Not if last night's waltz and the kiss in the kitchen before that were any indication.

"We have a familial connection," he hedged.

She shook her head this time. "People will believe the worst because it is almost always more exciting than the truth. I do not have the time or resources to worry about what the good people of Warm Springs think right now. Robert trusted me with his property and I must conduct my business as I deem expedient."

He supposed she was right. Under normal circumstances. But the prickle was still there, despite his view of the doctor's rapidly diminishing backside. Somehow, he'd have to make her understand that there were worse dangers than a bit of gossip.

She brushed by him then, ready to leave the discussion, and him, behind if need be. "I believe I've found the path I need, if you'd like to continue on with your own business," she called from the far side of a stand of brush.

A resonant kuk-kuk-kuk sound overhead had her pivoting to look up over her shoulder by the time he joined her. She shaded her eyes from the sun. "What—"

He put his finger over her lips, as fascinated by the rapid changing of her moods, and by his own swift shifts in her company, as she was by the large bird of prey in the sky.

"A goshawk," he spoke softly. There was a rustle in the grass a dozen paces away. The hawk sounded again. This time its quarry bolted across a small clearing and into the next cluster of weeds.

"A rabbit." She sounded as breathless as a child. He nodded.

They set off for the lake's edge far more companionably after that. Accomplished with a minimum of conversation, the walk and survey of the property was eye-opening for Michael. Could Robert's widow really be the young innocent she seemed at the moment? Or was she the money-hungry woman he had also

seen, concerned with the cost of just about everything
she came in contact with?

Warm Springs Lake was lined with weeping willows
that swept long tendrils down to the water and back
up to dance in the breeze almost in greeting, especially with the soft rustle that echoed over the water.

"Look at the geese." Amelia pointed to the center
where a family of snow geese swam in lazy circles.
"They squawk to keep track of one another."

"That's what families do. Or, so I'm told."

We have a familial connection. He was such a hypocrite.
When he looked at Amelia Mitchell he felt anything
but familial.

Ten

Amelia stared across the expanse of Warm Springs Lake. The weeping willows lining the shore were just as she had pictured them from Robert's description. The quiet chatter of their branches as they dipped toward the water and then were stirred to life by the breezes called out to her in welcome.

She shaded her eyes and squinted at the bright-white waterfowl swimming lazy circles in the center of the lake as they gabbled to one another.

"Look at the geese," she said, pointing them out to Michael as he approached. "They squawk to keep track of one another."

At least, that is what Robert had explained. She hadn't believed at the time she'd ever have need of that bit of trivial information. Need, or interest. But after watching the hawk and rabbit just now and seeing the deer at the Holmdale farm, she took great satisfaction in having a nugget to share about the natural beauty in the area.

"That's what families do. Or, so I'm told."

She looked back at him, trying to read his expression. To see if he was trying to needle her, or convince himself. "Point taken. I'll look out for you and you'll look out for me."

Her earlier question lingered. Was she safe from scandal in his company? Seeing him standing there with his mud-caked boots and work pants, his rough tweed jacket and open shirt collar, there should be no question. They were from two different worlds.

Despite that fact and all the other factors separating them, the answer still hung between them, no matter how he'd dodged around it by citing the fact that his aunt had once been married to her late husband.

They both knew that answer even without it being given voice. Not if the kisses they'd shared had anything to do with it. Not if he felt the same prickly awareness on his skin, the heightened tension in his muscles, whenever she was near. Not if the day, the room, the meadow, felt like a brighter place because the other one of them was also there.

Given those signs, scandal was the mere brush of a lip, an accidental sweep of fingertips, a waltz, away.

Their eyes stayed locked for a heartbeat longer than necessary for her to read all of that in his eyes. For him to see the same in hers. She seemed frozen where she stood. Frozen on the edge of all the distances between them. Distances that could not possibly be bridged. The debutante and the drifter, both displaced with too much to lose if they dared to reach for one another.

"Show me." She managed to get the words out. "Show me Robert's grave."

She had come all this way for that reason, for that reason alone. Not to stare longingly into another man's eyes and wish for something that could not be.

Something flickered across Michael's gaze before he answered. Disappointment? Relief? It didn't matter.

The distances between them were too great for either of them to close.

"This way, madame." He took a deep breath before he inclined his head at a rakish angle and made a swirling gesture with his wrist.

A short distance away, on a rise hidden among the trees, he took her to a small, fenced enclosure. The willows on either side whispered their soothing magic as he stood back and let her approach on her own.

The plot was meticulously tended. There was one stone marker in its center next to a length of freshly turned earth. Robert and Betty's graves. Side by side in death as they had been in life. As it should be.

"Oh, Robert," she whispered as she looked at the view of the lake. "You were so right. This is a beautiful spot."

She turned around to look at Michael, needing to share the moment with someone. Needing to share the memories that had drawn her to the man she had married. "They used to have picnics here. On this very spot."

Michael came to stand beside her at the wrought iron fence. "Who?"

"Your aunt and uncle. Even before they built the Grand Estate, they would come here and talk over their dreams. They planned the house, named all their children, and shared their lives. Right here."

"Betty and Robert had no children, Amelia."

"But they dreamed of them." A prickle of tears stung the corners of her eyes. "This is where he proposed and where he brought her every anniversary, rain or shine. This is where he laid her to rest. To wait for him until he could join her."

That's when she'd known she was going to marry Robert Mitchell. That she could be his mail-order bride in truth. When he'd told her his and Betty's story. A man who could love that deeply without hiding it was someone she had wanted to know. Someone she wanted to be worthy of.

"Look here." She rushed away from the fence to the trunk of one willow. "Here's where he carved their initials the day she said she'd marry him."

She traced her fingers over the initialed heart. There was a large *M* in the center with *E C* above for Betty's *Elizabeth Catherine* and *R T* for *Robert Thomas* below.

"He was going to put our initials together on one of the other trees." The words clogged in her throat as Michael followed her to the tree by the water's edge.

"Ha-oo-oo, ha-oo-oo." A quavering wail flowed across the water to fill the silence. She stepped back, colliding with Michael's shoulder. He grabbed her by the waist to steady her.

She looked up at his startled expression. "Is that—"

"A loon." He nodded. "What it's doing here at this time of year is beyond me. They don't inhabit the area at all during the winter."

"Just like Robert said." Tears were flowing freely down her cheeks now. She paid them no heed, trying to finish. "He loved to listen to them during the summer and told me he was sorry I would have to wait."

That was all she managed before she turned in Michael's arm, burrowing her head against the crook of his neck. He brought both his arms around her and held her tight while she cried. Held her long after her tears had stopped and she rested in the security of his embrace, listening to the steady beating of his heart. Held her without question or comment for as long as she needed.

How much time passed before she finally gathered herself together enough to pull away and look up at him, she couldn't say, but she did know that if she had needed him to stay there, holding her into the night, he would have done exactly that.

"Thank you—"

He stopped her by brushing his thumb over her bottom lip. "Thank *you,*" he said.

She couldn't think what he could possibly be thanking her for.

"Thank you for sharing this with me," he continued. "For showing me. I think I know Robert better. Robert and Betty, and you."

Tears gathered again at the understanding in his voice, the recognition in his eyes. She nodded her head, unable to speak past the lump in her throat.

He leaned down then and brushed his lips against hers, following the path his thumb had just traced.

His mouth lingered over hers, accepting her. This was not a kiss of passion or hunger, despite the fact that it touched both deep inside her. She clung to him as his lips swept against hers, tasting and teasing in gentle strokes.

She understood the yearning, the loneliness, the hope, held in such a soft encounter. Understood and welcomed, even as he stepped back and ended the kiss.

She shivered as much from the kiss as from the loss of his warmth and the stiffening breeze blowing off the lake to whistle past them.

"I should get you home. Are you ready to go?" he asked.

She looked back across the lake one more time and nodded. "As horrible as it sounds, I'm glad Robert had a place like this to come to. A place where he's surrounded by life, instead of getting lost in a granite garden with nothing but cold stone and death around him."

She took a deep breath of the fresh air tinged with a hint of the lake water and exhaled slowly.

"Who did you lose, Amelia? Who did you lose in such a place?"

"My father," she answered, somehow not surprised by Michael's perception. Her bitterness must be fairly transparent. "He died when I was eleven. I found him in the study, slumped at his desk. We buried him, if that's what you call it, in a granite-and-marble vault beside our church in Brookline."

"You were your father's princess, weren't you?" He fixed her with a troubled gaze.

She nodded, wary.

"That's why my calling you that is so raw."

Again, she nodded, waiting to fend off a figurative blow that was sure to hurt.

"And then what happened?"

This question caught her off guard. "I went to talk to him one day. Just woke up one morning and decided to visit, to say good-bye. But I couldn't find him. There were too many vaults and they all looked alike. It was so terribly quiet. And cold. There wasn't anything of my papa there. He wasn't anywhere."

She'd said enough. She'd said far more than she'd ever said to anyone. Even Tori, who'd been the one to

spot her when the news had come that she was missing so long ago. Tori had seen her from the window
in her father's rectory study, sitting on a bench, weeping, in the middle of the cemetery. Why had she
revealed so much to this man now?

"I understand." He surprised her again. This time
because there was so much pain in his voice. "I lost my
mother when I was eleven. Having seen this from
Robert's perspective, I wish we'd had such a place for
her. She would have loved it here."

Amelia nodded, sympathy welling. He'd lost his
mother when he was a boy just like she'd lost Papa. He
knew the devastation. He knew the loneliness of being
abandoned. She laced her arm with his and they
began the long walk back to the Grand Estate, bonded
in their common losses.

She looked over her shoulder at the wrought-iron
fence and the couple it housed.

Thank you, Robert. Rest in peace. She sent the prayer
heavenward. She didn't say good-bye. She felt certain
she would be back for other visits.

Michael stole a glance down at the woman walking
beside him. With her prim widow's bonnet and her
green cloak, Amelia Mitchell was the embodiment of
all the contrasts she evoked in him.

To say she was intriguing was far too tepid a word
for the fires of longing she ignited in him.

She was a little girl lost in a cemetery, scared and
alone, and a wife secure enough to embrace her husband's love for another woman. She was a debutante,
far more at home maneuvering the intricate balances
in a ballroom soiree, yet enthralled with the wildlife
around her.

In a Boston drawing room, he had no doubt she could freeze an overzealous admirer or inconsequential hanger-on with the lift of a brow, but in her own dining room she had listened to Festive's childish assurance that he'd been born in town, nowhere near the woods, as if the boy inside that man's body was the most important person in the room. She was a woman he could not afford to fall in love with even as she wormed her way into his heart.

The silence between them was heavy with the revelations they had just shared, the pieces and secrets of their lives divulged. What should he say now? How did one make small talk after such deep disclosures?

He released a heartfelt sigh and she looked up at him with a rueful grin. "After sharing such things, it's difficult to know what to say next, isn't it?"

He nodded. "Very awkward."

"Strenuous, even." She was teasing him.

"Tedious, more like."

"Laborious." She rose to the challenge, a gleam of delight dancing in the glance she slanted at him.

"Arduous."

"Grueling." She laughed softly and the sound skipped over his heart.

"You win." He joined in her laughter. "I've reached the limits of my vocabulary."

Tension eased, they walked further along. The hawk was back overhead, still riding the wind with its wings outstretched, screeching occasionally as it tried to scare up dinner. The little rabbit they had spotted earlier had gotten away.

Reaching the fence he'd just completed, she stopped and looked across the pasture. "What are you doing here, Michael? What brought you to the Grand Estate, to Robert? And how long will you stay?"

She looked up at him for what seemed a long time, but was no more than a breath or two. What to tell her? Or rather, how not to tell her? He wanted to demand the truth from her. What was she doing here? Why had she come? What had she planned for the future? But he felt like the very cad she'd declared him to be for wanting to know all those things while he could not share his own truths with her.

He stared into her cool blue eyes and wanted to tell her everything—what he was doing in Warm Springs, why this job, this manhunt, was so important to him. But he'd taken an oath and made a promise, both of which compelled him to keep his true purpose to himself. To lie.

He rested his hand on the top of a post. Perhaps the answer to his dilemma lay in telling her the truth, or as much of the truth as he dared.

"I took an oath before I arrived, and I made a promise. I'll stay until I've fulfilled them both." The truth and a lie, one and the same, depending on how you looked at them.

She wasn't satisfied. He could see the questions gathering force behind her eyes.

"What about you, Amelia? Why did you run away to marry a stranger? And now that you are here, how long will you stay?" He tried to deflect her questions with some hard ones of his own. If she answered, at least he'd have something concrete to relate to Marshal Taylor later.

Her gaze drifted back to the meadow behind his shoulder. "I wish I could say I was coming to something rather than running away. But that wouldn't be true."

Then she faced him fully again. "I didn't like my stepfather. He . . . he is in trade, a meat wholesaler. Quite prosperous and very generous, especially given that I was prone to referring to him as a butcher. I couldn't stand living in his house. I needed to escape."

"Was he—?" His muscles tensed, he gripped the fence post, ready to crush it if need be.

"Cruel? Crude?"

She supplied the very words he'd been about to form. Cold dread crystallized around his heart. Had he hurt her somehow, driven her from his home? He'd have to kill the man.

She shook her head as if answering his unspoken questions. But she also lowered her gaze as though there was something she needed to hide, something she was ashamed of. He'd distracted her from her quest for information about him, all right. Distracted and forced her into more personal revelations. He hated his job at the moment.

"Worse." Loathing laced the word. "He made my mother laugh."

Relief flooded through him. Relief and recognition. He remembered harboring a deep resentment for Eugenia when his father had first introduced her to Will and him.

"I'd forgotten how beautiful her laugh was because it had simply stopped the day my father died." Caught in her guilt, Amelia continued. "I . . . I was away this summer and when I came home after their wedding, the sound of her laughter, her happiness, made me furious. I couldn't stay in his house."

"You're talking in the past tense. Have you decided to go back?" Somehow the idea that she might actually leave the Grand Estate was far more devastating than he'd thought possible up to now.

"No." She raised her eyes to his again. Regret was etched in the furrow in her brow. "But I have come to terms with her remarriage. I'm glad my mother has found some happiness in her life."

"Even if the man is considered unsuitable in your social circle?"

She nodded. "I hope I get the chance to tell her one day, to apologize for how I left."

"You know . . ." He took her arm and they started back up the hill toward the Grand Estate's crude barn. "There is this remarkable device known as the United States Postal Service. You could use it to let your mother know how you feel. Does she even know where you are?"

"Not really." Amelia shook her head. "I sent her a telegram from Chicago the day Robert and I wed, but nothing since then. What I have to say needs to be said in person. I hope I get the chance to go home and see her soon, but I don't think there will be enough money for a trip to Boston and the new barn roof before next summer. I can't get there and back and still work on getting those horses for Festive to tend."

So, she didn't want to go back to Boston to stay, only to put things right with her family. He could understand that. Perhaps when his investigation was through, when he'd seen justice for Will, there was something he could do to help her. After all, he had a few family fences to mend himself.

Amelia second-guessed herself all the way back to the house. What had prompted her to spill her innermost thoughts like that? Especially to Michael, a stranger to her mere weeks ago.

She slid her glance over to his chiseled profile as they walked up the hill toward the dilapidated barn with its sagging roof. Toward the house and barn and people she was responsible for holding together. He seemed lost in his thoughts. He was probably horrified by all she had spilled out to him, by all she had revealed.

He was a drifter able to come and go as he pleased, as his whims dictated. He'd asked if she intended to stay, as if she had any other choice. Was he already planning his own escape?

She'd told him her secrets, far more than she'd ever revealed to any one person before. She was drained of all emotion and weary to her core. If he had not had her arm, her steps would have slowed until she collapsed in a heap. What had started as a way to clear the cobwebs from her head had ended by emptying her heart. How different from when she had started out with Dr. Walker.

They crossed behind the barn in silence.

"Odd," Michael said as he stopped and peered through the doors still standing wide open, as they had been earlier. He craned his neck to look back over to the corral. "Cora and Clara must not have returned from the Emporium yet. Festive hasn't put Becky back. Or the wagon."

"They left hours ago." Alarm raced through her. "Do you think they met with a mishap?"

"I'm sure not." His tone was light as he looked up at

the house, but his frown said otherwise. She reminded herself to breathe.

"Festive usually accompanies them to unload the wagon. Despite his youthful mind, he is really quite sensible and capable. Try not to fret."

He said this as he practically pulled her across the yard toward the house.

Her heart pounded. What could have delayed two elderly women who'd left chattering about the ingredients they were shy to make apple pies? Or rather, Cora had chattered and Clara had nodded.

"There they are." Michael mercifully slowed his pace as the edge of the wagon, already unloaded, came into view around the front of the house.

A few steps more and the relief pouring through Amelia was cut short.

"That's Dr. Walker's rig." She gripped Michael's arm. "Didn't he leave us saying he had an appointment back in Cold Springs?"

"Yes." Terse and to the point, Michael answered and was already moving at breakneck speed again. "Midafternoon."

They practically collided with Festive coming down the front steps.

"Miss Cora sent me to fetch you, missus," he said. His normally sweet expression looked pinched.

"Is she—"

"Thank you, lad." Michael continued on up the steps, taking her with him before she could finish her question.

He stopped, his hand on the doorknob, and looked down at her. He took a deep breath and smoothed the worry out of his expression.

"If it's bad news . . ." His voice was barely more than a whisper. "It's best coming from the doctor. Festival's quite fond of the Browns. They dote on him so."

She nodded her understanding and worked to school her own expression. Festive did not follow them back up the steps.

"Good girl," he said and stepped into the foyer.

"Well, there you are, dears," Cora exclaimed in a cheery voice from the landing above. "I just sent Festive to find you. Did you see him?"

"We saw him," Michael answered.

"Is everything all right?" Amelia craned her neck to try and catch sight of her diminutive tenant, to no avail. "We . . . we noticed the doctor's gig is outside."

"He's here." Cora's voice moved off. "He passed the Emporium at the most fortuitous time."

Michael tossed Amelia a puzzled glance. Had they both overreacted?

"Where's Clara, Miss Brown?" he called up the stairs.

"Why, she's in the drawing room with Dr. Walker." Cora's voice continued to drift down from the second floor. "He says she'll be better in no time. No time at all."

Better?

They turned together and walked across the foyer to the drawing room. Amelia was feeling more than a little foolish for all the fright hammering through her veins since they'd reached the barn. Michael pulled the doors open and preceded her into the room with a determined stride.

Josiah Walker and Clara were seated in the matching rockers by the window. A tea tray sat on the table between them as they looked up from their conversation.

"Did you have a nice afternoon outdoors, Amelia?" Clara asked. "Dr. Walker was just telling me about accompanying you at the outset. I hope you took care of her the rest of the time, Michael."

"As you can see, I managed to bring her safely home," Michael answered. He also managed to keep the tension, still evident in the set of his shoulders, out of his voice.

"We were not expecting to see you again, Doctor." He nodded as the other man rose from his seat. "At least, not so soon."

"Duty called," the doctor answered. "Good afternoon, Mrs. Mitchell. I hope you did not overdo on your expedition."

"I'm fine, thank you. But how are you, Clara?" Amelia asked. "We were concerned."

"Nonsense. I don't know what all the fuss is about." Clara waved her hand impatiently. "It was the smallest of mishaps, really."

"How small?" Michael and Amelia spoke at the same time.

"A mouse ran out of the Emporium's storeroom. It startled me and I jumped." Clara looked sheepish.

"Clara has been afraid of the wee things since we were young, dears. Screams something awful whenever one of them scoots across the floor." Cora bustled into the room carrying a plump pillow and a quilted coverlet.

"Will these do, Dr. Walker?"

"Just the thing." He took the pillow and bent down beside Clara. "If I may?"

Clara nodded and braced her hands on the rocker arms. Cora's hand covered her lips as she watched.

Amelia looked up at Michael. Could no one give them a clear answer as to what had happened?

Dr. Walker slid the embroidered stool that matched the rockers in front of Clara and placed the pillow atop it. Then he lifted her leg, ever so gently, and placed it on top of the pillow.

Clara's face crinkled with discomfort and he patted her hand. "The laudanum I gave your sister will ease the pain. But you should be in bed when you start taking it as it will make you quite sleepy. It's a potent opiate."

Amelia could give a testament to that fact, given her foggy recollections of the two days she was in Chicago after Robert's death.

Clara shook her head. "I want to stay here. Cora will need my advice on preparing supper."

"I told you I could manage, sister," Cora scolded as she placed the coverlet over Clara's lap.

"I don't believe anything is broken, but a sprain can be worse than a break sometimes." Dr. Walker turned and addressed Michael and Amelia directly. "She needs to keep it elevated and warm. No bearing weight of any kind."

"I'll carry her up to her room when she's ready to go," Michael said.

"For how long, Dr. Walker?"

"Hard to say. Depends on the swelling. Hot compresses, right away, should help. Keep that up until I stop back in a couple of days."

Amelia nodded. Hot compresses. She might not be much use in the kitchen but she had at least learned how to heat water. Thanks to Michael. And she'd do her best to help Cora with the cooking, too. It would be fun. "Thank you, Doctor."

She supposed it was selfish, but she was grateful he'd missed his appointment with Horace and then played escort for her as long as he did earlier—otherwise he would have been gone from the town before Clara's accident and she would have had no clue what to do to care for her tenant.

Yet another skill she lacked, but she really hadn't the time to indulge herself in enumerating her faults. She'd have to learn and that was it.

"I really must be going." Dr. Walker retrieved his bag and his hat. "Two missed appointments in one day. It would appear I will never achieve my goal."

"What goal is that, Doctor?" Michael asked in a tone underscored with suspicion, which Amelia easily recognized from the number of times she had heard it directed at her. She shot him a look but his face was as clear and innocent as a choirboy's.

"I'm looking to buy land." Dr. Walker put down his bag to answer. Most men liked to talk about their plans and dreams, she'd observed over years at a variety of soirees. Most men who were not content to drift from place to place, that is.

"I'd like to settle permanently in the area," he continued, "but my funds are limited. So far, I have been looking at land abandoned over the years as the frontier pushes westward. If you hear of any likely properties, let me know."

"Will do." Michael nodded even though it was obvious he had no intention of following through. It was really more how he said things than what he actually said that set her nerves jangling.

"I'll see you in two days, Miss Brown," the doctor called across the room, but the sisters were too deep in their discussions to hear.

"And I am still looking forward to next Thursday, Mrs. Mitchell. Good day to you." Dr. Walker donned his hat and nodded his farewell to Michael. "I can find my own way out."

"Good day to you, too," she replied. "And thank you again."

Next Thursday . . . next Thursday . . . her mind drew a blank and then she remembered her Thanksgiving plans, just as Cora and Clara's conversation dominated the room again following the doctor's departure.

"I told you not to fret, Clara. I will manage just fine. And I have Amelia to help."

"Cora, you know you burn everything you put your hand to if I am not right there."

This did not bode well for Thanksgiving. Not at all.

Eleven

Thanksgiving dinner was a disaster from first course to last.

And it was also a rousing success.

It all depended on whether the point of the meal was as a celebration of family and friends and blessings, or to serve as an example of fine dining.

At least, that was Amelia's observation as she sat, exhausted and exhilarated, at the end of the table after an arduous day. She'd been struggling to pull together a semblance of dinner following a long week with Clara confined to her bedroom or a chair in the corner of the kitchen—if Michael was home to carry her up and down the stairs—with Cora hovering beside her.

Amelia smiled down the length of the table at her tenants and guests manfully struggling to choke down the almost inedible meal she'd produced. The turkey was dry, the biscuits burnt. There were too many lumps in the mashed potatoes, not enough salt in the beans and the gravy was cold. As far as the food was concerned, the gathering was a genuine catastrophe.

Still, they all appeared happy to be in each other's company. Mama always said the mark of a social triumph was the noise level and in that respect, her first Thanksgiving at the Grand Estate was indeed a success.

There was Horace Salzburg scraping the black crust off his third biscuit as he continued a debate with Ethan on the likelihood of Stephen Douglas winning the presidency at the next election. On the same side of the table, Festive was telling Eleanor about his day at the Emporium.

Dressed in a suit and tie, Michael stood across from Eleanor, carving additional slices of turkey for anyone interested in second servings while Cora and Clara peppered him with questions about his religious up-bringing and the holidays he most enjoyed. He looked very handsome in his new clothes, although his unruly hair still wanted smoothing, and he seemed to be answering the deluge from the Brown sisters with good humor.

"Cora," Clara touched her sister's hand after he finished regaling them with a wild story of a Christmas spent in Philadelphia, "you know he is teasing. Not even back East would grown men dress like that and dance in the streets—carrying parasols, no less."

"They call it mummery." Michael continued his game. "It's an old tradition, and they are rewarded for their efforts with cakes and spirits.

"If you don't believe me, you should ask the good doctor," Michael protested as he returned to his seat. "He must have witnessed the same goings-on while he was there in his college years."

The sisters swivelled in Walker's direction just as he took another bite of turkey. He chewed under their watchful eyes, chewed and chewed.

"I'm sorry," Amelia said, horrified as he continued chewing. "Perhaps some gravy would help?"

He waved her off and reached for his goblet.

"Thank you, no," he answered after several swallows of the wine Horace had supplied for the feast. "Everything is delicious, even without cranberries. But I believe I'll save some room for dessert."

He lied with just enough honesty to make it believable. Perhaps that was a skill that came in handy for men of medicine.

"I'm afraid you've been misinformed, ladies," he addressed the Browns next. "My alma mater is nowhere near Philadelphia. Yale is located in my hometown in Connecticut."

"You're a Yale man?" Ethan spoke up from the middle of his discussion with Horace.

"Yes." Dr. Walker nodded. "I graduated just before I entered the cavalry. And you?"

"I attended Princeton, myself," Ethan said. "But a classmate of mine, Harry Stevens, was a professor in the English department there for years. Tragic loss last year, tragic."

"Yes, very tragic. I rather liked Professor Stevens. I was saddened when I heard the news."

"Quite right. Quite right," Ethan nodded, lost in thought for a moment.

He came to himself and looked around the table. And then back at Amelia. "If I may have a moment, dear lady?"

"Of course," she said. "I want to thank you again for trapping the turkey. I'm afraid my cooking skills did not do it justice."

"Nonsense. I merely built the contraption. Eleanor set it out and brought home our prize."

Amelia noticed that while not taking credit for the

catch, he did not dispute the stringy outcome. "Thank you, too, Eleanor."

Eleanor smiled. "My pleasure. I don't know where my appetite has gone these last days, but everything I tasted was delicious. Having this feast was a wonderful treat."

The seamstress's voice hinted at just enough of a cold so that she probably was not tasting much of anything. Amelia wished she could quiet the cynical voice in her head.

"Back to my point . . ." Ethan was using a very professorial voice and the attention at the table flew back to him. He raised his wineglass. "Along the lines Mrs. Holmdale began, I think we should all raise our glasses in salute to our hostess. When I think of all I have to be thankful for this year, you come foremost to mind."

Everyone raised their glasses. The crystal glinted in the candlelight like liquid stars.

"Here, here," they said together while heat crept across Amelia's cheeks.

Her gaze snagged on Michael's. She'd had precious little time for anything beyond trying to assist Cora and keep the Estate running smoothly this past week. Cooking, cleaning, organizing took all her energy and left her little time to dwell on all she had shared with him on the edge of Warm Springs Lake or to try to analyze his reactions. But of course she had done both of those almost constantly.

She'd hardly seen him, except in passing, but he'd been in her thoughts, and in her dreams, and as their gazes locked just now, she was certain she had been in his.

"Thank you all for coming." She tore her gaze from his and looked around at her company of new friends. "Next year I will try to improve my culinary skills and hope to provide you with better fare."

"Don't fret, dear. Dr. Walker assures us Clara will be up and about very soon." Cora leaned forward. "She'll make sure we do a better job next time."

"Cora," Clara protested.

"Does that mean we'll have something other than soup for supper soon?" Festive spoke up. Soup had been the only meal Cora and she had managed not to burn.

"Yes, yes it does. And that will be something we will all be thankful for." She laughed. "Shall we adjourn to the drawing room? I believe Festive and Cora have some music planned for us."

"An excellent end to an excellent celebration," Horace said and stood. "Thank you for including me."

Everyone started to gather their plates and silver. "Please leave those," she said. "We'll enjoy our night together and take care of the cleanup later."

Michael pushed the small piece of kindling he'd wedged in the back door out of his way and carried in his third armload of wood.

Dirty dishes lined the kitchen table. He was glad it was not his responsibility to get them all clean and put away. He was going to stoke the fires in the study and the drawing room to blazing in order to provide enough heat to last the night. Eleanor Holmdale had not looked at all well during dinner and he wanted to make sure she did not catch a further chill from any drafts.

As he passed through the back hall toward the drawing room, he heard Amelia in the dining room. "Thank you so much for helping me to clear off the table, Festive, but you've done enough. You go on to bed now. You have a full day at the Emporium ahead of you tomorrow, do you not?"

Michael peered in the doorway. Someone had turned out the oil lamps in the wall sconces, but there was enough light from the candles burning low in the table's center for him to see that she'd changed from her sedate blue gown to a simple white blouse and brown skirt covered by a voluminous gingham apron.

She'd let her hair down from the elaborate chignon she'd worn for tonight's special occasion. His fingers had itched to pull it free then, and now they yearned to bury themselves in the silky mass that spilled over her shoulders in an ebony waterfall, gleaming softly in the flickering candlelight.

"Yes, missus," Festive answered, looking troubled. He usually went to sleep far earlier than the current hour, but he knew there was more cleaning up to be done than one person could handle. "But I don't mind helping you finish up here. There sure is a mountain of dishes in the kitchen. You shouldn't have to do them alone."

"She won't." At the sound of his voice, Amelia almost dropped a covered vegetable dish as she jumped out of the halo of light from the candles. "I'll help Amelia once I get this wood stacked. You go on, Festive."

"Thank you, really." She faced the hall doorway, and him, more fully. Standing in the shadows, he couldn't see her eyes. "But I think I can manage to wash a few dishes on my own."

"Uh-huh." He was already turning away to deliver his wood.

"Good night, Festive. Sleep well," he called over his shoulder.

"Good night, Michael, Happy Thanksgiving," Festive called after him. "And good night, missus. Thanks for the party. I had a good time."

Amelia's answer was lost as Michael entered the study and bent to the task at hand. He might as well keep himself busy tonight—he had a great deal to think over, which portended little chance for sleep.

Horace had delivered a message before they sat down for dinner that his presence was required in Springfield, and soon.

That was good. After the concern Ethan had raised just now, before retiring for the night, he had planned to go anyway to set another line of inquiry in motion regarding Dr. Walker.

Thankfully, the solicitor also carried news of the arrest of the radicals threatening Senator Douglas. They had been apprehended near the senator's home, carrying the architectural plans for the structure and a description of the senator's daily routine. In the struggle, Bill Fallon had been injured. Salzburg had no information on the marshal's condition, only that the incident was being kept quiet to avoid whipping up public sentiment for either the abolitionist movement or those claiming to favor states' rights.

The good news from all of that was that Ben Taylor would no longer expect him to be giving reports on Amelia's activities or want him to investigate connections between her and the radicals. On the other hand, his tip that the money from the robbery which cost Will his life had been sent here to Warm Springs—and the last of the robbers was also supposedly to be in the area looking for the money—was growing stale.

He'd cleared all but two men from his list of possible suspects weeks ago. When he'd been in charge, Fallon had known Will and had given Michael a great deal of latitude in his hunt for his brother's murderers. This new summons could be Taylor telling him to call it quits in Warm Springs. He wasn't ready to go.

And it was no longer just because he'd feel like he'd failed Will.

The fire crackled as its flames licked the wood he added. He'd have to check back in an hour to keep the fire red hot, but he imagined he could help the reluctant widow get quite a few dishes done in that amount of time.

"Why don't you want my help?" He asked the question uppermost in his mind as he entered the kitchen just as she was going to take a steaming pot from the stove.

She spun to face him, her hair spiraling across her shoulders. She still clutched the towel she'd obviously planned to use in place of potholders. "You have got to stop doing that," she hissed.

"Doing what?"

"Sneaking up like that." She was seriously annoyed. "I almost dropped scalding water all over the place."

"Well, we can't have that." He advanced to the stove. He'd offered to help, not argue. "I'll do that for you. If you get scalded, we'll be down one more woman in the house and however will we survive?"

She wasn't angry enough not to smile at his weak joke.

"Soup for supper." She imitated Festive's slow speech without making fun of him. "Soup for lunch. Soup for breakfast?"

"Horrors." He laughed and took the towel from her. Lifting the pot, he moved quickly to pour half its steaming contents into the washbasins waiting in the sink, then set the cast iron vessel back on the stove.

"You weren't seriously thinking you could lift that pot full of boiling water, were you?" He frowned at her as the wall lamp over the sink added a fine patina to her porcelain skin. "I thought you had more common sense."

"I do have common sense," she protested, putting her hands on her hips.

"Well, next time, try lifting the pot while the water is cold first. Then you'll know whether you can manage it when the water is hot."

"Oh." The steam went out of her indignation. "That's a good suggestion. Very practical. Thank you."

He barely saved himself from laughing again as he realized she was entirely serious. Prim, but serious.

"Wash or dry?" he asked.

"What?"

"Wash or dry," he repeated. "Which part do you want to tackle?"

She looked over at the tall stack of plates and array of glassware and cutlery awaiting their attention and pressed her lips together as she contemplated her choice. "Wash."

She reached for the soap flakes and sprinkled them into one of the basins. He snatched her hand back by the wrist just before she plunged her hand in to mix them up with the water.

"Have you ever washed dishes, Amelia?"

"I've helped Cora all this week," she declared, attempting to tug herself free.

"Washing or drying?" He held fast.

That determined chin he'd come to expect rose a notch as she tugged harder.

"Drying," she admitted. "But I watched her wash as I dried."

"I'll wash."

He put the towel in her palm and released her. Next, he mixed cool water from under the sink into the basins to lower the temperature.

"Oh," she said for the second time. "I guess I didn't see everything she did."

"Uh-huh," he answered and reached for the first stack of plates.

They worked for a long time in companionable silence. At least it seemed like a long time to Michael. Ever since their walk by the lake he'd stayed away from Robert Mitchell's widow, afraid of what he might do if he spent any more time alone with her, afraid of what she might tempt him to do. He'd wanted her from the first time he'd seen her, widow's weeds and all. But the deep revelations shared by the lake made her that much more attractive, that much more dangerous, and he'd kept his distance as much for her sake as for his own.

He'd thought working together to do the dishes would provide enough distraction, enough occupation, to keep thoughts of holding her in his arms, of lacing his fingers in her hair, at bay. Instead all he could concentrate on as he scraped the plates, washed and rinsed them, then stacked them on the drainboard was Amelia's lips whispering against his under the willows, her scent filling his lungs, her heat warming his body as she pressed against him.

He blew out a long breath as sweat beaded on his forehead, partly from the heat of the water and partly from the struggle between his desire and his better judgement.

She chuckled softly beside him, startling him. His thoughts had centered around her so much this past week he'd almost forgotten she was actually here in the darkened kitchen with him. He turned his head to her.

"It's unbelievable, isn't it?" She looked over at the table and the stacks of remaining china and then back up at him. "I never realized how much work, how many dishes, went into making and serving a meal."

"You never answered my question," he reminded her.

"Your question?"

"Why didn't you want my help? Why did you think you had to do all this yourself?"

"Oh, that." She looked over at the dishes still awaiting their attention. "I guess it seems silly. I wanted this Thanksgiving to be a real thank-you for welcoming me into your home. It didn't seem right to ask my guests for help."

She smiled then and the lamplight added a sparkle to the depths of her eyes that stole his breath. To hell with his better judgement. He gave in to impulse and flicked some of the rapidly cooling water from his washbasins at her.

"What was that for?" She shook off the droplets that landed on her cheeks and chin.

"You think entirely too much, madam."

"Oh, really?"

"Really." He plunged his fingers into the basins, then shook them off again. This time he splattered her blouse as well as her face with droplets. "What have you done lately just for fun?"

She was quiet as she considered her answer. He dipped his hands in the water again. She darted forward with her fingers cupped and scooped a handful at him. He jumped back in surprise.

"This *is* fun." She laughed as he looked down at his soggy shirt.

"No." He shook his head. "This is war."

For a few minutes they frolicked with the abandon of forgotten youth. Responsibilities, regrets, caution cast aside as they splashed one another, laughing and shrieking like naughty children. By the time they both called a truce, they were breathless. Dishwater was everywhere. On the floor, in their hair. Their clothes were saturated, skin drenched.

Amelia collapsed against the sink, still laughing silently, her wet cheeks glistening and her eyes sparkling in the lamplight. Dampness pulled her hair into long strands that dripped over her blouse, gone from white to almost translucent with the moisture he'd flung at her.

One small droplet clung to the end of her nose. Without thinking he reached down and kissed it away. Everything he'd been holding back flooded though him. Everything from their walk, from the kiss they'd shared in this very kitchen, from their first kiss, his catching her in the bedroom, or carrying her home from the train station. Even from the first time he'd ever seen her—everything crested and broke inside of him with the force of a riptide.

He gathered her in his arms and poured it all into the kiss he pressed on her lips. Desire, concern, anger, apology, compassion in a dizzying mix he could no longer deny as he drank from her tenderness.

Amelia flowed into him, her hands cupping the edges of his jaw and drawing him closer. Her lips parted and she kissed him right back, alternating between his lips and small gulps of air before opening herself and letting her tongue dart out to seek his.

He wrapped his arms around her. His hands splayed across her back. If he could have pulled her inside himself he would have. Instead he met her tongue and suckled it, letting her explore his mouth at will.

Her fingers pulsed and massaged his neck and the back of his head, driving him mad as they urged him to kiss her, probe her, deeper and wilder.

He broke away long enough to sweep her hair away from her neck and to tilt her cheek to one side so he could kiss away the moisture still clinging to it. He nibbled a path to her earlobe and then back along her jawline until she moaned with an unmistakable passion that sent him back to her lips for another long drink of their sweetness.

Her lips clung to him and her hand clutched his shirt as their tongues met and mated. He wanted, he needed, to feel more of her. His fingers worked the buttons at her collar, fumbling with haste and trembling with his raging desires. Each of his efforts was spurred to increased urgency by her lips locking with his, her tongue darting along the edge of his.

When he'd laid the slender column of her throat bare he went back to the delicious process of kissing and licking her skin dry. He traced a line down to the base of her neck and suckled her there, feeling the heat of her on his lips, flicking her pulse point with his tongue, reveling in the surrender she sounded with each gasp of breath, each tiny moan of pleasure while he continued to torment her.

He wanted to bury himself deep in her, here and now. To sheath himself in her soft, hot depths and taste true pleasure on her lips as he pushed them both over the brink.

He braced against the sink and took her lips fully this time, plundering them with his need. His hand covered her breast; her nipple, already hard, demanded his attention as it thrust against his palm. He kneaded her resilience through the fabric and longed to caress the satin flesh within, to roll her nipple beneath his fingers, skin to skin.

She was pliant in his arms. Sensual and open, willing and waiting. He reached for the next button, grew impatient with the wet fabric and pulled instead. The buttons popped, whether from age or his insistence, he did not care, as long as he could tear the fabric aside and taste her fully.

He might have hesitated, had he thought she was inexperienced. Might have moved more slowly, but she was a widow. He was rapidly losing all control. He felt her tugging at his own buttons, pulling his neckline open to expose his flesh to hers just as urgently and he was lost.

He picked her up then, under both arms, not breaking contact with her lips until he'd crossed the small distance to the table and sat her on it. Not until he'd ripped aside the thin covering of her chemise and pulled her to him so that his chest was against her stays and her breasts cradled his chin. Only then did he release them.

"Oh, Michael," she breathed as he took her in his mouth. "Oh, Michael. Oh-oh-oh."

Her cries urged him onward as did her hands, and she clung to him and pulled him closer to her.

He suckled her, teasing her nipple with his tongue, tasting the sweetness, savoring her responsiveness as she swayed to the rhythm of his demands. He held her to him with one hand and cupped her other breast, alternately rolling his thumb over her and tugging her while he continued to suckle and ply the other with his tongue.

He looked up at her as he switched the attentions of his mouth to the breast he'd been manipulating. Her lips were full and parted with ragged breaths. Her eyes were alight with the fire of newly awakened passion and her skin glistened in the lamplight as her dark hair gleamed against its paleness.

He was heavy with wanting her. Raging to possess her. He suckled her harder and she threw her head back. Her hair brushed his hand as she rocked against him, seeking more. The soft silk whispers sent gooseflesh up his arms.

He grazed her with his teeth and laved her hard with his tongue.

"Michael. Oh, Michael." Her husky appeal, her wanton willingness, shot straight through him. He found the sound of his name on her lips almost irresistible. Almost.

He released her breast and gathered her close. Her breasts pressed hard against his chest. The heat of her scorched him straight through.

He took her mouth again. Tenderly, this time. Slowly, worshipfully, once more. He tasted the promise of ecstasy on her lips. Felt unforgettable passion from her tongue. And then he let her go.

She clung to him. Her hands clutched his shirt at the shoulders. She didn't protest. She didn't question. She waited.

For an impossible moment he was certain he didn't have the strength to step away, to deny what they both clearly wanted. But he was a deceiver. He was here, with her, based on a lie. And she deserved a man who could give her, and claim from her, total honesty. An honesty he couldn't offer. Not now.

He turned then and left the kitchen without a word, afraid that if either of them spoke, his effort would be undone.

It took Amelia more than a few moments to come back to herself after Michael left, to stop trembling where she sat on the table and pull herself together.

Her blouse was ruined. Her chemise was ruined. And even though she had precious few of either, she had no regrets.

No regrets beyond an empty questing, an unfulfilled longing awakened in the glorious embrace of Michael Thompson's arms. Or, more accurately, with the tender flicks of his tongue.

She giggled at that realization. Giggled as she looked at the mess they'd made of the kitchen and the shambles they'd made of her clothes. She might be able to mop up enough of the water to keep Cora clueless about what had happened, or what had very nearly happened, but how would she explain her tattered attire to Eleanor, who was working so hard to help her expand the very wardrobe she had just allowed to be casually torn asunder.

"No," she corrected herself. "Not casual."

There had been nothing casual about the passion in Michael's embrace, the promise of more on his lips. There had been nothing cavalier or careless about the way he had looked at her just before he left the kitchen.

"Quite the opposite," she said aloud.

There had been a world of longing and a lifetime of caring in his eyes before he walked away. That was why she was not sliding down into a well of despair. Why she knew that what was awakened this night would not disappear. That *he* would not disappear until it had been resolved between them.

One way or another, she told herself as she jumped down from the table and set about mopping up the water. The rest of the dishes could wait until morning—she needed to go upstairs and get out of what was left of her clothes. She didn't want anyone to slip on unexpected puddles, but didn't want to shock them or have them thinking something terrible had happened to her.

"Quite the opposite," she said again.

She gathered the remnants of her blouse together as best she could and pulled one of Clara's shawls around her shoulders to maintain her dignity before she exited the kitchen.

All the lights in the house were out and it was quite dark—the moonlight of the other night lost in the clouds, it would seem. She moved cautiously, not wanting to bump into anything and make unnecessary noise. She reached the steps and was just about to ascend when the study door opened.

Michael stood in the opening, silhouetted by a blazing fire behind him. He'd stripped off his damp shirt and stood there bare-chested, his muscles outlined, his face in shadow.

"Amelia," he said.

"Don't."

"Don't what?"

"Don't apologize. Don't thank me. Just, don't." It was as simple and as complicated as that.

She hadn't expected to see him until tomorrow at the earliest. Didn't really want to see him. No, she did want to see him. Right this minute. Especially standing there with his chest, his muscled arms, his broad shoulders making her fingers ache to stroke them.

She walked over to the study, reached her hand up to the back of his neck, and pulled herself up to kiss him.

Their lips brushed. His breath whooshed out of him and he caught her lower lip in his and clung to it, tasting the fullness and passion still lingering from their earlier kisses. There was no demand in this kiss, no pleading. It was just a kiss. Yet it promised so much more.

Her heartbeat quickened and she pulled away before things got too dangerous, too tempting.

"Good night, Michael," she said as she turned away.

"Good night, princess," he called after her as she walked up the stairs. This time she knew he did not mean the title as a cut.

This time she knew he really meant it as a compliment.

Twelve

"I'll stay with her for a while, Cora. I think Clara said she needed you downstairs. Something about dinner."

The look of gratitude Eleanor gave her as Cora made her way to the door convinced Amelia the small lie was worth it.

"Are you sure, dear? You know it wasn't so long ago that you were unwell yourself." The smaller woman put her hand on Amelia's arm as she walked by. "I don't know what we'd do if you had a relapse. You did all that work on that wonderful meal the other day, and then all the cleanup. You'll exhaust yourself."

She'd only done part of the work she was being credited for. After she had gone upstairs, Michael must have returned to the kitchen and finished the rest of the dishes, and the pots and pans. Everything had been washed and put away by the time the sun and the household had roused.

"I don't think sitting here just in case there is anything Eleanor needs will overtax me. I'll call you if I have any questions."

The morning after Thanksgiving, Michael had disappeared on one of his trips, but Amelia still held the certainty he would be back. He would be back to re-solve all that still lay unanswered between them.

"All right then, I suppose that will not be too stren-uous. Stay in bed, Eleanor—you know what the doctor said about rest. I wish you would take the syrup he left you. Maybe I'll bring you both up a nice, hot cup of tea in a bit. How does that sound? There is nothing quite so soothing as a cup of tea when one is overset or troubled. I'll be back." Cora was still talking at full stream as she moved down the hall.

Amelia closed the door behind her as she reached the back steps.

"Thank you." Eleanor punctuated the words with a cough.

Amelia couldn't help but smile.

"Cora Brown is a dear friend but there are times when she could positively talk a body to death." Eleanor coughed again, deep and congested.

Amelia bit her lip. The cough sounded worse, not better. Should she call the doctor back for another visit?

"Don't go making faces, Amelia. I'm not about to die just yet." The bout of coughing that followed this declaration put it immediately to doubt in Amelia's mind. She offered Eleanor a sip of water when it passed and she finally caught her breath.

"I've always had a weak chest. I used to scare poor Jacob at least once a winter." Eleanor handed the glass back with a weak smile. "This settles in, and some-times gives me an awful week or two before it goes, but it always goes."

She released a sigh that ended on another cough. She closed her eyes for a moment and leaned back against the pillows. Despite her assurance, Amelia did not like the older woman's pallor, nor the smudges of exhaustion evident under her eyes.

Amelia drew the chair Cora had just vacated closer to the bed and sat down while Eleanor watched her every move. "I'm glad to hear that this is not as serious as it seems. You have become a dear friend. I don't think my life would be the same without you in it."

"Why, thank you." Eleanor smiled that proper little smile that looked so like it belonged in an elegant drawing room. "I do believe I could say the same about you."

"Well, thank you, too. Now, don't you think you should take the medicine Dr. Walker left you?"

"Not until I have to." She coughed again and closed her eyes.

Amelia struggled to ignore the nagging worry etching the back of her mind. Eleanor was an intelligent woman; surely she was familiar enough with her own reaction to her illness that she was right to say her cough was nothing to be overly concerned with. Surely the doctor would have said something if there were truly any danger. For the second time in a handful of days she wished she had more practical knowledge about illness to be able to help one of her tenants.

Eleanor's eyes were open and fixed on her, waiting. Amelia struggled for something to say beyond her worries. "Those pictures are lovely."

She indicated the various small, framed sketches hung in a display about the room.

Eleanor beamed as her gaze flew to the pictures. "Yes, they are fine, aren't they? Those were done by my Jacob. I told you he liked to sketch. Go ahead and look at them."

Amelia hesitated. Clara had told her to keep an eye on Eleanor and allow Cora a chance to rest.

"Go on," Eleanor urged. "I'll not expire while your back is turned. Jacob loved to draw. He especially liked to draw our home and the surrounding countryside. And our deer."

Amelia followed the trail of pictures from one side of the room to the other. There were images of the little farmhouse where Eleanor and Jacob had lived. There was the meadow, in various seasons, with deer and without. And there were pictures of Eleanor. Young and beautiful, with a rather haughty expression on her face. Older, but with love shining pure and bright in her eyes. There were several images of hands entwined, one male, one female. Even those revealed the love of the artist for his subject. The emotion showed through so strong it caught at Amelia's throat. She traced the meshed fingers with a feeling of awe.

"Oh, Eleanor, they are truly lovely." She turned to smile at her friend. "He was a talented artist. And he very obviously adored his subject."

"Yes." Tears sparkled at the corners of Eleanor's eyes. "He was very talented. He poured himself, heart and soul, into every picture he ever drew. But then, he was like that in everything he did. He carved me the most charming set of animals to hang on our Christmas trees. Every year he added a new carving."

A fierce bout of coughing seized Eleanor, but she picked up her point as soon as she caught her breath. "I wanted him to put his talent to use. I wanted to take him back to Philadelphia with me. To introduce him to the right people and help him be the artist I knew he could be. I had big plans for him. Big plans for the both of us."

Amelia could all too easily picture the life Eleanor had planned. Art shows, commissions from the very finest families. A life of recognition and ease filled with gala events. All the things Amelia had expected and wanted all of her life.

A lifetime filled with important things.

Eleanor coughed softly. "I'm so glad he didn't listen to me."

The admission shocked Amelia. "What do you mean?"

"Come and sit beside me again."

Amelia took her seat and pulled it still closer to the bed. Eleanor reached for her hand.

"It's almost funny, Amelia. My life with Jacob began a long time ago and yet I remember each day as though it happened only yesterday. What I wanted so long ago was really only for me. It was a selfish dream. I wanted to take the man I had fallen in love with and somehow fit him into the kind of life that I had been given to expect. I wanted very badly to make him the sort of man I was supposed to spend my life with instead of the man he truly was."

She paused to cough for a moment and Amelia tried to keep her worry from showing. Eleanor drew a slow breath to continue, the dreamy look back in her eyes. "I was a very foolish and headstrong young girl. I don't know why he fell in love with me, but he did. It took me some time to realize that what I wanted was not the life he wanted to live."

She squeezed Amelia's fingers. "The man I was in love with was a farmer. He was a poet with the soul of a farmer who loved the land and would have withered if I had been successful in uprooting him. He sketched for the pure enjoyment he got out of making the pictures come to life. He got the same enjoyment from growing crops and watching his sheep multiply. He liked to dance in the evenings with only a music box for accompaniment. He asked me to share that simple life instead of the one I so foolishly thought I wanted."

Her gaze came back to the present and marked Amelia. "I loved him enough to accept him even though I was afraid I would not like the simple life he offered. Even in the face of my father's anger and my mother's despair. It was the hardest decision I had ever faced. And, it was the best decision I ever made."

"You were happy."

"I was the happiest woman. Even now, with Jacob gone and only my memories to keep me warm, I am happy. My life was wonderful and my memories are more than anyone could ask for in one lifetime. Ultimately, when I'd found the man I loved, the rest didn't matter."

Amelia's throat was tight and burning. She envied Eleanor the life she had shared with her husband. "Is that why you still go to feed the deer?"

"Yes. That and many more reasons. My commitment to Jacob and his to me was for a lifetime and beyond. I reaffirm that commitment every time I do what he loved. I feel him with me in the early-morning air and in the home we used to share."

She sighed again, dissolving into a the worst coughing fit yet.

"Eleanor, don't you think you should try that medicine?"

"Yes. As much as I detest the concoction the doctor makes for me, I should take it. Do your worst."

Amelia fetched the medicine from the bureau along with the tablespoon left there for just this purpose. She poured out two full spoonfuls and gave them to Eleanor, who made an awful face after each one. But she did manage to sigh without coughing once she had taken it. Amelia shuddered in sympathy, almost certain the awful-tasting laudenum-laced concoction was the same she had been dosed with.

"Nasty stuff, that. But it will do me in for a while." She lay back against the pillows, her eyelids already beginning to droop in reaction to the medicine.

"Good. You need to rest."

"Of course, you *would* side with him." Eleanor smiled with her eyes closed and there was no sting in her words.

Amelia drew the curtains, her gaze drifting out over the yard and the gray clouds lurking overhead. "It looks like more snow on the way—it's a good thing you'll be snug in bed."

"Take care of the deer for me, will you?" Sleep laced, there was still a certain urgency in the request.

"Eleanor?"

The older woman's brow furrowed and she moved restlessly against the bed. "I promised Jacob . . ."

"All right. I will take care of the deer. I know what to do. You rest. I'll go right now."

Eleanor stilled her disquiet and slid into sleep. Amelia smiled and soothed a hand over her brow. She was too warm. The fever on top of the cough increased Amelia's worries. If this did not lift by morning she would send Festive for the doctor again.

She opened the door to find Cora had returned as promised with teacups on a tray.

"Here we are, dear—"

"Shhh." Amelia placed a finger over her lips and closed the door firmly behind her. "Eleanor has taken her medicine and is asleep. I think it would be best if we let her rest for a while."

"Oh, yes, of course, dear." Cora smiled and linked her arm with Amelia's. "It was good you were able to convince her to take the medicine. Nobody likes Dr. Walker's mixtures—they taste awful and make one so sleepy, but they do seem to do the trick."

"I'd have to agree with you there." Amelia glanced out the landing window. The clouds were growing more numerous by the minute and the wind had started to pick up. She'd better hurry if she was going to carry through on her promise. After listening to Eleanor's reminiscences of her husband and the life they had shared it seemed very important that she not be the one responsible for any break in the woman's commitment.

"I guess it will have to be the two of us drinking tea. Will the drawing room do, Amelia dear?" Cora's expectant face turned to hers.

Amelia bit back a sigh. She could spare time for one quick cup of tea, surely.

"I can have a quick one, Cora. But I promised Eleanor I would attend to something for her."

"Ahhh." Cora set the tea tray on a side table and poured two cups. She handed one to Amelia. "You're going to go and feed her deer for her?"

At least she would not have to explain that to Cora,

who made it her business to know everything about everyone. "Yes. She asked me to."

"That's so good of you. I know she will appreciate it. As long as I've known Eleanor, she has fed those deer. Her husband used to feed them with her."

"So I understand."

Cora sighed. "There were never two people so much in love as Jacob and Eleanor Holmdale."

"Did you know Jacob?"

"Oh my, yes, dear. Clara and I have lived in Warm Springs for a great many years. Jacob Holmdale was a gentleman through and through, yet there was something about him that just needed to be outdoors working in the earth. He loved their farm. Their life together there was a happy one. That's why Eleanor has been unable to part with it."

Amelia felt a pang of envy for the other widow. Eleanor had been unable to part with her home; she went back there every day to remember her husband and the life they built together. The fact that those visits were not made in sorrow or bitterness for what she'd once had was so touching. Each visit was a celebration of what she and Jacob once shared together. Of what they still shared, even though they were parted.

Amelia finished her tea, trying to ignore the envy she felt for the strength and love Eleanor possesed.

"I really must go."

Cora peered out between the curtains. "Oh, Amelia, I don't know that you're going to be able to feed them today after all. There is a storm brewing—a big one, from the looks of those clouds."

Amelia joined her at the window. Her heart sank.

Even in the short time she'd taken to allow Cora a conversational outlet, the sky had darkened further. She could almost taste the coming snow on her tongue from inside the house. She shivered.

She had promised Eleanor. She had allowed her friend to take some much-needed rest, so essential for her recuperation by promising to fulfill the loving commitment Eleanor had made to her Jacob.

She tightened her lips and shook her head.

"I won't be long, Cora. If I hurry I can make it there and back before the storm really breaks. We have plenty of snow in Boston. I'll dress warmly and be just fine."

"Oh, dear."

"Don't worry, I won't be long." Amelia hurried into the hallway and retrieved her cloak from its peg. Her half-boots would do for the moment—there wasn't time to waste on hunting for others, if there were any others she could use. She would run all the way to the meadow and be back before suppertime.

"Amelia, I don't think this is wise. Surely the deer can wait for tomorrow."

She thought of her promise, and she thought of Eleanor's promise, and she thought about those beautiful creatures huddling under the trees, cold and hungry all night in the middle of a storm.

"Please don't worry," Amelia offered over her shoulder as Cora followed her into the kitchen. "I'll be back before you miss me."

"Don't worry about what?" Clara turned from the stove, where she had already begun to stir something that smelled heavenly. Chicken, onions, and more all stewed together. "And back from where?"

"She's going out, Clara." There was an edge of fear that came out as indignation as Cora reported Amelia's errand to her sister. "In this weather."

Amelia caught back a groan as she pulled the bag for the corn from its peg in the pantry doorway. Cora managed to make it sound as though she intended to trek into the next county.

"Amelia? What are you thinking? Festive can go in the morning," Clara said. "What about dinner?"

"Ladies." Amelia held up a hand and drew on her years of command in drawing rooms across the eastern seaboard. "I promise not to be long. Just as I have promised Eleanor that I would do this for her. Please understand. I will be back before you have finished your fricasee and help you with the biscuits."

They both gave her that owl-eyed look of concern that so marked them as sisters; then, finally, it was Clara who spoke as she wiped her hands on her apron.

"Take my shawl to protect your head from the wind. We'll be waiting for you."

"Clara—"

"She's a grown woman. She came all the way here from Boston on her own. She'll be back." Clara cut off her sister's squeak of protest. "Is there any tea left?"

Amelia made good her escape. She closed the kitchen door behind her without further argument and stepped out into the surprising, bone-chilling cold. She hugged her woolen cloak tighter about her. She would be only too happy to finish with this chore and be back inside the warm and cozy confines of the Grand Estate's kitchen—boiling, baking, or stirring any concoction Clara happened to think up.

"Enough of that." She hurried down the steps and

into the gathering gloom, stopping to fill the pouch with corn from the barn. She gave Becky a hearty scoop while she was there and patted her nose. "That will keep you for a bit."

She set out across the field along the route she had used when she trailed Eleanor that one morning. The wind stung her cheeks and tugged at her hair. She'd forgotten the shawl. She should go back, but did not want to face any further arguments. She just wanted to get to the meadow and be done.

A smile tugged at her lips. Who would ever believe the rather fastidious and authoritative Amelia Lawrence, a young lady given to commanding any party and who had honed the ability to cut any unwanted hangers-on to ribbons with her sarcastic derision, was rushing out into this kind of weather to feed deer?

Who indeed?

Well, perhaps Amelia Lawrence would never have imagined such a task and would have laughed at anyone who would. But it seemed that Amelia Mitchell was an entirely different person who had learned a thing or two about what was really important in the world. The thought warmed her despite the frigid air nipping her nose and cheeks. Would Lenore and Tori even recognize her?

Imagine . . .

The clouds moved faster as the wind whipped at her back, hurrying her along. She had to laugh as her feet fairly flew over the ground. She had told more truth than she intended when she'd claimed she wouldn't be long. At this rate she would return so quickly, both sisters would be stunned into silence.

And such a concession from Cora would be worth the trip.

The snow started as she reached the edge of the yard. Tiny little flakes. The silent landscape around her was filled with the soft sounds of tiny ice crystals pelting the ground.

She drew a deep breath and plunged onward. The faster she got there, the faster she would return. If she didn't get the corn sprinkled before the ground was covered, the deer would be unable to eat it or even find it. There was no telling how much snow there would be. Cora's dire predictions still rang in her ears. The icy clicking of the snowfall was lost now in the whistling sound of the wind as it gained force.

Eleanor's stories about Jacob and his pictures, about the changes she had wrought in her expectations and the happiness she'd found, kept playing through Amelia's mind as she hurried along. There was so much feeling, so much love, in the life she related to Amelia. Would she ever know such love? Or feel for any man what Eleanor had felt for her Jacob?

Michael Thompson's tilted grin and piercing gray eyes, his disrespectful manner and ability to judge just when she needed him the most, edged into her thoughts. The feel of his hands on her, of his lips and his tongue caressing her so intimately the other night, shivered through her unexpectedly. He'd looked so breathtaking, silhouetted in the study door with his shirt off the last time she'd seen him. Heat warred with the wind's wintery kiss caressing her cheeks and her lips, warming her despite the cold air.

The storm buffeted her, blowing her skirts up to blast winter's cold breath against her ankles. The ice crystals stung her legs and her face. Her teeth chattered as she tried vainly to keep her skirts down and her feet moving despite the cold and the nipping edges of snow dousing the tips of her boots. She still had time. She had to have time. She couldn't let Eleanor down.

She reached the meadow at last. Snow dusted the ground and skirled in small whirls across the opening. She ignored the temptation to dump her corn on this spot and head home—she marched forward from the edge of the trees.

The wind whipped stronger out in the open than it had before, and the snow pelted her relentlessly as it came sideways, hitting bare skin with each lift of her skirts. It was icy and oh-so-cold. Her teeth were just chattering constantly now. It was time to drop the corn and return. She sprinkled the feed as best she could, great handfuls of the stuff, enough to be seen against the snow.

She lost her footing and fell to the ground as the wind picked up stronger and rushed at her, knocking the breath from her. Her hands sank into the snow, cold and icy as her skirts fluttered about her. Enough was enough; she had followed through on her promise to Eleanor; she had kept the commitment. Now she needed to get out of here before the storm worsened so much she couldn't reach her house.

She had to push to her feet three times before finally gaining her footing as the wind pelted her with a vengeance. It was darker now than it had been when she'd first come out. She wished she had thought to bring a lantern of some sort with her. But she hadn't and wishing would not help now.

She bundled the empty corn sack into a ball and thrust it into her pocket as she turned back the way she had come, directly into the wind. It whipped her without mercy, blasting the hood from her head and shrilling past her ears. Her hair came loose beneath raging fingers of cold air and streamed behind her. Fear tugged at her. The snow slanted sideways first, then directly at her, changing direction with each whimsical change in the wind's breath. She could barely see in front of her between the wind and the snow.

Dear heaven, Cora had been right. This was no mere storm.

It had more the look of a blizzard. She'd read news stories of people lost in blizzards out in the wilderness and never being seen again. Read them with little regard, safe in the warm confines of her mother's salon. She'd actually wondered how someone could get lost in a storm and freeze to death.

Fear tugged tighter. That couldn't be her, could it? Her simple desire to carry through on her promise to Eleanor had not placed her in some kind of danger. Not really. She tamped back her fears and forced herself onward. After a few minutes she stumbled and fell as the ground level rose unexpectedly in front of her.

Tears sparked at the edges of her eyes and her breath burned in her throat. There had been no downward slope on her way to the meadow from the Grand Estate once she left her yard. The ground was fairly level all the way there and back. If it was her hill, she'd surely see a light from the house. The wind had been at her back on her way to the meadow; she had thought having it blow directly at her meant she was going the right way. Had the wind changed its course?

So where was she?

She thrust a fist to her mouth, in part to blow a little warmth into her cold fingers and in part to keep the hysteria rising hard and fast inside from streaming out of her.

Think, Amelia, think.

If there had been no upward slope on her way to the meadow, she had somehow gone in the wrong direction. She needed to picture the meadow as she had seen it the day she'd been here with Eleanor. Clear, crisp sunshine, the open expanse of meadow, the trees, the graceful and quick deer coming down into the meadow. That was it. She had gone in the opposite direction she'd intended. Not good, but at least she had figured it out. She could not trust in the direction of the wind then as her guide. She would have to trust in her own sense of direction. She swallowed hard and pushed to her feet again.

What use had a young woman at the pinnacle of society ever had for a sense of direction? All the streets had names, didn't they? All the carriage drivers knew which way to go, didn't they?

Again hysteria bubbled in her throat.

What she wouldn't give for a knowledgeable carriage driver and a warm lap robe!

If she had one here at just this moment, she would know exactly what to say. She smiled despite the cold. Very good, then.

"I wish to go home by the most direct route. No dawdling." Firm command laced the words despite the wind's determination to whip them away into the darkened sky.

The snow continued to fall and her feet were cold.

She was not accomplishing anything staying here and wishing her circumstances away.

"Just go, Amelia."

She drew in a deep breath, blew it out, and forced herself forward in the opposite direction she had taken. Not an easy task, given the weather's determination to pelt her from all directions and threaten to knock her to her knees. She kept her feet by bending forward and making a smaller target of herself and praying she would reach something that looked familiar.

She could see the faint outline of trees in front of her and hurried her steps. Then the ground sloped away from beneath her and she slid down, forcing snow into the backs of her half-boots. Tears clogged her throat. Her direction had been wrong again. There was no downward slope. She had no idea where she was or where to begin again. She squeezed her eyes shut and pulled her knees close.

Her mental image of the meadow, with Eleanor at her side, did nothing to help her this time. She had slid down. How far? Three feet? Ten? She couldn't say; shock had jolted her as she slid and in that moment she hadn't been sure when her fall would stop or even if it would.

Now what?

Tears dripped down her cheeks and she brushed at them, impatient with her own weakness. Crying wouldn't help her. She had to think. If she truly had become one of those poor souls lost in a blizzard, then she had only herself to count on. Only herself and the members of her little family back at the Grand Estate.

Her Grand Estate.

A smile tugged through the tears. Cora and Clara knew where had gone. She wasn't really alone. Despite her fears, she wasn't really that far away from home. Someone would come for her.

Michael would come for her.

Thirteen

Michael would come for her.

That certainty brought enough warmth to brighten her spirits.

She gathered her cloak closer, blessing Eleanor for the quilted depths of her gift, and resolved not to move any further. Her slide downward had at least taken her out of the major portion of the wind's pelting. The snow still fell around her, but if she kept herself warm she would probably survive the night.

She shuddered. Survive the night?

No, there was no use torturing herself with the outlandish fears forming in her mind. She would stay right where she was and listen for anyone calling her name. She would listen and watch for a lantern. Eventually, everything would be all right. Eventually, she would be all right. All right and warm.

Michael stamped the snow off the edges of his boots as he gained the shelter of the back pantry with an armload of wood. They would need a dozen such loads to stave off the chill from the wind howling on the other side of the door.

He was only too glad to be back at the humble

lodgings of the Grand Estate. It might not be the most glamorous place in the world but it held all the warmth a man could ask for. And then some, if you counted the lovely proprietress who would drive any man mad with wanting her.

He smiled despite himself. It was a madness any man would welcome. The image of Amelia Mitchell, her breasts bare and gleaming in the lamplight, her lips parted by passion, her hair streaming over her shoulders, had haunted him throughout his trip to Springfield. He'd reported to Marshal Taylor, he'd checked on Bill Fallon, but his thoughts had been centered on the woman who welcomed his kisses and allowed him to walk away without melting into hysteria.

Had she missed him as much as he had missed her while he was gone?

Amelia Lawrence Mitchell was steadily winding herself around his heart and his soul. Not something he had time to pursue fully at the moment, but when this mission was over, when his promise to Will and to his father had been completed, then . . . then he would see just what lay between him and the lovely widow and just where their future might lead.

That time might be very soon. A halting, incomplete deathbed confession in a Kansas jail had sent him to this town looking for the last of his brother's murderers, Joseph White. Only one likely candidate remained. His trip to Springfield had eliminated Otis MacNamara as a suspect when they had finally found the former patent medicine salesman's partner and learned his name. Oscar McKinley, MacNamara's real name, had been in a Rhode Island jail the day Will was robbed and killed.

That left Josiah Walker to be cleared or caught. He was close, very close. Then he might have a future to offer a woman. To offer Amelia Mitchell.

He reached for the kitchen doorknob and it turned on its own beneath his grasp.

Cora and Clara both stood in the doorway.

"Oh, Michael, we're so glad you've come back."

"At last, dear, at last. We've been so worried."

"She's been gone too long."

She *who?* He had a sick feeling that he knew. Whatever they were trying to tell him, they tumbled over one another in their rush to get it all out.

"We tried to stop her, dear. But she was so determined."

"Cora, we've got to let him at least get into the house or he'll never understand." Clara took her sister by the arm.

"Oh, yes, of course—come in, dear, come in."

The sisters backed out of the doorway with a nervous rustle of skirts. Their owl-eyed concern was more pronounced than ever, underscored with the worried wringing of their hands.

His stomach knotted. He tried to get to the heart of their fright as clamly as possible. "What is it? Who is in trouble?"

"Amelia, it's Amelia." Cora looked ready to cry. "She wanted to help Eleanor so badly. She wouldn't listen to reason."

"And, of course, it's her house, and she's a grown woman."

They were winding up again. Michael held his hand up for silence. This was getting them nowhere and only served to tighten the tense knot inside him.

"One at a time, ladies, please. Clara?"

She drew in a breath. "Amelia promised Eleanor she would attend to the feeding of the deer. She left just before the storm started. It's been too long, Michael, and she hasn't returned. And she didn't take the shawl I told her to."

He raked a hand through his hair, already crusted with melting snow. Cold fingers of alarm dripped down into the collar of his shirt and down his back. Deer? No shawl? Was she out there in only her dress? "What would possess her?"

"She wouldn't be dissuaded. We both tried."

"Yes, we did, dear, and she just wouldn't listen. She wanted to feed Eleanor's deer because Eleanor—she's dreadfully ill."

"Ill?" he interjected. "Amelia?" Had Amelia had a relapse and wandered into the storm in a fevered state?

"No dear, pay attention. Eleanor is ill. Amelia promised to be back in time to help Clara with dinner. But it's long past time to help and she has not returned."

Fear iced his gut as the two sisters finished their report. Amelia was out in this storm somewhere on some fool errand.

"I'll find her." He turned back toward the door.

"We knew you would."

"Take this with you." Clara's hand on his elbow halted him before he could open the door. She handed him a leather satchel.

He raised a brow—he didn't have time for any distractions. Or extra errands. Not now.

"There is food and water in here, Michael." Clara's steady blue gaze held his. "We knew someone would go out after her if you did not come back tonight. Ethan and Festive will be home soon."

She patted his arm. "You'll need this. And you'll need it for Amelia when you find her."

He nodded, glad of the steady tone in Clara's voice. He clutched the bag. "I'll find her. Ask Festive to bring in more wood when he gets home. Tell him and Ethan to stay put. We don't all need to be out in the storm."

"Of course you will find her."

"We'll be waiting, dear, and praying every moment."

Their voices drifted out into the cold after him. He knew where Eleanor Holmdale went every day. He'd made it his business to know what all of them did every day. It was part of his job. He'd felt so wrong spying on his neighbors, his friends. Now he was glad of it.

He cursed under his breath as the darkness and the snow swirled together, obscuring his vision. He ducked into the barn as soon as he found it and grabbed the lantern he kept on the ledge there. With a quick strike, light glowed forth. It might not make much of a dent in the storm, but it would be better than nothing and might serve as warmth should the need arise.

He pushed back out into the swirling wind and snow.

His gut tightened. Even in the short time it had taken him to receive the news from Cora and Clara, the storm had worsened. Amelia was out in this somewhere. Alone, and probably frightened.

What if he didn't locate her?

His curse whipped away on the wind. If only his raging worry would follow. No good ever came of allowing doubt free rein. He would find her. He had to. Experience was on his side and something else.

Hearing the report of her missing from the household when he had expected to find her there, clouds of dark hair and cool blue eyes contrasting with the warmth of her kisses, had clenched his gut and told him something he had only just begun to suspect.

He needed Amelia Mitchell in his life. Whether his stubborn little widow wanted to let him into hers or not. He needed her.

He pushed forward, holding the lantern in front of him and gritting his teeth every step of the way. He had to find her because he couldn't face the consequences of failure.

It took him more than an hour to reach the meadow, an hour of steady, slow progress and gritted oaths that were more prayer than curse.

The meadow was a sheet of pure, undisturbed snow.

Despair edged his thoughts again. She wasn't here. And she had been nowhere on the trail leading to the meadow. At the time she left, she would surely have been able to make her way here. So where was she?

He held the lantern in front of him, swinging it slowly from one side to the other as he advanced into the blinding snow. Would she have thought to take shelter somewhere? Could she have found shelter? She was a city girl.

He cupped his hands to his mouth. "Amelia! Amelia!"

The wind snatched her name from his lips with greedy fingers and snarled around him like some great beast. He tried again, ignoring the fears surging inside him. She would not survive in this fierce weather alone, his delicate, house-bred society girl.

He had to find her.

He moved forward again and then noticed the slight dips in the snow. Footsteps? There was corn, too. In a snow-covered little mound.

He gritted his teeth, uttered another short prayer and followed the dips. They were evenly spaced and varied from side to side. They were footprints wind-blown and very nearly disappeared, but footprints nonetheless.

They had to be hers.

He followed them to the edge of the trees and called again. "Amelia! Amelia! Answer me."

The wind laughed in his ears. But underneath, the faintest sound.

"Amelia! Amelia!"

There it was again. His throat tightened and he hurried off to the left, lantern swinging in wild arcs.

"Amelia!"

"Michael!"

He half-slid, half-dove down the hill and there she was, mantled in snow from head to foot where she crouched in the partial shelter of the slope, her back against a tree. He laughed in spite of the predicament they were in and pulled her into his arms.

Her lips were icy and shivering beneath his, but it didn't matter. He'd found her.

"Oh, Michael, I just knew you would c-c-c-come for me."

"I came." He helped her to her feet. She couldn't stay out here—she was already half frozen. With the snow ever increasing, it was an iffy matter to get her back to the Grand Estate. They were closer to Holm-dale farm than they were to anything else. "Come on."

He drew her into the shelter of his arm and held

the lantern out in front of them. It was slow going and Amelia was sluggish on her feet after sitting for so long in the snow. Though they were close to the farmstead, he guessed it took them an hour to navigate the blinding snow and wind. Amelia drooped at his side as they reached the steps.

"Where . . . are . . . we?" Her ragged breath tore at him.

"The Holmdale spread. I'm sure Eleanor won't mind if we take shelter here."

"But the Grand Estate. C-c-c-cora, Cl-cl-clara."

"They'll understand." He opened the door and pulled her inside, out of the killing weather. The immediate cessation of the wind's battering roar created a deafening silence. Their breath mingled in cold white clouds as they stood for a moment.

He held up the lantern and gazed at Amelia's face. Her eyebrows were frosted with snow and her lips were bluish-gray. Not good. But at least she was alive and she was with him.

"We have to get you warm."

"That sounds g-g-g-good." She smiled at him, but it was tremulous and unsteady as her teeth continued to chatter.

He propped the lantern on the table and drew her over to it. "Keep your fingers close to the lantern. I'm going to get a fire going."

"But w-w-w-wood?"

"Eleanor always keeps this place stocked and ready as though she and Jacob might return at any moment. There will be plenty of wood." And hopefully enough kindling for him to start a roaring blaze with no delay.

True to his observations of Eleanor, there was

plenty of wood; the kindling was sparse, but enough to start the fire. In moments, bright orange-yellow flames licked upward, spilling warmth into the cold interior of the Holmdale kitchen.

He pushed to his feet and went to Amelia. She was still chattering, but the frost on her eyebrows had started to thaw. He reached for her hand—it was warmer. "Come to the fire—you need to get warm."

She crossed to the fireplace with him in a silence broken only by their footfalls on the fine wood planking in the farmhouse. "Let's take off that cloak and have you sit down."

He drew the sodden garment from her. It was weighted down with snow. She must be exhausted just from the weight of it.

She sank to the floor in front of the fire and held her hands out. "Lovely."

His groin tightened at the husky sound of her voice. He took the cloak back toward the door, draped it across two chairs, and added his own. They sagged in snow-covered dismay as the windows rattled. If possible, the storm was worse now than it had been only moments before. If he hadn't reached home when he had, if he hadn't gone right out after her, if he hadn't seen the footsteps already filled with snow—myriad disasters played through his mind, each ending with Amelia frozen to death as he failed to reach her in time.

He shuddered and turned back toward the fire and the vision in damp black serge that even now hunkered down, trying to chase the icicles out of her blood.

She was alive and she was with him and that was all that mattered at the moment. He shook the rest of the snow out of his hair and went to stand by the fire and warm himself as well. Firelight flickered warm, golden light over her face. She was wet and bedraggled with hair hanging in snow-sodden ringlets. She was beautiful.

"Are you feeling better?"

"Yes. At least my teeth have stopped chattering." She offered him a smile. He couldn't help but smile back.

"I . . . we . . . were all worried about you. Do you have any idea of the scare you've put into the . . . people that care about you?"

"I'm sorry."

"Amelia." He knelt down beside her. "Why did you go out in this weather? You could have waited—"

"I had to." She didn't let him finish. "I needed to. For Eleanor."

"I'm sure she would have understood that you couldn't go out with a blizzard breathing down your neck."

"Perhaps." She held her hands toward the fire for a moment.

The flames backlit her slender fingers, making her seem even more vulnerable. He swallowed hard as she turned her gaze back to his. He had so nearly lost her.

"You're probably right. Eleanor would have understood, but I didn't know there was a blizzard coming. We've had many nights with clouds and even snow that turned out to be nothing more than a dusting. I thought I could accomplish what I needed to, hold to Eleanor's commitment for her, and return with no harm done." She swept her damp hair back from her face and tucked it behind her ears. "I wanted to do what she needed done."

Who would have suspected his haughty, pale little widow with her society airs and her inability to so much as boil water would brave a winter storm to feed a few deer who were probably much more adept at feeding themselves than she was? He could have laughed at the absurdity of it all. He could have railed until he raised the rooftop. He bit both reactions back.

"Michael?"

"Yes."

She reached for his hand and laced her own much-warmer fingers through his. "You saved my life tonight."

He knew that. Had known it ever since he'd found her huddled in a near-frozen ball at the meadow's edge. But somehow hearing her say the words aloud tightened the lump in his throat and brought back the dull taste of fear.

"I—"

"No." She placed her other fingers over his mouth, stilling any denial he might offer. "It's true. Without you . . ."

She shuddered. He could feel the reverberation through their linked hands. "Without you, I wouldn't be here and . . . well . . . I just wanted to . . . thank you."

She scooted to her knees and leaned toward him. Her mouth, so much warmer, so alive, touched his. Her hands rested on his chest. Fire ignited low in his belly, making the blaze in the hearth a pale thing in comparison.

He groaned, needing her in his arms. Needing to blot out all his frozen fears by her very real warmth.

He reached out and pulled her closer. Her gown was soaked.

He drew back from her mouth with regret. "Amelia, you need to change out of that wet gown."

She smiled, mysterious and soft, sensual as hell.

"Yes, I do."

She pushed to her feet; the grace so second nature to her had returned as she warmed by the fire. He could only sit back on his heels and stare at her. She undid the buttons on her serge jacket and shrugged it to the floor. His mouth went dry.

Her white cotton underblouse was every bit as damp as the jacket. It clung to her like a lover, molding the full curves of her breasts, clinging to the corset underneath. Reminding him of Thanksgiving night in the kitchen of the Grand Estate.

The memory of each taste of her soft flesh burned his mind and his soul. Desire swelled hot and heavy. He wanted to tear the sodden garments from her body and take her here before the fire as though she were some temptress of old and he the warrior king come to claim her.

She stood before him in her damp finery and snow-fresh skin as though she awaited just that. He fisted his hands at his sides and struggled for reason against madness.

"Amelia." He meant her name as a warning. It sounded far more like a plea.

"Do you think there is anything here for me to change into?"

It was the last question he expected her to ask. He wanted to kick himself for the debauched nature of his thoughts and intentions. She had practically frozen to death, and here he was, ready to tumble her for his own pleasure as soon as she was warm enough.

What kind of man was he?

If he hoped to prove himself a lecher and a cad, he was definitely on the right path.

"I'll look," he told her, his jaw tight despite himself as he pushed to his feet. "You stay here by the fire."

He grabbed the lantern off the table where he had left it and stomped into the darkened depths of the farmhouse. In a few moments he had located the bedroom with its big four-poster bed, still fully made and draped in a quilt with loving care. His thoughts easily provided suggestive images of just what he could do with that bed and the lovely young woman awaiting his return by the crackling hearth.

He cursed beneath his breath and turned his attention to the large trunk at the foot of the bed. It was unlocked. He threw the lid back and perused the contents.

"Oh, Michael, you found them." Amelia appeared at his elbow. She reached around him and retrieved several delicate-looking, carved animal ornaments. "Eleanor told me about these. Jacob made them for her. What a talented man he must have been."

"Indeed." He shifted the container the ornaments had been in to the side and uncovered a gown. He grabbed a handful of lace and satin. "Change into this."

She set the ornaments carefully back in their box and took the gown from him. Her face turned up to his, her eyes aglow. Did she have any idea of the effect she had on a man when she looked up like that?

"It's too lovely. I wouldn't dream of wearing this without Eleanor's consent."

"I'm sure Eleanor will not mind you managing to stay alive another day by changing your wet garments for this."

He used the sternest tone he could manage under the circumstances as the tempting alternative of putting her stark naked under the covers of the bed behind them occurred to him. Dressed would definitely be better if he wanted to maintain an honorable facade.

"But Michael, this isn't just a gown, I think this is her wedding gown—"

"Just change. I'll leave the lantern here with you." He turned on his heel and left her behind in the bedroom with her wet and bedraggled outfit, her all-too-tempting mouth and the inclinations clamoring in his soul.

No, to be strictly correct, the inclinations came right along with him, riding his soul and pricking every nerve he possessed.

He gritted his teeth together and lengthened his strides, providing ample space between the two of them. There would be no well-intentioned boarders lurking in the darkened depths of the farmhouse to keep them apart. Not tonight. He would have to count on his own inner strength and his patience. And his patience was already stretched to the breaking point, between the fear he'd known earlier before he'd found her to the fetching glimpse of her shapely form by the fire.

Damnation—was there no relief for the things she made him feel? For a moment he was tempted to ransack the old farmhouse for some whiskey, brandy, or even some homemade brew—anything to deaden the urges she'd awoken so easily. But then, if past history was anything to go by, liquor would not be his friend. It had a tendency to loosen the reins he held on himself and would no doubt encourage him to follow his true urges. To make love to Amelia. To make love to her and never stop.

He groaned aloud and rested his forehead against the frosty windowpane still being pelted by icy snow and glacial winds. He counted slowly to ten, then to twenty. He let his mind dwell on the wind outside. And the other matters he'd come to Warm Springs to solve in the first place.

The gaps and inconsistencies in Josiah Walker's history sprang to mind. He was almost certain now that Otis was eliminated as a suspect; the doctor was his man. He just needed confirmation.

What he wouldn't give to discuss all of this with Will.

It would be better if he just ignored Amelia and sent her to bed. Surely she could manage a night in the big bed in the farmhouse bedroom. He'd start a fire in the smaller hearth, settle himself in here for the night, and they would both sleep easier.

Fourteen

I'm sure Eleanor will not mind . . .

Michael's words echoed in Amelia's mind while the
gown's satin and lace pooled, cool and silky, against
her fingertips.

Long strides etched with impatience took him out
of Eleanor and Jacob's bedroom and into the murky
shadows beyond the lantern's reach. A cold stone of
worry solidified in her stomach even as she told herself his tension shouldn't twist her into convoluted
knots. The needs and disposition of Warm Springs's
town drifter and ne'er-do-well shouldn't matter one
whit to her. If anything, she should find him an object
of interest. A specimen worthy of study. And then only
if she had time to spend on such pastimes.

Her lips tugged into a smile. It didn't seem to matter
to her rebellious heart what she should or shouldn't
feel. It didn't matter to the desires he awakened in her
what her status in society had been or if he'd never
known any societal status whatsoever.

A shudder rippled through her. Memories of his
kisses in the late-night sanctity of Clara's kitchen to
the last in the study door sizzled through her with a
rich, slow sensation that took her breath and heated
her cheeks.

She buried her face in the cool satin for a moment. Each exquisite touch was burned into her mind, her heart, her very soul. His thumb tracing her lip, his tongue plundering the depths of her mouth, his hands on her breasts, his arms cradling her.

Playing harmony to the fiery mixture within her were all the things Eleanor had told her today. The life Eleanor had been given to expect, and the one that made her happy, were worlds apart. Eleanor had loved her Jacob very much. She had gained everything she desired by giving up what she thought she wanted. For Eleanor, escaping the bonds of propriety and expectation had given her more than freedom and a respectable home.

She'd found love enough to last a lifetime. To last two lifetimes.

Amelia's throat ached as she sighed and draped the gown carefully on the oversized bed that had known the married nights of Eleanor's life. Against every plan she'd ever made for herself and every direction she had been given throughout her life, she found an envious longing inside her to live that kind of life. To know the same kind of love and to share her life with a man who knew her to her soul and loved her anyway.

And of all people, the man she wanted to know all this with turned out to be Michael Thompson, a rootless drifter by his own admission.

The knowledge twisted her heart as her fingers traced the tall, slender bed spindles of the four-poster. It didn't seem to matter that her choice was this mysterious drifter with a background he refused to share and a propensity for disappearing at the oddest times.

Her mind could all too easily picture Michael's lanky frame filling the space just as he had filled her heart.

He would look virile and dangerous against the pillows.

Each touch he gave her would be sensual and understanding.

She knew that to her depths, but it didn't stop the thrill of scandalous fear tracing her spine. Fear and certainty. She bit her lip. She had known in her very soul that Michael would find her tonight.

Even as the cold had closed in around her, urging her to rest and promising her peace everlasting, she had known.

She had known, and he had come.

Cool air brushed her as wind battered the windows and she shivered in the chill. Standing here wet all night debating the rights and wrongs of what she felt for him was surely a recipe for pneumonia and she wasn't up to drinking any more of the doctor's concoctions.

She tugged the buttons open on her wet blouse and shrugged it the floor. The moist and chilly confines of her skirt and underpinnings followed suit, leaving her with nothing but damp skin, thoughts of Michael, and the needs growing between them. The scandalous image of presenting herself to him in nothing more than her own flesh teased her thoughts.

What would her heroic Mr. Thompson do then?

Fresh heat flooded her cheeks. Perhaps she hadn't quite journeyed as far from propriety, hadn't become as scandalously free, as she thought. She rummaged in the chest for the undergarments to go with the wedding gown. After her third pass through the chest she sat back on her heels and faced the truth. There was nothing else she could wear, save a quilt.

A quick survey of the armoire in the corner and a larger chest by the window revealed no other clothing.

She eyed the gown on the bed for a moment longer as cool air played over her bare skin, raising goose-flesh and anticipation in its wake. So be it. It was the gown by itself or nothing at all. And as far as she had come from the self-absorbed debutante she'd left in Boston, she wasn't quite up to nothing at all. The gown by itself would be scandalous enough. She pushed to her feet and ran her fingers over the old lace.

"This will have to do. Eleanor, I hope you really do understand."

The satin and lace rustled over her with a comforting sigh and slid downward in a single cool, silky-smooth caress to puddle about her feet. Without the layers of petticoats needed to fill out the voluminous length of the skirt, fabric spilled over the floor around her, its creamy highlights shimmering in the lantern's glow. She scooped the skirt up over her arm and gave in to the tug of vanity calling from the tall, oak-bound mirror in the opposite corner.

The image flickering back to her made her gasp as her hands measured the bare expanse of skin still visible. The lace barely covered the edges of her shoulders and the tops of her breasts. The satin of the gown began only where modesty demanded before falling sleekly to the ground. Which was worse? Bare skin or this gown?

Scant as it was, the garment provided barely a modicum of modesty. If anything, she looked like a woman ready to tempt sin itself. Perhaps she would be better off staying hidden here in the bedroom.

When she turned to view the back, a second gasp escaped her, heightening her tension. There was no way to close those tiny little buttons by herself. She would have to ask for his help and provide him an all-too-clear view of her nakedness in the process.

Her pulse thumped faster and her breath quickened with a startling realization. The gaze her reflection shared with her was expectant and glowing. She was face-to-face with her deepest desire. The memory of Michael's hands and lips against her skin and the taste of his sense-drugging kisses swirled through her stomach in a hot spiral.

Ultimately, when I'd found the man I loved, the rest didn't matter. Eleanor's explanation confirmed it.

She was going to seduce Michael Thompson, drifter and handyman.

She placed her cool fingers over her hot cheeks. Amelia Lawrence, the toast of Boston?

"Yes."

Another smile tugged. Wouldn't her mother be surprised? Look at what she'd learned. What was it Mama said when Amelia had scorned her marriage to the butcher?

It doesn't matter what you think of his occupation, Amelia. What matters is the love we share. Nothing I shared with your father, God rest him, or with any man, compares to what I feel for Patrick. I'm sorry, my dear, but all the things I've taught you have been wrong. It took heartbreak and scandal for me to realize that recognizing and embracing love when it's offered is all that matters.

Perhaps one day you will understand.

"Oh, Mama," she whispered, tracing her fingers over the cool and perfect surface of her reflection. Her pride in the contained life she had once lived was as remote and lifeless as the mirror's icy surface. "I think I understand."

She scooped up her skirt and turned away from the mirror and the past and the vainglories that had once been everything to her. *Recognizing and embracing love when it's offered is all that matters.* She gathered up her courage, along with the lantern, and left the bedroom.

When she reached the end of the hallway, Michael stood with his back to her, watching the snow blow and drift outside. She shivered, more than glad to be out of harm's way. Courage and anxiety warred within her as she set the lantern down beside her on the table next to the delicate, carved music box Eleanor was so fond of. Yet another sign of love from her Jacob.

"Hello, Michael." At first he didn't respond. Had her nervousness made her greeting too soft for him to hear?

Then he turned to face her.

"Amelia, I really think—"

He stopped as his gaze settled on her. He stood outlined against the drifting snow outside the window, tall and sure as firelight flickered over him. She'd never known a more beautiful man.

Oh, Mama, I think I do understand.

His gaze traveled over her, warming her to her toes. She was all too aware of the image she presented and the unspoken message her appearance would offer. Which was just as well because her throat had constricted and she wasn't sure she could speak. Her heart pounded as his gaze moved over her again, slower and more thoroughly.

As the silence stretched, she needed to say something, anything, to fill the void. She swallowed twice before finding her voice again.

"It's a little bit long without petticoats." She picked up the hem and shrugged, offering him an awkward smile. He didn't so much as move.

"But it is lovely, isn't it?" She twirled around in a circle, providing him a view of her back and the row of undone buttons.

"Yes, lovely." His voice was husky and low, rasping against her heart as she completed her pirouette. She could no longer stand the distance between them.

She walked toward him, watching his face as he watched her. Fire danced in the dark, steely gray of his eyes and his jaw worked at her approach. Each step slid cool satin against her heated body and heightened the nervous tension clamoring within her.

She stopped in front of him, her heart hammering wildly in her ears at her own boldness.

"Thank you for being my hero, Michael Thompson." She dipped into a curtsey. "I'm glad we found shelter here in a house that knew so much love. Jacob and Eleanor Holmdale were very lucky to have found each other."

She straightened again, warmed still further as the hot look in his eyes matched the rising warmth inside her. For a moment longer, her heart hammered in her ears. Then she smiled up at him and presented the bare length of her back for his inspection. "Could you help me with the buttons before I fall right out of this gown?"

"Buttons." The single word sounded halfway between prayer and curse.

For the longest time she stood frozen, waiting for him to help with the buttons or rip the gown from her body. Tension tightened within her until she wanted to scream. Then his fingers brushed her skin. She sucked in a breath as he traced the length of her spine. Her eyelids closed as the brush of his fingers spiraled desire into her middle. She shivered, unable to control her reaction.

"Michael." She breathed his name in a single whisper filled with the passion he unleashed so easily. He unfastened the first button at the bottom of the row as her heartbeat drummed in her ears. Then he transferred his attentions to the next button, his fingers swirling a caress against her spine.

She sighed as heat shot clear through her. And then again. Two more buttons and she was shivering beneath each brush of his fingers.

She was breathless when he finished. His fingers lingered against her skin for just a moment and then were gone. The loss of his touch made her ache. She turned to him and was caught in the dark glow of his eyes and the rising tide of her own desires.

"I've never been a hero, princess," he told her. "I'm just a man."

His hands closed over her shoulders and pulled her into his arms. Her satin skirts sighed against him even as pure feminine triumph surged through her middle.

"A man," she repeated as he bent toward her. "That's just what I need."

He covered her lips with his; pure heat swallowed her as she moaned. This was exactly what she wanted—needed, with each breath. There was nothing tentative or soft in the touch of his mouth on hers. His lips molded her own, taking command and making sure there were no barriers between them, no doubt. Here was a man who knew what he wanted and had every intention of getting it. The heat invading her body demanded she give him anything he asked.

And more.

His tongue stroked hers, bold and sensuous. She moaned and twined her arms around his neck. There would be no one to stop them. Nothing to break them apart

Good. She wanted him to make love to her and blot out the fear she'd lived with for too long, the loneliness she'd never recognized until he'd touched her. Tears sparked behind her eyes. His hands traced her back again in slow, sinuous circles and then lower still. And he was teasing her lips, sucking first one and then the other into his mouth, tracing her mouth softly with his tongue.

"Michael." She could only breathe his name. "Oh, Michael. Dear God."

His mouth left hers to forge a trail of kisses over her cheek, her neck, her collarbone. His hands slid over her hips and gripped her tighter. The satin slid, cool and slick, over her heated skin.

She clung to his shoulders as his mouth moved over her bared skin, lower and lower. His breath stirred the lace and warmed her beneath it.

"There *is* nothing beneath this gown." His heated gaze caught hers again and surprised a husky laugh from her.

"No, there isn't." She could barely speak. Her skin was on fire with wanting him, and he was worried about her undergarments.

His jaw worked for a moment and then he set her from him. He meant to deny her, to deny them both. Her ne'er-do-well drifter intended to do the honorable thing.

"Dance with me, Michael." She used the offer to break off any platitudes about temptation and taking advantage of her. Now was not the time. She wouldn't listen to that logic now. *Now* was the time for the two of them. Perhaps the only time.

"Please?"

"Here?" Agitated confusion etched his voice and creased his brow. "Now?"

"Yes." She smiled, pulled away from him, and reached for the little music box she'd seen earlier. "Eleanor and Jacob used to dance here in the evenings. They danced to celebrate."

She twisted the little knob on the box. Music tinkled out, delicate and slow, as ethereal as the feelings she had for him. She scooped up her skirts and held out her arms.

The crease in his brow edged downward and he frowned at her. Clearly he was bent on saving her from himself. But she didn't want to be saved.

"What did they celebrate?"

"Life. Being together." She almost had him. She could almost see his defenses crumbling. "Please, Michael, one dance."

He sighed and stepped toward her. Wind rattled the windowpanes and she didn't care.

"What are we celebrating?" He locked his thumb with hers as their hands slid together. The calluses on his hand rubbed against her softer flesh. She could remember all too clearly their last waltz in a room filled with onlookers. And the thought of his kisses that had played through her head even then. His other hand settled at the small of her back, branding her with the warmth of his fingers.

She slid her hand to his shoulder, her breath uneven at his touch.

"Life. Being here together," she told him as he pulled her closer and swept her easily into a waltz. "Love."

Love. She let the word fall from her mouth even as everything inside her trembled and screeched for her to take it back, but she refused to guard her heart. Not tonight.

His fingers tightened against her back. "Love?"

"Yes." She nodded, tilting her head back to hold his gaze. "Don't you feel it all around us?"

He raised a brow at her even as his fingers splayed against her spine and brushed against her bare skin. "Is the storm your idea of love?"

She sucked in a quick breath at the contact and for a moment lost the direction of her thoughts. "The storm? No, not that. It's this house."

"An odd perception of love, surely?" But he was smiling at her now.

She smiled back. "You can feel it in the warmth of the fireplace, the bed with a view that stretches for miles, the music box still waiting for one more dance."

"Obviously you are paying more attention to these details than I am." But the glow in his eyes belied his words. "What is it you feel from these things?"

"A chance for happiness," she told him honestly.

"Amelia—"

"Shhh." She cut off the warning tone in his voice before he could go any further and slid her fingers into the hair at his nape. It was cool and soft, curly and rebellious. "Not tonight."

"Tonight more than any other," he said, but his gaze brushed her lips.

"No, Michael, tonight belongs to the two of us."

His gaze came back to hers. "The two of us?"

Her courage wavered again, but she refused to give in. "There is no one here but us. There is no one to know what passes between us. Tonight is ours. I don't want to share it with propriety and doubts. I don't want to share it with could be's and should be's."

The music had stopped, but they were still dancing, slowly and far more closely than would ever be considered proper anywhere in polite society. It didn't matter.

"For a drifter, you have a fine dancing manner," she told him.

"For a widow, you are exceptionally beautiful," he offered back. "What do you want, Amelia?"

"Tonight is ours, Michael." She swallowed and took courage from the blaze of desire in his eyes.

"I want you to make love to me," she told him before the fears inside her could rise up again.

"You would tempt the morals of a saint." The frown returned to his brows again even as he pulled her closer still. "And heaven knows I am no saint."

His mouth covered hers and she sighed. His hands slid over her back, tracing the bare length of her spine to stop at the buttons he had closed such a short time ago. Her skin seemed to sizzle beneath his touch as he tasted her mouth and the honesty of her words.

"Tonight, you're mine." Low and soft, like a vow.

She shivered against him as his words rang in her ears, burning to a cinder any doubts she'd had about seducing him. He'd said nothing about his plans beyond the morrow, but it didn't matter. Nothing mattered but this night and this man. Tomorrow would have to take care of itself. She lifted her chin and held his gaze with a smile.

She pushed up on her tiptoes and pressed a soft kiss to his mouth in return. With total honesty, she repeated his claim. "And tonight, you're mine."

Fifteen

Tonight, you're mine.

The sound of his words echoing back to him shredded his best intentions.

He'd wanted her from the first moment he'd seen her, swathed in black and oh, so pale. Each touch, each kiss, had burned his soul and blackened whatever honor he laid claim to.

In the deepest recesses of his mind he knew he should release her, should tell her she would feel differently in the morning, and send her back to the bedroom alone. But he couldn't seem to take his hands from her body or deny his own fiery needs.

She pushed up on her tiptoes and pressed a soft kiss to his mouth. With total honesty she repeated his claim. "And tonight, you're mine."

"So be it."

The words gritted from him almost with a will of their own. He kissed her again, claiming her mouth as fully as he intended to claim her body. He sifted his fingers into the cool dampness of her hair and tilted her head to better accommodate him. She shivered beneath his touch and her hands slid down over his chest and then around his waist to cling and pull him closer.

He had never wanted any woman as he wanted her.

Never burned to possess any woman as he now needed her. Tonight he had almost lost her. Now she would be his.

He scooped her into his arms, every soft inch of her torturing him with longing as he held her close. The wind rattled the panes and swirled on in the world outside as though demanding he release her. But tonight nothing mattered beyond the two of them. And the night that belonged to them both.

His strides took them easily down the darkened hallway. He stopped when he reached the bedroom. Awash in a snow-silver glow, he could all too easily picture her against the downy depths of the large bed. His desire for her, already pounding with painful intensity, heightened still further.

He smothered a groan and kissed her very softly as he released his grip on her legs to let them slide down over his body. Her arms were looped about his shoulders and her body pressed intimately and fully against his own. Desire pounded in his blood as the vee of her legs cradled the rigid evidence of his intentions.

"Michael."

His name on her lips was erotic and enticing.

His fingers strayed down the silky length of her back to the foolish buttons that had given him so much hell just a few moments ago. It took far less time to release them than it had to fasten them. He punctuated the opening of each button with a kiss that drugged them both. When at last the gown was open, the deep vee in the back went the length of her spine—and more. He stepped back from her. Her eyes were wide and glazed with the passion he knew her capable of.

"Mine," he repeated. One tug at the shoulders and the gown slid from her in one long sigh, revealing her to his gaze.

She was every bit as breathtaking as he'd known she would be. Her breasts were full and high, her nipples tight and tempting. Her waist tapered to the rounded swell of her hips. She stood straight and proud for him, unabashed by his lengthy perusal and unashamed to stand before him in only the beauty God had given her.

"You are beautiful," he told her, wishing he could find better words. He cupped her face and caressed her lip with his thumb. "Incredibly lovely."

"Thank you," she whispered, so soft and ladylike despite her nakedness and the certain knowledge that he intended to make hot, sweet love to her all night.

He pulled her back into his arms and kissed her softly, tasting her passion and her willingness. The way she twined hers arms around him to press herself closer showed him that and so much more.

He slid his hands over her soft skin from her shoulders, down over her back and to the rounded, resilient flesh of her buttocks. She gasped at that intimate contact, then shivered against him as he cupped and stroked her bare bottom. He sucked her lower lip into his mouth and teased it with his teeth as she shuddered against him.

He needed to kiss her everywhere at once. To touch her and feed the burning need inside him. He trailed kisses over her chin, her neck, and then lower as his hands continued to knead her flesh and coax little moans of pleasure from her.

He bent and pressed long, slow kisses to the

rounded swell of her breasts, so full and soft and eager. He swirled his tongue over the tight bud of her nipple. She cradled the back of his head with one hand and clutched his shoulder with the other.

She was every bit as sweet as she had been the other night when he'd gone mad from wanting her. He'd walked away then and earned a night of torture for his efforts. There would be no walking away tonight.

"Michael." Her fingers laced into his hair and held his head to her breast as he opened his lips and drew her nipple in. "Oh, oh, Michael."

Tonight he would have her. He'd meant every word when he asked her if this was truly what she wanted. There would be no going back now. She was his.

He transferred his attentions to her other breast, eliciting further moans from her, even as the need burgeoning inside him demanded relief.

He allowed one hand to trace the full, soft length of her side, her thigh. Then he slid his fingers through the dark, springing curls at the juncture of her legs. She sighed and then shuddered as he dipped his fingers further between her soft thighs to stroke the hidden depths of her. She was wet and slippery against his fingers.

"Michael-oh-Michael." His name tumbled from her over and over.

Pure male pride surged within him. She was his.

He stroked her with his fingers, echoing the rhythmic suckling at her breast. She shivered and clung to him as he drew the taut nipple deeply into his mouth, tonguing her as his fingers stroked the hot, slippery flesh between her thighs. Her knees began to give from his attentions. He smiled and edged her back onto the bed. She fell back with a sigh and he stood for just a moment to look at her once more.

Splayed before him, trembling with the sensual anticipation he had awakened in her, with her breasts upthrust and her legs parted, she was sin itself. Welcoming him. Inviting him. Awaiting anything he would choose to do with her.

He pulled open the buttons on his shirt, no longer able to stand the confines of fabric or allow any barriers to be between them. He shrugged it to the floor. Then his hands went to his trousers. Her eyes followed each movement as he undid his belt and the buttons to release his aching flesh.

Her gaze flickered over him, a slow and intimate caress. He kicked free of his trousers as her eyes locked with his.

"You're . . . so . . . big."

He gritted his teeth as her words of appreciation made him swell larger still. He nodded, all speech impossible, glad she showed no reluctance.

He bent to his knees beside the bed and splayed his hands over the soft expanse of her belly, her hips. She sighed and closed her eyes at his touch. He kissed her thigh, then the softer-than-soft skin of her belly as his hands coaxed her legs apart more fully. He traced his fingers over the dewy center of her and she shivered. And then he dipped his head to taste her innocence. He swirled his tongue over the sensitive flesh awaiting him.

"Michael. Oh." She stiffened beneath his touch and moaned his name. "I . . . oh . . . please"

She squirmed and he slid his hands beneath her to cup her buttocks. Her legs slid over his shoulders—

soft, silky skin surrounding him as he tongued her. Fast, slow, over and over, his own flesh straining as he sought her release. He wanted her to be more than ready for the night ahead. His tongue flicked her sensitive nub and lower to her feminine depths, sipping her sweetness.

Her release was not long in coming as she moaned his name and quivered beneath each stroke of his tongue. When he sucked the pulsing nubbin of flesh into his mouth, a wordless scream escaped her and her hips bucked against him.

As the echoes of her passion died away, only the sound of the wind and her ragged breathing broke the silence.

He lifted his head to view her, sated and limp, her eyes aglow as they locked with his.

"How do you do that?" she whispered, the ghost of a smile flitting at the corners of her mouth.

He couldn't hold back a laugh. She was everything he'd known she would be. Responsive, passionate, his. Sensual, innocent, and eager.

And there was so much more yet to come, to share. He joined her on the bed and kissed a pathway from the indent of her belly button up to the pale skin of her throat.

"My beautiful Amelia." He kissed her mouth, tasting her release and the passion still untapped inside her. "There is more. Much more. We have all night to explore each other."

He pressed his body down against hers. He could barely hold back.

"Lead on," she whispered against his mouth as her

arms slid around his neck and her legs cradled him against her. "Lead on."

He kissed her slowly, letting her feel every inch of his body against hers, enjoying the warm heat of her soft flesh against him. He couldn't wait much longer. Her legs slid over his hips and her center pressed, wet and soft, against his manhood.

He groaned, stiffening his spine as the desire to thrust blindly into her ripped at him. He held back with effort.

"Michael, are you all right? Did I hurt you?" So soft and innocent an inquiry, and yet she had been married, if only for a few nights. Surely she knew.

"No, beloved. You are everything I desire." He kissed her even as the muscles in his arms trembled. Then she rocked herself against him once more. The soft, wet silk of her body teased him again and he shuddered. "I have never felt more alive."

He managed a slanted look down at her. Her eyes sparkled back at him as a smile curved her lips. She teased him again, brushing slick heat against him. He took her lips in a fierce kiss, branding her as his own. He pushed forward with his hips, opening her to his possession. And met a barrier he'd never expected.

Shock etched the edges of his arousal. His little widow was a virgin! He'd known she was inexperienced, but not entirely untried!

"Dear God, Amelia." Words failed him as the pleasure of her tight sheath around his erection tore at his sanity. He stopped his entry. He should be gentle, he should move slowly. This was her first time and he did not want to frighten her, to hurt her. Should he stop? Could he?

She rocked against him, blindly demanding action. Instinct took over, pulling his thoughts from the ramifications of what he was doing as he pushed through the barrier of her innocence and made her his own. Wholly and completely. His, and his alone.

She winced beneath him.

Buried completely in her soft, sweet body, it took all of his will to keep from driving himself over and over into her softness and finding the release he so desperately needed.

"You didn't tell me. I would . . . I wouldn't—" he began.

She leaned up and pressed a kiss to his mouth. Her breasts brushed his chest. "I didn't want you to stop. I want this as much as you. This is our time. Our night."

"Dear God—"

She kissed him again and he groaned, needing the taste of her, the feel of her, more than he needed his next breath. More than he had ever needed anything in his life. He pulsed, wanting to move within her, but still he held back.

"I need you," she whispered. "You feel so incredible inside me. Make love to me. Don't stop."

"Gladly." The word gritted out of him along with any remorse he was capable of feeling as her words released him. He took her mouth as he took her body. Slow and sweet, stroking her and coaxing her to feel everything he was feeling, to enjoy the melding of their bodies as fully as he did.

After a few moments a moan came from her and

then another, but it was not pain she released as he thrust his body into hers. It was pleasure.

Desire rocketed through him, heightening his need and blinding him to anything but the ageless drives of his body, the demands of hers. His thrusts came faster, harder, and she welcomed them, locking her legs about his waist and echoing his rhythm.

"Oh, Michael, oh, Michael." Wonder etched her tone.

He tasted his name on her lips as the rhythm riding the two of them demanded more and more of him. The pressure building inside came higher and faster, searing his flesh and burning any lingering regrets to cinders. Then her body convulsed around his, rippling over his erection, undulating hot pulses of pleasure directly into his very soul.

He surrendered completely then to the needs that drove him, and thrust himself into her softness over and over again, faster and faster, harder and harder, until he was sure he had reached her very core. The pressure of all she evoked in him reached its zenith and carried him over the edge after her.

In the aftermath only their breathing, ragged and deep, broke the silence. Somewhere amidst the sound and fury of their lovemaking the outside wind had died away and the storm was a memory.

He lifted his head from the crook of her shoulder and gazed down at her. A wash of snowy light drifted over her features, worshiping her pale beauty.

"Amelia—"

"I wanted you so very much," she interrupted him. "Please don't spoil our night by apologizing for taking what I willingly gave you."

Her prim tone, even as she lay pinioned beneath him, made him chuckle despite the circumstances.

"Oh." She shivered and her body clenched around him. "I can . . . feel you laughing . . . inside me."

He kissed her, overcome with tenderness. "Why? How?"

"How could I explain and still honor Robert?" Her fingers traced the planes and angles of his face. "How could I explain to anyone that the mere thought of . . . engaging in the marital act . . . killed him. He never . . . we never . . ."

She blew out a quick breath. "Well, you know that by now."

Yes. He knew that she had just surrendered her virginity to him. On purpose. With no promises. No questions. Only a sincere and earth-shaking desire that humbled him.

"If I had known . . ."

"You wouldn't have made love to me." She quirked a knowing brow.

"I would have been more gentle with you," he corrected. "I would have taken more care and made certain you enjoyed it as much as I did. That you were completely ready."

"Oh." She smiled at him and squirmed a little beneath him. Her body clenched his again and the after-echoes of pleasure shot through him, making him suck in his breath. "You did that. I . . . did enjoy it. You were wonderful, Michael. Everything was wonderful."

He realized with a clarity that struck him clear through that he could stay right here with Amelia for the rest of his life and not regret a single moment. His throat tightened. Somewhere along the way, while he'd been telling himself he was only investigating a case, that his mission was totally focused on solving his brother's murder, Robert Mitchell's virginal little widow had wrapped herself around his soul. There was so much he wanted to tell her, to explain.

He kissed her then, letting the things he couldn't say spill over from his heart as he molded her soft mouth beneath his. She was exactly what he hadn't wanted. A debutante. A lady. And still she was everything he wanted. Desire sprang to life again inside him.

"Amelia, I need you—"

"Oh, Michael," she interrupted yet again and her body clenched around his, rippling hot pleasure through him. "I need you, too. I think you're going to have to make love to me again. This night is ours."

"With pleasure." He told her as he pressed a kiss to her lovely lips. She was right. The night was theirs and all of the explanations could wait until tomorrow.

It was cold and the room was filled with bright sunshine when Amelia opened her eyes. For a moment she couldn't fathom where she was. The bedroom. The curtains. None of it looked familiar. And then the events of the previous evening thundered through her memory in a blaze of passion and tenderness.

Extra tenderness, she thought wryly as she struggled to sit up. She was sore and aching in parts of her body she'd never felt before. They were delicious aches. Warmth curled her toes and shivered over every inch of her body. She had made love with

Michael three times through the night. Twice the first time and then a third time when they woke in the wee hours, already locked in an embrace. And in between she had slept in his arms.

She closed her eyes and stretched. She had enjoyed every minute of the night, awake or asleep. Even the first time, when the invasion of her body had caused pain, it hadn't lasted beneath his tender touch and the passion deep inside her. And despite the ache between her legs, she would willingly do it all again.

She giggled at the unladylike direction of her thoughts and looked up to find Michael fully dressed, watching her from the doorway with the heartrending lopsided smile that had first been her undoing.

"Michael." Heat flooded her cheeks. He was dressed, she wasn't, and he'd been watching her remember their time together. She smiled at him then, refusing to be embarrassed by what they had shared, by what he'd observed. "Good morning."

"Good morning indeed, princess." His boots rang against the floorboards as he approached the bed. "The snow stopped sometime during the night. The wind drifted it high in some places and low in others. I think we'll be able to make it back all right."

He stopped next to the bed and his fingers brushed her cheek, gentle despite the report that their time together had ended. Well, she had asked for no promises and he had offered none. So be it.

"Everyone back at the Grand Estate must be worried sick about us."

"I'm sure they are. Clara packed us some stewed chicken last night. It may not be the usual fare for breakfast, but it will have to do until we get back to the house."

How quickly it was all ending. Last night had been theirs, but now it was morning.

Sorrow tugged at her heart and she wanted to weep. Not for the loss of her virginity. Heaven knew, she should have lost that many weeks ago. But for the loss of the intimacy they had shared along with the passion. She had foolishly hoped they would be able to spend the day here. Perhaps even the following night, before the real world intruded and she had to face her life again. Blasted snow—why couldn't it have continued for another few days?

"I think your clothes are dry." He gestured to the neatly folded pile on the chest. How long had he been up? And what had forced him from her side? Had he been so anxious to leave?

For a moment she was tempted to throw back the covers and see how he would react to her nude body. Would he drop this careful facade of capability? Would he take her in his arms and whisper the sweet things he told her last night? Would he make love to her again?

"You'd better get dressed. I'll wait for you out in the other room." He stroked her cheek again, belying the no-nonsense tone of his words, and then bent to brush the softest kiss against her mouth. "Better hurry, princess."

With that he turned on his heel and left her, his boots ringing against the oaken floorboards in the distance.

So much for shocking him with the temptation of her body. Irritation flooded her and she wanted to scream and vent her frustration. For heaven's sake, they'd made love last night. All night. She'd given him everything she had to give and he was . . . he was . . .

She sighed.

He was no different with her now than he had been before she had satisfied his sexual appetite. It was she who had been changed by the experience. She who had risked her heart and soul to love him.

"Enough." He obviously didn't hold the same depth of feelings for her. She pushed back the covers and got to her feet, ignoring the tender twinges in her body. Life was a risk. Love was a risk. She'd been willing to accept it last night when her body and soul had been clamoring for him. She wasn't going to stand here now like an insulted virgin and decry the fates.

She managed to dress, glad for each layer of clothing that would insulate her from him.

She joined him at the small table by the windows as he dipped hot stew into two bowls from a pot he had warmed by the fire. She sat carefully, refusing to squirm as she ate. It was delicious, filled with rich broth and vegetables, as all Clara's meals were. They ate in awkward silence and she hated it. Hated her weakness. Sometime during the night she had become a sack of emotional nerve endings. And no matter the temptation, she was not going to give in and create a scene. She'd gotten what she asked for and that was that.

"Tell me something about yourself, Michael." There—she could be casual, impersonal.

"Like what?"

She shrugged and scooped another bite. He wanted to be distant, let him be the one to squirm. "Where you were born. Any brothers and sisters? Will they turn up at the Grand Estate some day?"

"There's very little likelihood of that. My sister is still at home. My brother was killed some time ago."

Killed? "I'm sorry."

She looked up to find his gaze fixed on her. She'd been playing petty and brought up something painful. "Really."

He shook his head. "You couldn't know. I . . . I don't talk about Will much."

"His name was Will?"

Michael nodded. "He was killed in a robbery. What about you?"

"Me?"

He took a bite of stew and chewed it slowly before explaining. "Any brothers or sisters?"

"No sisters. I had a brother, too." She tried to sound casual.

"I'm sorry."

"Don't be. Jonathan's not dead. He just embezzled money from his partners and left my mother and me penniless to face the scandal while he fled to Italy."

"So every man in your life so far has let you down. In one way or another. Your father, your husband, your brother."

She guessed that was one way of looking at it. All the men in her life *had* left her. Robert and her father through death, her brother through perfidy. And Michael? She looked up to see he'd already gone back to eating. At least this man was not giving her any false expectations. It felt like he was already gone.

That was enough conversation for now. Awkward silence was infinitely better.

When the stew was finished, he gathered both bowls and stacked them into the sack he'd brought with him when he rescued her last night.

She blinked.

Was it only last night he had rescued her? It felt like a lifetime had passed between the cold, snowy vista she'd been lost in and the bright, sunlit morning.

"It'll be a hike," he told her over his shoulder as he banked the fire in the hearth and gathered her cloak from the back of a strategically placed chair. "Cora and Clara will be frantic."

"I know." She lifted her chin and met his gaze, striving for an even tone and the casual air he maintained. "I can do it. I don't want them to worry any more than they already have."

"That's my girl." He pulled the edges of her cloak around her and his fingers brushed beneath her chin. She tilted her head back to look at him. For a moment she stood lost in the unfathomable depths of steel-gray. Her fingers itched to curl around his waist and she wished he would pull her closer and kiss her as he had last night.

Then he dipped his head and pressed a kiss to her mouth.

Not the passionate demand he had given her last night, but soft and gentle.

"Let's go, then." He whispered the words against her lips.

"The ornaments," she whispered back. "I want to bring them for Eleanor."

She hurried from his side to the bedroom that had known the sound and fury of their loving last night.

She opened the chest to find the wedding gown folded neatly away once more.

Just how long had he been awake? She smoothed her fingers over the gown's lovely fabric and then gathered the box with the ornaments in it into her arms.

Despite their intimacy last night Michael Thompson was still just as mysterious and unknown as he had been before. What kind of a man was he? What drifter made such tender and passionate love to a woman and then took the time to fold and care for an old wedding gown?

"Amelia?"

"I'm coming." She closed the chest and pushed to her feet, pausing for just one last glance around the bedroom. This place would always be special for her. Even if Michael Thompson eventually drifted on to other towns and other women. Because this is where she had fallen in love and known the first touch of her lover.

What was it she had thought to herself last night?

Tomorrow would take care of itself.

Well, it appeared that tomorrow was here and she was the one who would have to take care of it. She left the bedroom behind along with her hopes and memories. Now she would face the real world. And see what could be made of it.

"Are you ready?" Michael was at the door, his coat buttoned and the sack slung over his shoulder. He looked every bit a man ready to head out on his own.

"I'm ready," she answered as she joined him.

For whatever might come.

Sixteen

Sunlight glinted off fresh snow, piercing Michael's eyes and forcing him to squint and shield his vision as best he could. His footsteps crunched along in the snow in perfect harmony with Amelia's.

Every moment of the night they'd just spent together was etched in his mind and heart. He'd waited as long as he could to wake her, wishing he could stay forever in the little oasis of time and space they had created for themselves at the Holmdale farm.

But wishes could not abate his mission or the tasks he'd vowed to complete when he first convinced the head of the U.S. Marshals to allow him to operate this investigation. Only the tug of finishing the investigation, of finally bringing his brother's murderer to justice, had forced him from her side. He'd spent those hours checking the trail out beyond the house to determine if they could safely make it back to the boarding house. He'd packed away the satin gown Amelia had worn for him, tempting him beyond sanity last night. And he'd watched her sleep.

That part had been the hardest, and yet the best. She looked so beautiful. Soft. Innocent. Alluring beyond all measure. He wanted to wake her and tell her all the things bottling up inside him. All the things he'd thought never to tell any woman. To wake her and make love to her all the day long. But his mission came first. So he had contented himself with watching her and reliving every moment of her passion and her honesty in his arms, until those cool blue orbs had opened and she'd focused on him standing in the doorway.

At that moment he could easily have forsaken duty, honor, and anything else she wanted from him, left it all behind in the dust just to be with her. It had taken every ounce of will he possessed to turn and walk away once she was awake.

That will had been further tested when he'd seen the hurt in her eyes at the impersonal distance he needed to keep if they were ever going to leave the Holmdale farm. One night in the snow, a town might forgive any woman but two, and she would be ruined. He did not know how long it would be before he would be free to remedy such a scandal. He had another promise to keep first.

Her eyes had held the hurt of the distance he put between them but her behavior had been impeccable. She had asked for a night and was expecting nothing more. She was accepting so easily so much less than she deserved. All because of him. Him, and a louse of a brother. She could forgive her father and even poor Robert for dying, but how does a girl forgive the betrayal of her own brother? The calculated disinterest of her first lover? When he was finally free to tell her how deep his interest truly was would she understand?

She trudged in the snow beside him, her hand linked with his out of necessity rather than passion. They didn't have time for either one of them to fall or slide down some hidden embankment. They didn't have time for him to try and smooth things over with her.

He had to get Amelia back to the Grand Estate and then catch the 9:40 for Springfield. He'd sent out his inquiry about Dr. Walker's tenure at Yale when he'd made his last report, then detoured to visit the ailing Fallon, only to arrive back in Warm Springs to a summons back to Springfield just as the storm broke last night.

If Josiah Walker really was the man he was looking for, the sooner he knew for certain, the better off for all involved. If the man was Will's killer, he had already spent way too much time in Amelia's company and attending to the boarders in her house for his comfort.

The Grand Estate rose out of the snow before them. He stopped for a minute to let her catch her breath.

"Oh, thank heaven," Amelia panted beside him. "Somehow it seems a far longer trek in the snow than in clear weather."

Roses bloomed in her cheeks and nipped at her now as her breath plumed the icy air in front of her. He squeezed her hand and barely managed to keep from drawing her into his embrace. In the full light of day, with the house only yards away, was not the time to give in to his own desires. There would be time for that afterward.

If she was still willing.

Michael rested his head back against the courthouse wall. He'd left Amelia behind in the warmth and gratitude of her little makeshift family. Cora and

Clara had been only too happy to fuss over her and to provide the information that Eleanor was doing much better. If only their cheerfulness could erase the haunted look in Amelia's eyes.

He cooled his heels in the hall, waiting for the information that could bring the culmination of the past two years' work. What was the holdup. He'd been waiting for the better part of an hour.

The door opened.

"No, thank you, Senator Douglas," Ben Taylor's voice boomed. "Good luck in Washington. The U.S. Marshal Service is at your disposal."

An imposing gentleman in an immaculately tailored suit emerged. He was imposing in demeanor, if not in stature. Michael stood out of respect. It wasn't every day a United States senator walked by.

Marshal Taylor poked his head out the door a second later. "What are you doing still out there, Thompson? Time's wasting."

Michael walked into the office. If anything, the stacks of papers on the marshal's desk had gotten larger since his last visit.

"How did you find Fallon when you went to see him?" Ben asked as they shook hands.

"Irritable. Fretful. Brusque. In other words, almost completely recovered."

They both laughed, and then it was time for business.

"You were right about that quack doctor, Mike." Ben settled into the chair behind the huge desk and rocked backward a bit as he perused the report in front of him.

Tension tightened in Michael's gut. He'd been right all along. "What did you find out about him?"

Ben straightened in his chair. "We checked out the lead you gave us about Walker's graduating from Yale. There never was a Josiah Walker enrolled in Yale's medical school. Nor are there any other records of a Josiah Walker that match his description or the timing he's given you about his past and whereabouts." Ben looked up from the report and his hard gaze met Michael's.

"However, a Joseph Wright enlisted in the cavalry and served as a doctor's assistant right after Joe White escaped from jail. I had a couple of men track down some of Joseph Wright's comrades in the army. All of the reports came back the same. He's the spit of our escaped robber."

Michael's gut tightened even more. He leaned forward, listening, but already halfway back to Warm Springs.

". . . Skinny fellow. Dark hair. Green eyes. Never went to school but could charm the ladies with the best of them. That sound like your doctor?" Ben fixed his astute glare on Michael.

Michael nodded, anger rising.

That was exactly the man who had ingratiated himself into Amelia's household. The thought rang alarm bells along Michael's spine. Suddenly it seemed he had been gone far too long and the trip back to Warm Springs would take a lifetime.

He pushed to his feet. "I've got to go."

"Mike—"

"I'm sorry, Ben, but if Josiah Walker is the man I want, I've got no time to waste. He's been looking at property in the area for months; he must be closing in on where the loot is hidden if only through elimination."

"It's been years since the robbery and your brother's murder. If this guy is our man, we'll get him. Let me arrange backup for you so you don't go into this alone and saddle us with another funeral."

"No. This man is too close to some people I care about. One woman in particular. If he truly is the man who killed my brother, I can't take the chance he might hurt anybody else."

"All right. I'll follow with some men on the next train. How's that?"

Michael nodded and turned for the door, and Amelia.

"One more thing, Deputy."

He turned back with great reluctance. Everything in him wanted to leave—now, an hour ago, last week. That prickly feeling of danger was riding him hard. "Yes?"

"Does the name Holmdale ring a familiar note?"

As he directed his feet down the long hallway at the federal building and back toward the train station, fear still gripped his gut—enough fear to choke off anything else and set his mind firmly on the man he'd come to find. Josiah Walker alias Joseph Wright alias Joe White. Will's murderer.

"Your time has come."

"I think I'll bring some more of Eleanor's things over here for her." Amelia turned away from the windows and the crisp, snow-laden afternoon outside to pour tea for the doctor. "She brightened so when I brought back some ornaments her husband had carved for her."

"I had a professor who insisted people always fared better in their homes," Josiah observed. "He was adamantly opposed to the establishment of hospitals."

"That's what I thought. I can always return them later, but I thought having more of the things she loves about her will help ease her until she can get back to her usual routine."

Dr. Walker's visit was a welcome interruption to her ongoing cycle of thoughts over Michael. He'd disappeared so quickly after they returned to the house. With no explanation, as was his wont. Why had she expected anything different? He'd never explained his disappearances before. Surely one night of soul-shattering intimacy was no reason for him to change his patterns.

"Really? You're going to go out to the Holmdale farm? I've always wanted to see the inside of that place."

She'd obviously piqued the doctor's interest.

"The inside?"

"Why, yes. Eleanor tells me her husband was quite the artist. I've seen his sketches on the walls of her bedroom upstairs. I was hoping to see some of his larger drawings. I'm certain there are some at the homestead. Besides, I'm hoping to buy a place near here and from what I see of the outside, that farm is just what I'm looking for."

"There are some lovely drawings. He was very talented. But I don't think Eleanor has any interest in selling."

"She may change her mind one day, and I have nothing to lose by asking. I just want to get a glimpse at more of those lovely drawings. Please allow me to accompany you." He favored her with a smile most women would find charming, but it was not nearly lopsided enough to appeal to Amelia.

She bit back the further denials that formed all too easily on her lips. She had hoped to return to the farmhouse alone. She understood now, more than ever, Eleanor's need to return to the home where she'd shared so much love with Jacob Holmdale. She could regret her scandalous night there, but all she wanted was a chance to relive it.

Amelia wanted to stand in the bedroom doorway and remember every exquisite touch, every tender word that had passed between her and Michael. Their one night was over, but she wanted to touch it again. That was selfish and probably very maudlin, especially in light of her expressed desire to make Eleanor feel better. Eleanor had glowed when she saw those Christmas ornaments. She had touched each one and probably would love having other momentos here with her. By taking the doctor and his buggy along, she would be able to bring more things back to her friend.

That decided it.

She set her teacup back in the saucer with a determined clatter that would have set her mother's teeth on edge. "I would be delighted to have your company, Doctor. Let me just tell Cora and Clara where we will be going."

"Oh dear, do you really think you should be going out now? You've only just returned home," Cora said as the sisters entered the drawing room.

"Cora, let her get some things for Eleanor."

"But the snow, dear."

"I'll be fine. The snow is over. Please don't fret. Dr. Walker has kindly offered to accompany me, so I will not even be walking. He will take me in his buggy and then give me a ride back."

"The doctor is going with you?" Cora and Clara gazed at her with that wide-eyed interested look the two of them could affect with such precision.

"Yes, and we won't be long."

"What shall we tell Michael?"

"Hush, Cora."

The question halted Amelia in her tracks. They had been careful, or so she thought, to act as though nothing untoward had happened between them during their night away from the Grand Estate, but somehow dear Cora had guessed.

"Tell him I've gone to pick up some things for Eleanor," she offered over her shoulder, unwilling to face the curious gaze again. "Or tell him I've gone out for the afternoon. It really doesn't matter."

"—told you not to say—"

"—know he will be concerned—"

Bits of the Brown sisters' conversation drifted after her. It really was none of Michael's business where she went or who she went with, just as it apparently was none of her business where he'd taken himself off to.

She grabbed her cloak from its peg in the hallway as the doctor followed her. He took the cloak from her with a gentlemanly flair and swirled it around her shoulders. It was the kind of move she would have appreciated at one time. The kind of flair that would have had her smiling her best smile up at him and enjoying his charm to the fullest.

Now, all she could think of was steel-gray eyes and rumpled red-brown hair. The kind you wanted to run your fingers through and smooth into place.

"Shall we?" The doctor smiled at her, unaware of his lack of effect on her.

"Certainly." She accepted the arm he offered her as he ushered her out into the cold air. It was remarkable how much the snow had melted.

Their ride to the Holmdale farm was accomplished much quicker by horse and buggy than her prior walking visits, which eased her discomfort about having anyone accompany her. There would be time enough surely to come back here at her leisure and relive her lovemaking with Michael. Today she would concentrate on the task at hand—retrieving items for Eleanor.

Dr. Walker kept a flow of entertaining chatter going through the trip and even indulged her by letting her spread more corn for Eleanor's deer. He was the epitome of a gentleman. Everything she had once expected to find in a man she might love and nothing like the reality she had found in Michael. Why, then, did she find the doctor's company so unsettling?

The doctor held the door open for her as she preceded him into Jacob and Eleanor Holmdale's house.

"Ah, a lovely little farm home." He gazed at the pictures on the walls with avid interest and she was glad she had allowed him to come. Jacob's art should be appreciated. Eleanor would surely be pleased by the doctor's interest.

"But it looks as though someone still lives here."

His comment brought heat to Amelia's cheeks as he followed her into the bedroom. The bed she and Michael had slept in was still rumpled. Neither of them had thought to smooth the covers or change the sheets to hide the evidence of her lost virginity. Social ruin hovered.

"Yes, odd," she managed. A quick glance told her that at least there was no blood showing to pique the doctor's interest further.

"I believe this is the chest the ornaments were in— perhaps there are other carvings in it." She knelt beside the chest and spoke louder than necessary in order to draw the doctor from his scrutiny of the bed.

He responded as she had hoped and joined her beside the chest. She opened it, only to confront once again the lovely satin-and-lace wedding gown. Her fingers spread against it for a moment, lost in the memory of her dance with Michael and the feel of his fingers against her skin.

"This is . . . must be Eleanor's wedding gown. And there's a nice quilt under it. I . . . just thought she might like to have that as well. Or a painting from the kitchen. But what to choose?"

"No doubt she would enjoy having a selection of her mementoes with her. Why not take them all and let her choose. As you said, you can always bring back anything she does not want."

The doctor leaned down, perused the chest for a moment longer, and slid his hands into the grips on either side. "It doesn't look too . . . umph."

"Are you all right?"

"Yes." The doctor didn't even glance at her as he answered. His entire focus was on the chest. Odd that he would be so intent on moving it. She was grateful for his effort to do so, but still it was odd.

"It's . . . heavier than I expected," he told her over his shoulder. "Where did you say she got this?"

"I didn't." Amelia smiled as his glance swivelled sharply to hers. "But I believe it was a gift from a cousin the last time she heard from him before Jacob died. A distant relation of her husband's, somewhere in Kansas."

"Ahh." Again that keen interest focused on the chest for a long moment. When he turned back to her, his charm had resurfaced and his eyes were sparkling. "I'm quite certain we need to get this to Eleanor. Perhaps I can talk her into selling me this chest. It is precisely the dimensions I have been looking for to hold my journals. I shall speak with her about it this very day."

"All right."

"Excuse me, my dear. I shall need a bit of room in order to move this out to the buggy."

She nodded and stepped aside, her gaze once more caught by the rumpled pillows and the indentations of two heads. This bedroom all but screamed her guilt to anyone who cared to look.

Thank heaven the doctor was so preoccupied with his need to purchase the chest from Eleanor. If there was anything she had learned from this visit, it was not to bring anyone with her the next time she came.

That, and that she would need to get back here before Eleanor was fully recovered in order to put the bedroom back to rights.

The doctor bent and strained for a moment before managing to heft the chest up in his arms. His face was rapidly reddening and sweat dotted his brow.

"My dear, if you could . . . get the doors before me."

"Of course." She hurried out into the hallway and toward the front door. Obviously he wouldn't be able to carry it far. She felt guilty for allowing him to carry it at all, but he seemed determined to take it with him.

She stopped long enough to pick up the little music box. She would tuck that into the chest once he had it safely stowed on the back of the buggy.

Crash.

Apparently he hadn't made it. She hurried out the door after him.

"Dr. Walker, are you all right?"

Fear clutched her as she skidded to a halt in the doorway. He stood beside the broken chest with a pistol leveled steadily in her direction. Gold coins, banknotes, and a heavy bag imprinted with the words *Payroll* and *U.S. Marshals Service* spilled in disarray on the porch.

She felt sick. What was so much money doing in the bottom of Eleanor's chest? Was it Eleanor and Jacob's?

"Quite all right." Dr. Walker nodded toward her with the same charming courtesy he had always displayed. "Better than I have felt in years. Thank you for asking, my dear. I am so pleased to have recovered what is mine at last."

"I . . . don't understand." Perhaps if she played the innocent, flighty widow, he would let her go. He could tie her up and leave her here. Money did horrible things to people. Look at Jonathan's dishonorable actions, her own brother. "The chest is Mrs. Holmdale's."

"Your lack of understanding is truly unfortunate. I like you, Mrs. Mitchell. In fact, I find you quite attractive. I was hoping to pursue that attraction to its logical conclusion. Widows are usually so desperately lonely. So very in need of a doctor's special . . . treatment. However," he gestured toward the broken chest and its unexpected contents, "circumstances appear to dictate otherwise. I am sorry."

He sounded as though he were apologizing for breaking a luncheon engagement or for appearing late for tea. She felt quite ill.

"I still don't understand."

"Very well, I shall explain it." He waved the pistol again. "This is money from a payroll stolen from the U.S. Marshals some time ago. It has taken me quite some time to find it again."

"And you are going to return it to them?" She knew the answer even as she voiced the question, but couldn't stop herself from offering the vain hope anyway.

He chuckled as though she had offered some witty repartee. "No, no. You see, my dear, this is my property. I worked to relieve the marshals of this payroll. I have been hunting this money since it was hidden. Sent to the area for safekeeping by my compatriot. I am very glad to have found it at last. This is one of the few locations in this dratted town that I have not had the pleasure of searching, since he died without telling who he sent it to."

"So Eleanor had no idea—"

"No." He moved a step closer. She backed up. "It really is a pity I can't afford any witnesses. You were kind enough to offer me the opportunity find this. Not only that, but you led me directly where I needed to go and saved me countless hours of fruitless searching. I am in your debt for that."

"Then you will—"

"Release you?" He shook his head. "No, I'm afraid not. It's a pity. Truly. But I cannot take the risk. The Holmsdales may not have known what they held, but you do. I've gone to a great deal of trouble to set my life up and become Dr. Josiah Walker, man above re-proach. I'm not about to be fingered as a thief now."

He'd come closer as he spoke and now stood too close for comfort. His nostrils flared as he looked at her. "You are quite lovely, did you know that, Amelia? I should very much have liked to get better acquainted."

He leaned in closer still and pressed his mouth to hers. His lips were chilled and stiff. She whimpered beneath his kiss, afraid to move as the cold metal of the pistol pressed against her side. He pulled his mouth away, but the gun stayed in place.

"Yes, a true pity. You are tempting, but such is not to be the case."

"What . . ." She swallowed, unable to form the question.

"What do I intend to do with you?"

She nodded as tears pricked the backs of her eyes.

"Why, kill you, my dear," he said in that conversa-tional way, as though she would understand perfectly. "It's the only way. But not here." And then the pistol slammed against the side of her head and blackness swallowed her whole.

She awoke to the rocking pitch of the buggy and clip-clopping rhythm of the horses' hooves. Her head pounded where he had struck her with the pistol, but she was alive. Tears blinded her for a moment as self-pity rose up inside her. How on earth had she gotten herself into this mess? Had there been something in the doctor's manner, something in his behavior to in-dicate he was a thief and a murderer?

No. Right up until the moment the pistol showed in his grip, there had been nothing to indicate he was anything more or less than the charming country doctor he appeared to be. Whoever he was, he was an accomplished actor.

Oh, Michael.

By all her old standards, he came up short compared to Dr. Walker. But she'd learned so much since coming to Warm Springs.

Tears burned again and she blinked them away, wishing she had stayed at the Grand Estate and waited for Michael before journeying back to Eleanor's home. But the temptation to go and get it done had been too much. A sob welled up inside her and she gritted her teeth to hold it back. The doctor or whoever he was couldn't know she was awake. She quickly replayed the last few moments in her mind. No, she had made no sound and had lain perfectly still. He wouldn't know. And that would be her only chance, the only weapon she had. She would have to be ready to put up a fight.

If she wanted to live.

"When did she leave?" Michael gritted the question out as all the demons from the fourth ring of hell battered his mind. Amelia was alone with the man who had killed his brother.

"Well, I don't know, dear. I'm not sure I noticed the time. We asked her what to tell you. She told us just to say that she'd gone out for the afternoon."

"Cora, she said to tell him she'd gone to the farm to pick up some things for Eleanor."

"I know, but I don't think she really wanted him to know that—"

"When did she leave?" He directed the question to Clara this time. She stopped her argument with Cora and looked at him for the first time as if realizing there was more to his question than idle curiosity.

"She left about an hour ago, Michael." Clara put a hand on his arm. "Is she in some kind of trouble?"

"I hope not. I really do hope not." He squeezed Clara's hand, then rushed out the back door and into the barn. Becky snorted in surprise as he saddled her.

"Sorry, girl, we've got work to do." He grabbed his rifle, badge, and revolver from their hiding place among the haystacks and swung up into the saddle. "Yah."

Becky took off at a gallop as the blue-and-purple skies over Warm Springs heralded the coming twilight. Amelia and the doctor had been gone more than long enough to get to the Holmdale farm by buggy and return. He knew in his gut she was in trouble.

He only hoped he would reach her in time to stop it. To stop Josiah Walker, or whatever other name he might choose, from hurting another person he loved.

Seventeen

Amelia's pulse increased its frightened tempo, keeping pace with the speed of the gig. Dread ached in her throat. Her nerves stretched taut with waiting in the darkness.

How far had they gone? How far would Josiah Walker take her before he'd gone far enough to kill her? She prayed an opportunity to escape would appear. She hoped she would be ready when the time came to act. She would have to fight for her life. For the life she desperately wanted. The future she wanted.

Images of Michael threaded her mind in tight circles. Standing in the doorway, laughing under the covers, bending down to kiss her. For all the darkness surrounding her, she understood the term *heartache* in a wholly new light.

She wasn't ready to lose the love she'd just found with him. She wasn't ready to give up on the chance they could find happiness together.

And she wasn't ready to give up on herself.

Her ire rose with each thought of what Dr. Walker was trying to take from her. Good. She would need her anger to help her fight for the very things she did not want to lose. She would need every ounce of courage she could muster.

The gig slowed as the terrain beneath the wheels grew uneven. She bounced around in the dark, thrust first to one side, then the other. He was pulling off to the side of the road to do away with her. How far had they come from town? How far were they from any town? How much longer did she have to live?

Panic swirled her stomach with nausea. For a moment, small sparks danced before her eyes and the temptation to just give in and black out gripped her hard.

Then she shook herself and summoned every bit of resolution she could.

She had to be ready. She had to be ready. She had to be ready. The litany played through her mind and heart as she held herself immobile.

"Noooooo!" she shrieked as loud as she could as he opened the boot.

She sprang at him, throwing the full force of her determination to live into her leap for freedom, and screaming her intention to do just that. This man wanted to kill her. She was not ready to die. Surprise was her only weapon.

It worked.

He fell back and lost his footing. The pistol fell from his fingers, parting the snow with a soft thud. Should she grab it?

He was between her and it and she had never so much as touched one. She couldn't afford to waste time. She pushed to her feet, gathered her skirts, and ran.

Snow, now slushy, now hard, impeded her progress as she raced toward a stand of trees up ahead. She could hear him cursing behind her.

THE CHRISTMAS KISS   303

They were in a wash of some kind, isolated from the road and whatever lay on the other sides of steep crests. The perfect spot for a murder. Her murder. She rushed onward, seeking shelter. Praying for help. Praying she was not heading in the wrong direction to find either.

Breath burned hard and fast in her lungs, straining as the icy air rushed in and out. Her feet slipped on the snow and ice.

"Please, please, please," she prayed as she ran. The snow soaked the hem of her skirts and made them heavy and wet, slowing her even more.

"Stop!" His command held none of the charming inflection he'd used on her previously.

Fear iced her spine and drove her onward.

"Come back here!"

But her killer wasn't waiting for her to obey, any more than he was going to let her disappear into the gathering gloom. He was gaining on her.

Her heart pounded wildly in her ears. She couldn't seem to make her feet move any faster than they already were. Pain pounded in her head. Icy fire burned in her chest.

"Oh, please." Tears streaked her face as she ran, all but certain he would catch her. Soon. Then what?

She rounded a tree, only to skid down an unexpected embankment. Panic seized her as she slid into a wall of solid muscle.

The barest squeak of fear escaped before a warm mouth covered her own, silencing her.

She struggled for just an instant longer until her body recognized what her mind had yet to comprehend. She relaxed against him and he lifted his head.

She'd never seen anything as soul-warmingly beautiful as the lopsided smile he gave her in the midst of such danger.

"Michael." She breathed his name, then buried her face in his thick wool overcoat. She'd never been so glad to see anyone in her life. "How—"

"Hello, princess." His thumb skimmed her lips and stopped her questions.

He pressed another quick kiss to her temple, then straightened. A curse sounded nearby.

"Stand behind me." His ragged command brooked no argument.

She obeyed immediately, but peered around his shoulder to see that blackheart, Dr. Walker, cross the treeline and skid to a halt with his pistol pointed straight at them.

"US Marshal, give up your weapon!" Michael's voice rang clear through the wooded thicket as he leveled a rifle at the doctor.

Clouds of breath puffed from Dr. Walker, but the pistol remained gripped in his hand. Silence stretched as the world seemed to await his next move.

"You're not the first deputy I've dealt with, Thompson. But I will be the last fugitive you hunt if you do not stand down. That goes for your pretty little paramour, too, naturally."

Amelia felt tension ripple across Michael's shoulders at the doctor's easy contempt. But he held his peace.

"Was loving her sweet? I'm a rich man now. Perhaps once I've disposed of you, I'll keep her around for a few weeks and sample her charms for myself." Walker continued his taunts.

"We both know that's not going to happen." Deadly intent edged Michael's rebuttal.

"Put down your rifle, and I'll let her live."

"When you robbed that payroll in Kansas, you shot the deputy marshal in charge as soon as he surrendered his weapon."

The doctor spread his hands. "He got in the way. It couldn't be helped."

"He was my brother."

Michael's rifle blared, the report deafening in the quiet woods. The doctor clutched his forearm, his pistol falling useless to the ground.

"Stay here." Michael pushed her behind a tree, then stalked up the embankment and stood over the doctor. He recocked the rifle and for a moment she thought he would kill the man cowering on the ground in front of him.

"It couldn't be helped. We didn't want the marshal. We only wanted the money," Josiah pleaded. "Eustace shot him."

Michael raised the barrel of the rifle and nudged it closer to the doctor. "That's not the way the others told the tale."

The man shuddered. "It was an accident. We came for the payroll. We almost had it, too. The deputy rushed me and the gun went off. He was dead before he hit the ground. I swear it's the truth."

Michael stuck the butt of the rifle on the doctor's shoulder and forced him onto his stomach. He moaned in pain but otherwise didn't move as Michael circled metal cuffs around his wrists and closed them with a solid click.

"Tell that to your judge and jury." He dragged out

a handkerchief and wrapped the wrist where his bullet had grazed the doctor. Then he dragged him to his feet. "You're under arrest."

"Are you all right, Amelia?" he called.

"Yes." She hurried to his side and he brushed a quick kiss to her temple.

The fierce look in his eyes told her more than any words could possibly convey. He had come very close to pulling the rifle's trigger that second time. She was grateful he hadn't, grateful he was all right. That he'd found her and she was alive.

Her mind spun with questions and answers too numerous to sort out. "Michael, you're a United States Marshal?"

"A deputy marshal." He nodded. "I couldn't tell you before this. I couldn't tell anyone."

"A deputy marshal," she repeated, trying to wrap her thoughts, everything she had thought she knew about him, about them, around this revelation.

Again he nodded. "Charged with apprehending Deputy U.S. Marshal William Thompson's murderers, and recovering the federal payroll stolen along with his life over six years ago."

He shoved the rifle into the small of the doctor's back and edged him forward. "We have so much to talk about, Amelia. I have so much to tell you. But this is neither the time nor the place. Can you wait a little longer, sweetheart?"

She nodded, still too stunned by this news and grateful for their survival to mind much of anything. She was alive. Michael was alive. They would have a later. Nothing else mattered.

"Good girl." He put one arm around her and kept

the other one with the rifle trained on his prisoner. "Let's get you home."

She didn't think she'd ever heard a better suggestion.

Bound and gagged in the back of the wagon a little while later, there was nothing the doctor, or as Michael explained when they'd first reached the Grand Estate and had quieted everyone's fears, Joe White—escaped convict, thief, and murderer—could do but wait to be escorted to jail. In Kansas, where his worst crimes had been committed. That, apparently, was Michael's job.

He drew her away from the drawing room windows and turned her face to his. "I have to go."

"I understand," she lied, knowing it was what he needed to hear. They were alone to make their farewells.

He was a U.S. Marshal, not a ne'er-do-well or a drifter, or any of the things he had told her before tonight. He wasn't even Betty Mitchell's nephew. She wasn't sure what that made of them or the night they spent together. What did he truly think of her? What did he truly want from her?

Yesterday, she would have thought she knew the answers to those questions, and the hundreds of others swarming in her heart. Right now, she hadn't a clue about much of anything.

She was numb with it all.

In a few minutes she would be watching him walk out of her life. She only had so much strength to stand here and do that without crying. So she kept her questions to herself and told him she understood everything he had done and everything he had told her about what he'd yet to do.

"I don't think you do understand." He saw right through her. Somehow that made this all the harder.

His fingers stroked her cheek. His thumb brushed her lips. And then his mouth covered hers, soft and sweet and gentle. Tears burned the backs of her eyes. She would miss him so terribly. "I'll be back, Amelia."

"Of course you will." She nodded, not believing a word.

He had no reason to come back. The reason he was in Warm Springs, his investigation, was through. He'd caught his man and now he would have other men to track. Other criminals to bring to justice. That was who he was.

Deputy U.S. Marshal Michael Thompson had important things to do and a life somewhere that had nothing to do with a penniless widow and her love for him. It wouldn't matter just how desperately she wanted him to stay when the scales of justice needed him to keep them balanced.

He tipped her chin up and his steel-gray gaze probed hers. "I love you, Amelia Lawrence Mitchell." His words, his intentions, rang true.

"And I *will* be back."

Her heart lurched with that impossible promise. He kissed her long and slow and sweet again, echoing the passion and desire they had discovered in this house, that they had built and explored in the snowbound shelter of the Holmdale farm. Part of her wanted to throw her arms around him, to beg him to stay, to plead with him to take her along with him. But that was a part of her neither one of them would want to live with for long. He had responsibilities he could not ignore and so did she. She had the Grand Estate to run.

She pulled back and looked up at him for a time-less moment. Her breath hitched in her chest. Then she reached up and smoothed the rumpled hair on his brow back into place, just as she had been aching to do since the first day she had seen him.

She offered him a smile. Perhaps for the last time.

"Go on, then," she urged. "You'll never get back here if you don't hurry and leave."

He brushed the pad of his thumb over her lips again and nodded once as he gazed into her eyes with such a solemn and sincere look it nearly unraveled all her resolve.

With that, he strode from the room, leaving her with her blood singing in her veins and hope lodged uncomfortably against her ribcage. Right next to the shattered pieces of her heart.

"The tree is lovely, don't you think, Amelia dear? Truly, those ornaments of Eleanor's make all the difference. Those creatures her husband carved are divine. And the lace bows you added make it ever so elegant."

Cora's conversation washed over Amelia, drawing her away from the window and the darkening sky outside. Each puff of snow reminded her of Michael, of the one precious night they had spent together. But then there was very little here that didn't remind her of Michael. He was everywhere. And never farther than a heartbeat from her thoughts.

She had only to look at the elegant, carved ornaments of the wildlife around Warm Springs that Jacob Holmdale had made for his wife to think of the lovely wedding gown she'd discovered beside them and the night that had passed between herself and the man who had been a U.S. Marshal on the trail of a thief. A thief and a killer.

"Amelia, dear. Are you listening?"

"Yes, Cora," she answered. "They are lovely. The tree looks grand. You and Festive worked very hard."

She returned Cora's smile and brushed her fingers across the spruce tree's soft, pungent needles, but her thoughts were already flowing back to Michael.

Three weeks had passed since he had kissed her in this very room and promised to return. Three long weeks.

"I think we should hang the mistletoe right over there, dear, don't you?"

"What?" Amelia roused. "Mistletoe?"

"Yes, dear, over the door."

Cora did not seem to mind that she was not really paying attention, but the mention of mistletoe took her right back to the first time she'd seen Michael. She'd forgotten until now. He'd been talking to that young girl at the train station, the one who said something about Christmas and coming home. She must be the sister he'd mentioned. It was all jumbled, but Amelia was certain now there would be no Christmas surprise for her. No Christmas kisses. If Michael was anywhere other than doing his job, he would be home in Chicago.

Amelia shook her head. "No mistletoe. Not this year. It's getting late. Where are the others, Cora? We won't want to keep Horace waiting when he arrives."

"You're so right, dear. We don't want any delays tonight. I'll just go hurry them along, shall I?" Cora bustled out, leaving Amelia alone in the too-quiet room.

Where was everyone? She roused herself from her private torment long enough to wonder what was going on. Everyone had been so busy all day. So many comings and goings, hushed whispers and hastily shut doors. Holiday anticipation building in her little makeshift family. Some truly delicious smells emanating from the kitchen promised a real feast, at least. Thank goodness, Clara was back in charge of all culinary affairs.

Whatever was afoot must be plans for tomorrow. Her first Christmas in her new home. Her first Christmas to share in the traditions and customs of her new family. She felt a tug of longing for her mother, for the life she'd left behind. Perhaps by now her mother had received the letter Michael had suggested she write to her. She hoped Mama would answer.

Three weeks, her thoughts revolved again. She'd known then, despite the stubborn hope still lingering inside her, that he wouldn't be back. There was no reason for him to return. No reason but her.

And she wasn't sure she was reason enough for any man to return, especially not a man who was also sworn to uphold the law and protect the citizenry.

She and her boarders would gather in the drawing room without him tonight. It was Wednesday, after all. Christmas Eve. Family night. She smiled in spite of the melancholy tugging at her spirit. In a few minutes, Horace Salzburg was going to arrive with his capacious sleigh and team and whisk them all to Christmas Eve candlelight services.

There was a loud knocking at the door.

"Cora," she called. "Horace is here."

The knock sounded again. Louder and more insistent. She walked out into the foyer.

"Hello," she called upward. "Mr. Salzburg is here. It's time to leave for church."

Still no answer. No flurry of footsteps overhead. Where was everyone?

She opened her mouth to call louder as she headed to the stairs. A third spate of knocking changed her direction. It really was rude to make Horace wait on the porch when he had been kind enough to offer them a ride.

She thought she heard someone on the steps behind her. At last. She turned to look over her shoulder as she pulled open the door. "I'm sorry, Horace—"

"I'm afraid I'm not Horace."

A familiar voice interrupted her. Familiar, and much loved.

"Michael," she breathed, and turned toward him.

Before she got his name all the way out he had his arms wrapped around her.

"Hello, princess."

He found her lips then, and covered them with his own, cutting off the need for any other greeting. He pulled her close and filled her heart, filled her soul, with all the love she'd been missing so terribly since he'd gone.

When he finally released her enough to catch her breath, she looked at him for a long time to make sure this was not another dream. He looked so very handsome there in the doorway with the snow falling behind him and the lamplight from the foyer bathing his face.

He wore a new overcoat of smoothly brushed gray worsted. Highly polished boots gleamed at the end of dress trousers. Had he gotten a promotion for a job well done? It didn't seem to matter to her; it only mattered that he was standing there, holding her and giving her his lopsided grin as he examined her, too.

"You came back," she said at last.

A shadow flicked across his features. "I told you I would. I'm sorry it took this long."

"It doesn't matter." She shook her head. "You came back."

All the fear and longing she'd carried since he'd left melted on the rising flames of hope spreading through her.

"May I come inside?"

"Of course." She stepped back and drew him with her into the foyer.

"Amelia, I have so much to tell you." He broke from their second kiss. "So much to explain. But first, I have something very important to ask."

"You don't have to tell me, or explain anything. We have plenty of time."

"I do have to tell you," he said. "But just for the moment the asking comes first. I put everything together to surprise you, then realized I never asked you how you felt."

"I love you." She gave him the words he'd said to her before he left. The words that had given her the strength to continue to hope, to function, while he was gone. "And I always will."

"I know that, princess." He smiled and hugged her. "I know that because it's how I feel about you." His breath flowed warm over her temple, just as his words warmed her soul.

He stood back to look at her again. "I want the world to know how we feel. Marry me, Amelia. Marry me tonight. Everything's arranged."

"What?" She wasn't sure she'd heard him right. Wasn't sure she'd heard him at all.

"Yes. Say yes." The barest whispers floated down from the hall above.

"Marry me. Tonight. Right now. Everyone is waiting."

Logic dictated that she not rush. Practicality demanded they detail how this would work. He needed to roam. She needed to stay put. The last time she'd flung herself into hasty action, that day it rained and she had found the ad in the newspaper cart she knocked over, she ended up here and . . . and . . .

She ended up here.

"Yes." She flung her arms around him and kissed him hard, heedless of the cheers from her tenants clustered on the landing above them.

The next hour passed in such a whirl she had a hard time grasping all the details he'd worked out ahead. For every question there was a ready answer or the solution right at hand.

She stood in the narthex of the church at the heart of Warm Springs, dressed in the satin-and-lace gown Eleanor Holmdale had worn on her own wedding day, and clutched a bouquet of silk roses, hand-twisted by Cora and Clara. Her arm twined through Horace Salzburg's—he had beamed when he'd said he would be honored to escort her down the aisle.

Candles gleamed in the windows and in tall stands that lined the aisle between the pews packed with the faithful, with her neighbors. Festive and the Brown sisters would play as she trod the fairy-tale path that led to the altar. Eleanor would stand up with her, and Ethan with Michael. Both radiated pride as they waited up front.

That's why the delay in starting the ceremony was so puzzling.

"Where's Michael?" she whispered as the guests swivelled from time to time, trying to catch glimpses of the bride.

"He had a last-minute detail to attend. Don't fret, he'll be here anon." Horace patted her hand.

What detail could possibly be left?

Everything was perfect, everything thought of. She was overwhelmed by his thoughtfulness. She'd been surprised when he had introduced her to his father and his stepmother and his sister, Katie, the girl she had seen with Michael at the Chicago train station the day they met. They were staying with Horace for the week. She smothered a laugh. She couldn't picture it, but they seemed content as they sat in the front pew.

William Thompson had a firm handshake and familiar steel-gray eyes. His wife was a slender woman, immaculately coiffed and gowned, a woman who was everything Amelia had once aspired to be, a woman who wished her all the best as she thanked her for making Michael so happy. They'd even revealed their pleasure that with his brother's case resolved, Michael was considering leaving the marshals service.

That was something she and Michael would have to discuss.

The only twinge she felt was when she looked at the

pew opposite the one where the Thompsons were seated. The one her family should be occupying.

Before her regret could fully form, the doors opened behind her with a gust of cold air, revealing a sight that sparked fresh tears at the edges of her happiness. There stood her mother, dressed in crimson and fur, clinging to her stepfather's arm.

"Mama." She flew to her mother and threw her arms around her, very unceremoniously, and not at all the proper thing to do. But it felt so right. "Mama, what are you doing here—how did you know?"

Her mother hugged her right back with no thought to decorum as she chuckled, "Your young man made all the arrangements. I couldn't miss this wedding. He loves you very much, Amelia. I hope you will both work to make each other happy."

Amelia looked at her stepfather, still standing quietly at the door to let her have a moment alone with her mother. The man she had been so childish about. "Thank you for coming, too, Mr. McCorry. For leaving your business interests long enough to escort my mother here."

"Nonsense, we're family." He waved off her thanks, but she could tell he was touched from the smile that creased his broad cheeks above his whiskers. He winked. "I do believe my little butcher shop can get along without me from time to time."

The tears that had hovered since she'd opened the door an hour before spilled down her cheeks at his easy forgiveness.

"Did you get my letter?" she asked her mother.

"It arrived just as we were leaving." Her mother dug in her beaded reticule and pulled out a dainty, lace-edged handkerchief. "Your great-grandmother carried this on her wedding day a century ago. A lady should . . ."

". . . always carry a handkerchief, I always say," Amelia finished the timeworn advice. Both of them laughed.

"Thank you for coming all this way." She hugged her mother again. "I am so sorry for the way I left."

"I read your letter on the train, over and over. We'll have plenty of time to talk later. We're being housed with the rector and his wife, I believe." Her mother nodded toward the altar. "I think they are ready for us to take our seats."

Michael stood at the front, waiting. Her breath hitched. She was going to marry him. Tonight.

Her mother made her way down to the front pew on her husband's arm. Michael had thought of everything to give her a perfect wedding. She didn't feel as if she deserved this much, but she was not going to waste the gift.

She was so happy. Her love for Michael was bigger than she had ever believed possible. She would try with everything within her to keep that happiness alive for both of them for the rest of their lives.

"It's like a fairy tale," Cora sighed.

"It is exactly what she deserves," Eleanor added, a twinkle lighting her eyes. Amelia returned her smile and smoothed her fingers over the lovely satin wedding gown Eleanor had shared with her.

"She looks like a princess," Festive added. Then he put his fiddle under his chin and began to play.

Amelia took Horace's arm again. She daubed her tears of joy with Grandmother Abigail's handkerchief and noticed that there were very few dry eyes in the house as the congregation turned to look at her.

Michael made the perfect picture of a storybook groom, impeccably dressed, hair smoothed into place just as she'd always thought it should be, with a light in his eyes she knew was meant just for her when she joined him at the front of the church.

"Are you ready?" he whispered.

"Almost." She reached up and tousled his hair. "That's better. Now, everything is perfect."

She awoke the next morning to the sensation of her new husband nibbling at her earlobe as the early morning sunlight streamed through the window.

"Guess what I found." His husky tone tickled her neck.

"What did you find?" she asked as she arched back against Michael's chest without opening her eyes. They'd made love until the stars had twinkled out and the dawn's first fingers edged the horizon, signaling the beginning of their first Christmas together.

"Open your eyes, princess," Michael insisted with a chuckle that rumbled in his chest. He tugged harder on her ear and then flicked the edge with his tongue.

A delicious shiver raced through her. She loved him so. "What could possibly be so important?"

From the answering quiver against her backside as she snuggled closer, she could almost guess. She turned to seek his lips and he pulled back. "Look up, Amelia."

She opened her eyes to see a fresh bunch of green

leaves surrounding a center thick with gray-green waxy berries dangling over her head.

"Mistletoe." She laughed and stretched above the coverlet to touch his offering, but he held it out of reach.

"Uh-uh." He smiled. "First, you must surrender a kiss, my princess. A very special kiss."

She chewed her lip, pretending she needed to consider carefully whether to grant him such a boon. "A Christmas kiss?"

He nodded, that lopsided grin of his lighting his eyes and making her heart tumble now as it always would. "Our first one. On our first Christmas morning. The first of a lifetime of Christmas mornings."

"Oh, Michael." Joy flooded her heart. She'd found her own true love. They would make their own memories to share. She pulled him to her, confident she could show him just what he could expect every Christmas morning . . . for the rest of their lives.

ABOUT THE AUTHORS

Elizabeth Keys is the pseudonym for Mary Lou Frank and Susan C Stevenson, who live in southern New Jersey. Recently named "Best Up & Coming Author" by *Affaire de Coeur* magazine, these lifelong friends enjoy creating tales of achieving your heart's desire through love's special magic.

To learn more about books by Elizabeth Keys, visit www.elizabethkeys.com.